THE ROOM UPSTAIRS

Ranjini said goodbye to Sarath the day before she left for Ceylon. Her fli[illegible]eave at eight thirty and [illegible]ng, I found her and [illegible]n.

[illegible]feld! I've got one or [illegible]e when you're [illegible] out and into my [illegible]

[illegible]rown skirt and n[illegible]ooked dull and d[illegible] and unflattering. My round Russian face did not improve with make-up, and my eyes looked small and narrow. What a contrast Ranjini and I must seem! Beauty and the Beasts if you took Rosenfeld into account. My spirits drooped as she tripped gaily into the room.

'We're ready to leave. Come on!'

I felt like an old brown suitcase, stuck in the front with Ranjini sitting between us; like Cinderella and her ugly sisters. I wished it was after midnight. How many more fairy stories would I be telling myself before we put her on the plane?

THE ROOM UPSTAIRS

Norma Levinson

For Rachel –
the last of
the bunch!
Love from
Norma xx
Oct. 1988

NEW ENGLISH LIBRARY

For Jean, With Love

First published in Great Britain in 1984 by
Century Publishing Co. Ltd

First NEL Paperback Edition November 1985

NEL Books are published by
New English Library,
Mill Road, Dunton Green,
Sevenoaks, Kent.
Editorial office: 47 Bedford Square, London WC1B 3DP

Printed and bound in Great Britain by
Cox & Wyman Ltd, Reading

British Library C.I.P.

Levinson, Norma
The room upstairs.
I. Title
823'.914[F] PR6062.E92/

ISBN 0-450-05806-9

Chapter One

I took a last futile drag at my sodden cigarette and threw it inaccurately at the dustbin standing on guard outside the mortuary. The rain had seeped into my shoes, down my neck and into my bone marrow. I pushed the rubber doors open with my carrier bag and turned left down the dark, icy corridor towards Nightingale. I sent out three Valentine cards yesterday, but all I received in the post this morning was a *Reader's Digest* advert.

I stretched my mouth at Sister as I dripped into the ward and managed to get past her without being turned into an insect. You should hear her sometimes, shouting at the nurses, her face twisted with ill temper; and then, within a second or two, beaming sycophantically at Mr Gavin and Mr Groves, the consultants. I hung my coat in the washroom after giving all the children a big Hello, and started titivating myself in the mirror, just in case . . . but it was one of those days when I looked as ugly as sin, no matter what.

'Hello, Teacher,' called Staff Nurse, coming in to bang around with the bottles and the bedpans. 'You look divine. What a shame you've just missed Agiba's round!' Staff Nurse is disturbingly observant. 'I shouldn't bother with your hair, though. You've probably caught nits from Patrick Weekes, and you don't want them spreading to your clothes, do you? We washed his hair today and it was positively *crawling*. Alive and *crawling*, I tell you. You're always slobbering over that kid, so I'd better give you some special shampoo to take home. Here,

I'll put it into this sample jar. It's only had wee-wee in it.'

My scalp started itching and tingling. 'I'll kill you if I've caught them!' I screamed at her, tearing at my sopping hair in panic as I felt the dicks crawling down my neck. 'Why didn't you wash his hair before? He's been here two months hasn't he? What's the matter with this place?'

'Oh, for heaven's sake, stop flapping. It's only raindrops running down. Whoops! Just a minute, though – there's a big daddy one on your shoulder.' She had a paroxysm over the edge of the sink as I ran at her insanely, shrieking at her to take it off. She eventually recovered from her little joke. 'God, you should have seen those things wriggling about in the bowl!'

'Oh, shut up. Give me the shampoo. And incidentally, I make a fuss of Patrick only when he gets a word right. Is it my fault that I'm such a good teacher?'

I picked up my bag of books and went back into the ward. It's lovely and bright in here with pictures on the wall, and toys and books scattered around. There's a big aquarium fixed into the far corner and a canary in a cage over there. Most of the children are jumping around on their beds or on the floor. Dawn ran up to me and I lifted her up and gave her a roundabout. Tara didn't get up from the armchair though; how pale and ill she looks today. Neither Dawn nor Tara are expected to see the year out. David's got Still's disease and will always be a twisted and helpless cripple; and what's going to happen to Kevin, with his grotesque, jutting, erudite forehead, and a face that shocks me, even after all this time? What will happen to him when he goes out into the grim, gaping world, with people seeing him for the first time? If they can't do anything for him here, perhaps he'll die. But Kevin will live. It's beautiful Dawn who is dying of cancer, and my clever, pretty Tara, who has Wilm's disease and is wasting away before my eyes. But there's Colin and Patrick who have only got fractures and rattle away on the weighted tractions, flipping paper aeroplanes and chewed bubble-gum at each other. They'll be okay, in a month or so, back at home, running about and forgetting all about it. I'll miss them all when they go.

'Come on, monitors! Get mobile! Bring your chairs and books over here. Hurry up, you big fat things, you great lumps!' I hauled them around. Dawn perched on Colin's bed, and I eased myself comfortably on to Patrick's, then remembering something, I jumped off rather quickly and forced my backside into a child's armchair at the foot of the two beds, with the children all around me. We had news and a chat first, and David told me how Patrick threw his Plasticine on the ceiling, and lessons were under way.

I taught fractions, with a few tangerines taken from various lockers, and the one who shouted out the correct answer ate the fraction. Whenever I felt slightly peckish, I gave them a difficult one, and then it was my turn for a juicy seven twelfths. I did a turn with an orange, to represent the earth, and I took off the earth's crust and handed out the lava and volcanoes, making sure no one was left out. We revised the four-times table to the tune of 'Gaudemus Igitur Juvenes Dum Sumus' and the five-times to the merry notes of 'The Star Spangled Banner', with a cock of the thumb at the USA.

We managed to fit in as much noise as possible, while Sister was having her morning coffee in some hidden sanctum. We practised our new song, 'The Trout', and acted out our well-worn 'Tailor and the Mouse' in joyous chorus. Then it was time for reading and story-writing, and I grouped them as far as possible, and spent several minutes with each child. It's surprising how quickly they learn, even dull, cabbagy Colin; and Tara wrote feverishly, as if she knew that there wasn't much time.

Tara isn't a cabbage: Tara is a rose which has blossomed into a beautiful, fast-fading bud, and is thirsty for the few drops of water that are scattered around her tender, stricken roots. She listens faster than I talk, her face tiny, white, intense, and I can see the shadow of death as clearly as my own hand.

David and I had a short session of our chess game, and, at last, it was story time, and everyone was clamouring to tell me where I left off yesterday. The strange narrative has been going on for weeks now, about a frightful child, full of malice and charm, who always emerges from her evil-doings, victorious. I invent it as I go along, and when I get stuck, I say, 'And guess what happened then?' Sure enough, someone comes up with an act of hair-raising mischief, and so the story continues. I wonder what Her Majesty's Inspector would say if he knew how little time I spent on formal arithmetic, compared with the time spent on our monster story! But my timetable is fixed for emergencies and I can always do a nifty switch if he calls. The children gathered close around me, leaning against my knees, staring up at me. I watched their big, round eyes; heard Dawn squeal with excitement; I looked at Kevin's face, and for a moment or two it was just like all other little boys' faces.

At last it was time to break off because the orderlies were bringing round the loaded lunch trolley. I waved goodbye to the children, and made my way to the staff canteen for my cheese sandwich, the crossword, a cigarette and a cup of tea.

It was still coming down in torrents, so I did a detour through the covered meat market. The stench is horrible, but I'm quite used to it by now. When I first saw the great columns of bloody meat hanging up, I swore I'd never touch a morsel again in my life. I was practically a vegetarian anyway. I'm on speaking terms with all the meat porters I pass. Sometimes I get, 'Can I carry your bag, darling?' or 'Cheer up, sweetheart, *I'll* take you out tonight!' They look like men from another planet in their ankle-length white shirts, stained rusty with dried blood, and their peaked stiff caps.

I crossed over by the ghostly remains of Gamage's, getting

splashed by a passing taxi, and waited with the poor and deprived for the number eight bus, which is one of those that comes in droves of six every fifty minutes, destined for the Beechwood Hospital for Nervous Diseases. It took ages, because we went through Oxford Street, and then there was that eternal jam, where they've been pulling up the Edgware Road for the last few years. I used to like that area very much. Sometimes I wonder whether it's my increasing dislike of the hospital that is changing my assessment.

I jumped off the bus and walked a few yards down the road to the German bakery. They sell plaited, burnt loaves there, of such utter deliciousness that, German or not, I must enter, zombie-like, and buy. I walked back to the main road, tearing off satisfying lumps of hot crust, waiting for the lights to change, my mouth crammed with joy. I could hear Jack, barking and growling even before I saw him, dancing back and forth in the entrance hall like a distracted puppy, waiting for me; now prancing about under the notice board, with all the queer Dickensian names on it. Jack and I have often laughed over them:

Lord Woodhead - OUT
Doctor Jelly - OUT
Doctor Wildblood - OUT
Doctor Yawner - OUT
Doctor Duck - OUT

I pulled off a hunk of bread for him and he mixed it with snot and spit and finally pushed it into his bubbling, tormented mouth. I told him I wouldn't be a sec, and popped along to the office to get my towel, then crossed over to the Ladies to have a wash and an Anadin. But I need more than that, today. A luxuriously perfumed bath and a treble whisky, more like. As soon as I set eyes on Jack, I invariably feel exhausted and hopeless. For the next few hours, Carl and Jack are to be my sole companions.

Carl is aggressive and intelligent, but academically very backward, and although he isn't yet certified, I think he will be, shortly. He's fourteen, with hard, black eyes and a stocky, strong frame. I don't like him and he doesn't like me, or anybody.

Jack is below average intelligence, so I'm told by the psychiatrist, Mrs Raymond, who believes faithfully and immovably in IQ tests. He's small and underdeveloped for his fifteen years, and afflicted with violent and perpetual twitches. About every minute he suffers a paroxysm of barking and growling and yelping, and I find myself taut and nervous, waiting for the next frightful row, immediately after one fit has ended. It comes as a sort of relief from suspense. Now that he's reached puberty, he's started what is known as involuntary obscenities, so that with a swear word every five seconds, barking every minute and non-stop Charlestons, there isn't much scope for the light of knowledge.

I leant against the sink for a minute, smoking nervously, hoping to steady myself for the fray, and read the new graffiti on the toilet door. Under the now stale 'Shitbag nigers get out', some bright spark had scrawled 'Sweetie pie, we are here to stay'. And this loo is supposed to be for the hospital staff only. I took a wet, soapy paper towel and rubbed off 'Shitbag' to 'out' inclusive, then walked out bravely to my pupils and descended in macabre fashion to the underground gym, where I conduct my school for two. We pulled our chairs up to the enormous polished table under the basket-covered electric light, hardly worth a candle in this huge, gloomy room, but it's the only empty place in the hospital. Carl was scraping his chair backwards and forwards making a noise to set my teeth on edge, digging his elbows into my ribs. 'Don't scrape your chair, please, Carl.'

'It's the chair! It's the sodding, fucking chair! I'm not moving. Look, you lying bugger, it's the chair, I'm telling you!' he bawled in my ear.

'Get another one.'

He dragged his chair across the gym with that same excruciating, nerve-chilling row, and kicked another one towards me. Finally, he was settled down, scraping wildly again. I mustn't lose my temper. He can't help it. It's not his fault. He's had a rotten life. He was expelled from school for throwing a desk at the headmaster's face and breaking his nose, so be careful, otherwise you'll get that knife he uses to cut leather in occupational therapy, right in your throat. Let him continue to scrape his chair and dig the knife into the polished table. How loathsome and repellent he is. I want to slap his hard, cruel, cocky face until I'm tired of doing it. 'Get out!' I shrieked, high and horrible. '*Get out* before I throw you out!' He rushed off, glad to get away from me, kicking the chair agonisingly against my knee. I gave Jack a cigarette, and we lit up and had a few puffs to steady ourselves, and Jack played nervously with the zip of his trousers, barking and swearing and trying to tell me how crazy Carl acts in occupational therapy as well, and that he must have pinched the leather-cutter from there.

We ate the rest of the loaf and started a game of Scrabble, and I sat there, mesmerised, wondering whether his favourite four-letter word would appear on the board. Come to think of it, I'd got the right letters for it, and I felt strangely tempted to put them down, but I'd better not risk that sort of shock therapy.

I became aware of loud kissing noises going on outside the half-open door. Thinking it was the fat pig of a kitchen porter trying to be sexy, I sent Jack over to close it. The next thing I knew, Carl had charged in, howling like a wild animal, his eyes black and dull and spit shining on his chin. He picked up a chair, jabbing Jack in the face and chest. I tried to separate them: one must try to pin the arms down, hugging the child tightly, but Carl is as strong as a tiger and whoever it was who told me to do that should be compelled to demonstrate now. Carl lifted the chair high in the air and brought it crashing down on my left arm with which I was shielding my head. I shouted at Jack to run for someone.

I talked to Carl quietly during the everlasting minutes I was alone with him. His face was ugly with violence and hatred and he jabbed and banged me with the chair repeatedly. It was impossible to wrench it from his grasp. Suddenly he threw the chair into my face and grabbed the knife from the top of his trousers. The chair was to the side of me, but I was afraid to lunge across to get it in case the movement maddened him. I backed away from him using my hands and arms as a shield. I believed he intended to kill me or blind me. He held the knife, blade pointing upwards, with knowledge and assurance.

Sister rushed in followed by Dr Feber, Jack and a psychiatric social worker called Violet. To my mind she's right round the bend, and I've often thought I might go funny like her. Sister yelled at Carl and the other three tackled him from behind, and held him, kicking and screaming, on the floor. Jack was really in there, doing his bit like a boy scout, and I was just leaning against the table rocking with laughter. Carl got his foot under Sister's skirt and kicked it up. I was doubled up with the painful stitch of uncontrollable laughter when, without warning, I started screaming and weeping, making more noise than all of them put together.

Dr Feber and Sister hauled Carl back to the ward and I walked to the office with Violet, still screeching like a potty old hen. The outpatients sitting in the corridor were all staring at me thinking, no doubt, that I was one of the prize patients, but there was no stopping me. Violet pushed me into a chair in the office, telling me to shush for Christ's sake, then dragged a bottle of Johnny Walker out of the desk drawer, so I got my whisky after all. She swiped me right across the face, poured out a good measure into a cracked teacup and handed it to me, taking a couple of swigs from the bottle herself. I never said Violet was anything but a good sort.

My arm suddenly started hurting terribly; my legs felt like bent pins, and I was all set to go off the deep end again. I didn't feel well at all. A nurse knocked on the door and took me to the X-ray room. I had two cracks in the bone in my left wrist, and the nurse wrapped it up for me. I told Violet what happened and she wrote it down.

Dr Feber came in and said, 'Why didn't you get hold of him, pin his arms down and hug him tightly? You couldn't? Then why didn't you give him a good hiding?'

I told him to go to hell before I gave him one on the nose. I drank the rest of my whisky, Violet helped me with my coat and I went out into the corridor where Jack was waiting, holding my bag.

'How are you, Miss?' he asked, decorating his question with the usual words, but I hardly heard them.

'I'm better, thank you, Jack. Heavens what a terrible performance I gave. What you must think of me!'

'You're not used to things like that,' he said. 'You don't want to cry and get upset. You're just not used to it, that's all. I am, though. I'm used to seeing people act like that, but Carl's the maddest person in this place. I hate him.' He fished in his pocket with difficulty, and pulled out a crumpled packet of ten. We sat opposite the NO SMOKING sign, smoking. 'Did you see how he kicked up Sister's skirt? All her drawers were showing.' He giggled. 'I'll be glad when I leave this dump and go home. Will I be glad!'

I didn't hear the swear words at all, now, nor the barking. 'You're going to an institution in Wales, Jack,' I thought. 'You're incurable. You're going to be the sort of man who shouts foul language at people in the street. You're going to frighten the girls and old ladies on station platforms with your vile abuse; amuse youths; disconcert; disgust; your tenderness and sweetness perfectly hidden beneath a coating of obscene filth.' He saw me to the door and I gave him a wave with my good hand. 'See you tomorrow, love. About one thirty. Ta-ta.'

I tried to read the Woman's Page on the bus going home, but I felt too shocked and depressed to concentrate. The faces and voices of the children churned around in my head. How was Bernadette today? I forgot to ask. She wasn't in her cot at the end of Nightingale. I'd concentrate on Tara and prolong her life by the urgency of my hopes, the strength of my will. Perhaps a faith healer could help; an acupuncturist; a witch; mass prayer. I've got my own life to lead. I mustn't think of the kids all the time, otherwise I'll end up in a private room in Beechwood.

The rain had slowed down into a misty drizzle as I hopped off the bus at Notting Hill Gate, and I pulled up my coat collar, which reminded me of the dicks making cosy nests in my hair. How was I going to wash it with one hand? I bought some celery and cheese flaps for my supper, and stuffed them awkwardly in my carrier. There's *An Affair to Remember* showing at the Classic. I'd seen it before, with my sister, and she screamed out loud in the cinema when Deborah Kerr got knocked down, and I spent the rest of the time incapable with hysterical laughter. Maybe I'd go over to see it again, with Cassy and Rina, my two actress friends who lived in the horrible flat downstairs. God, I'd not felt so depressed for ages.

I lived in a nasty flat with an Australian singer called Kate. She drifted in from Gundagai – a friend of a friend with whom I was sharing then. Kate gradually took over. She was unable to adjust to the ten-hour time change, sighing pathetically when the loathesome Northern Equatorial light penetrated the curtains. Soft music or a whispered conversation would cause her unendurable torment, which could only be alleviated by hourly cups of weak tea. During the late afternoon, Australian time, she would burst into tears about the way her current man was being beastly to her. We would give her kind advice in turn, but Kate never took anything we said to heart, thinking, no doubt, that we hadn't the faintest idea how to get along with men anyway, since we didn't have any success ourselves, that she could see. The only time she ever went out was at night, when her lover was free to adore her. I used to tell my friend to give her her marching orders, but she didn't have the moral courage. At last, it was she who left. Kate stayed. She gets on my nerves.

There were no cards or letters on the hall table. Nothing ever seemed to come by the second post for me. It was fifty-seven steps up to Kate and my damp, poorly heated room, yet from the outside the house looked grand and rich.

Was ever book containing such vile matter
So fairly bound!

It was, indeed, a lovely Edwardian house, with a dark green door set behind massive white pillars and a brass knocker and an antique bell-pull that didn't work. The Minister of Aviation used to live in luxury next door to us, until he became Foreign Secretary and went to live next door to Harold Wilson. It faced a private, beautifully kept square, where well-bred children with names like Penelope and Sebastian played well-bred games with beautiful au pair girls. There were a few owls in the square too, which Cassy and Rina maintained were actors pretending to be owls. Their toowit-toowooing was too theatrical to be genuine.

Although we lived among the rich and celebrated, everyone at number eighty-four lived in poverty and obscurity except for Kate, who was rich and lazy and comparatively successful. Polly, the landlady, was the poorest and most disorganised of us all. She never paid the bills, so the phone and electricity were cut off once a quarter. As I went to work regularly, I was considered eccentrically hard-working in that household.

Kate stayed in bed all day long, topping up with Mogadons and a sprinkling of Soneryls and Librium capsules; well, actually it couldn't have been quite all day, because while I was out, the rubbish bin in our shared kitchen got filled up with miraculous speed. She was a sort of secret dustbin filler, and of course that was all right with me, provided she emptied it occasionally; but Kate was always in bed or doing a concert rehearsal by the time I got home, to find it spilling over. Today, she'd really done herself proud. The greasy yellow bin was overflowing on to the kitchen floor and it stood in an obscene puddle of wet tea leaves and banana skins.

Dark, strange emotions gripped me for a moment, but I controlled my rage with difficulty, picked up the sodden paper bag with my one arm and descended the fifty-seven steps. You have to go out of the front door, turn right for a few yards and then climb backwards down the rotting wooden area steps to the dustbins. It had to happen, because the bag was already breaking all over me and the thing collapsed right on the pavement – tin cans, old food, the lot. I threw the remainder over the area steps and kicked the worst of it towards next door and took off my coat and shook it out in the street. I must try to keep calm, concentrate on slowing down the hammering pulses; mind over matter; behave with dignity and decorum. I rushed like a madwoman up the everlasting stairs and kicked open Kate's door. She sat up in panic, opening her swollen ping-pong-ball eyes.

'You lazy, good-for-nothing slouch! You vain, untalented humbug! I loathe your disgusting laziness. Your caterwauling makes my blood run cold. You're vile! You'd better find some other fool to share this muck heap with you, because I'm leaving!' She sat up, holding her head, her mouth hanging open, looking satisfactorily ugly, as I slammed the door to.

I rushed down the stairs to Polly's kitchen on the ground floor, banged on the door, and walked in. Polly was sitting on a tall, wooden stool in the middle of the room surrounded by dirty washing and babies, completely engrossed in *Fanny Hill* which I'd lent her.

'Polly, I have something to say to you.' I like Polly and was sorry I was so nasty to her today, and apologised later. 'I want my book back immediately,' I snapped spitefully. Even the screaming twins shut up to listen. 'I am leaving and you're lucky to get notice. The leak in the ceiling has never been attended to, the bed is broken and the rent is exorbitant. That zombie up there makes me sick. I am also sick of looking after your incontinent twins. Also, I am sick, sick, *sick* of putting money in the meter and then having the electricity cut off.' I banged out of her kitchen and leapt up the stairs, two and three at a time to my own. I washed out a dirty cup Kate had left on the draining board, put on the kettle which actually heated up, so the bill must have been paid; stole two spoons of Kate's coffee and selected all the chocolate biscuits from her assortment, leaving all the plain, dull ones. I went into my cold, hateful room to sip my coffee and simmer down, but instead I started to cry. I went on for ages and ages, not knowing why. I thought of Joseph, and was, at once, overwhelmed by more misery.

Polly tapped gently on the door, and I wiped my face quickly and shouted for her to come in. She could tell I'd been crying, because my face looked like a swollen-up turnip. 'Here's a cup of tea for you,' she said timidly.

'Thanks. I'll drink it after I've finished this coffee. You can hang on to the *Fanny Hill* for a bit, and I'm sorry I was rude about the twins, but I am leaving, really, Polly. I'll be buying my own place.' To tell you the truth, I didn't actually know what I was talking about, as all I'd got was three hundred and sixty pounds in the building society, which was left from what I made in the days when I could write stories.

'What have you done to your arm?'

'A boy hit me with a chair and I've got dicks in my hair from that Dettol-smelling dump I go to in the mornings. I'm depressed and at the end of my tether.'

'Have you got the curse?'

'No. I've just finished with it.'

'That's it! Some women suffer terribly with their nerves just afterwards. I mean, the whole of the body's chemistry goes berserk! With me, I go mad ten days before I'm due. Three weeks back, Amy was whining and I just went out of my mind. I bashed her so much I nearly went crazy with guilt afterwards. The doctor gave me some pills for it. Do you want to . . .?'

'No! Just leave off! I'll feel better in the morning.'

Polly went down after a while, because the twins were bawling again and she could hear Cassy and Rina calling to her. 'Coming! Coming!' she trilled. I could hear her clip-clopping down the bare part of the staircase. She was six feet two and always dressed in little black numbers or neat polo-neck sweaters and well-cut black skirts. She wore enormous dark-rimmed spectacles and three-inch-high heels on her huge feet. Her husband, who had a posh job in the Commons, was five feet nine inches. I liked the way Polly made one feel so abnormally undersized.

I finished my coffee and took my cold tea down to the pay phone in the hall as soon as I heard the girls go into the kitchen. Polly was eager to give them the latest bulletin on my activities. I rang my parents' number. Ma answered in her phone voice, which changed directly she heard me. I didn't fancy the cheese flaps any more. She asked me if I'd come over for supper and I told her I'd got a bad arm and I needed my hair washing. She was only too eager to oblige. Then I said, 'How about us buying a house and letting it, and I'll be the landlady and collect rents which could pay off the mortgage.' She thought it sounded like a good idea, and I told her I'd see her later, and rang off.

My mother and father live in the middle of a long road in a small house squashed painfully on either side by identical small houses. It belongs to the synagogue, which like a benign yet ever-watchful landlord surveys our comings and goings from the other side of the road, narrowing his eyes on high days and holy days. I'm the fourth of five children and my brother Orde, still a schoolboy, is the only one at home now. Quite often I go there on Friday night to spend the Sabbath Eve and Day with my parents and brother, the lighted candles and the fish and salad, with a pious visit to our landlord on the Sabbath morn; yet whatever the occasion, whenever I turn the corner of Bolsover Road my pace lightens and quickens, and like one of Pavlov's dogs, I begin to think of food – always apple pie with a little pastry leaf on the top. Delicious, fresh, generously proportioned, fattening, melting apple pie, with the top of the milk falling over it and sitting next to a good cup of tea, and my heart warms in anticipation.

Orde loped along the passage in answer to my knock, and I watched him through the letter box, smoothing his hair in front of the mirror before he graciously allowed me to enter. I could see my mother in the scullery, perched on a short metal stepladder which she claimed, totally falsely, was more comfortable than an armchair, turning over a piece of fish in the wobbly black pan on the gas stove.

When Orde finally opened up, his hair looked exactly the same frizzy mop it was before. I've got a lot in common with him, but you'd never think it, hearing our combined voices, usually raised in unison, yet understanding each other very clearly. My accent is broad East Yorkshire and his is impeccable BBC. He was only seven when my parents moved from Hull to London, but there's nothing hybrid about him now, ten years later.

He put my coat over the bannister. 'Dad said "Ach" when Myrtle told him you were going to buy a house, so he'll be able to blame her if it doesn't work out.'

He always calls Ma Myrtle. It isn't her name but he thinks it suits her. It does. He smiled to himself, for Orde treats our parents as if they were a couple of characters from Dickens, and he is aware of all their little foibles and weaknesses, measuring them up with indulgent but stunning accuracy. Ma shouted hello to me over the noise of the hissing oil, and I shuffled into the living, dining, everything room. Dad was listening to the wireless, which whistles and crackles, but he likes it that way. They don't have a television, but if they had it would flash and star and stripe.

'How's your arm?' he shouted above the din, and Ma came in with a big piece of pie on a blue plate, a cup of tea on a green-flowered saucer and an unopened bottle of gold-top milk, so that I could pour the cream myself, to be going on with until supper. Orde's homework was spread all over the table. He always brings tons of books home to give the totally false impression that he works hard; he's a fraud, and he knows I know, because I was and am exactly the same. I used his physics book as a table mat. The wireless noise was beyond human endurance.

'Why can't you get a new wireless, for heaven's sake, Dad?' My father, with poorly veiled delight, for he is the world's most successful damper of enthusiasm and enjoys practising his art, turned a loose knob, croaking, 'Five minutes ago, it was a new house you wanted.'

Ma came in and forked out her knitting from under a chaotic pile of newspapers and letters. She's knitting a green doll's dress for Malachi, one of her grandsons. Jessie, next door, looked at her askance when Ma told her it was for Malachi, who likes dolls, and not for his sister Miranda, who doesn't. She's never in her life knitted anything for herself.

'Tell us about the house idea!' Orde gave a fond little smirk and Dad the tiniest shadow of a sneer. 'There's money in property these days. You can't go wrong if you buy a decent house in a good area. And you know, Sam, we should start thinking about our retirement. We can't go on for ever. We're nearly sixty, remember.'

'I remember, I remember!' snapped Dad. The sneer got more apparent. 'Who's got money for property? Since when has anyone got money?'

'Amongst all of us, we must have quite a stack. I'll work it out right now.' I pulled a bit of Orde's file paper towards me. One side was covered in fancy signatures of his name – Orde I. Lazarus; I. Lazarus; O.I.L.Y., Israel Lazarus: just plain 'Lazarus' in case he gets into the House of Lords, and bang in the middle, in different writing, 'Smile, if you're wearing pink panties'. I just couldn't prevent my face from cracking in two, before I turned over to the clean side. I wrote: 'Leah Lazarus – four hundred pounds.' I knew I could somehow rake up the odd forty, to make my building society figure look round. Ma looked over my shoulder and jabbed me with the needle-knob.

'We've got a few hundred in Ernie. Write that down.'

'What's a few?'

'One thousand five hundred, isn't it, Sam?'

'What! You've salted away all that money on your lousy wages!' I couldn't get over it! Orde uttered a great shout of amazement, which made us all jump.

'Yes,' said Dad. 'We don't waste our money on unnecessary luxuries like wirelesses and tellies.'

'I've saved all the money I earned at Hilda's,' Ma said, knitting madly. 'We've never gone short these last few years. It was really for going to see the girls, but we put it in Ernie for the time being.' I wrote down: 'Ernie, one thousand five hundred pounds.'

Dad, of course, had absolutely no other money, but eventually he grudgingly admitted to having started a policy for Orde, when he was born, to mature when he was eighteen, to the tune of one thousand pounds. Orde and I were both stricken speechless.

'Well, you know,' said Ma, embarrassed, 'I was nearly forty-three when he was born.' All those present were fully aware of this fact. 'I mean we didn't know whether we'd be around to see him through.'

'I've got eleven hundred in the Halifax, from what we got from the house in Hull, that includes interest.' Dad had actually volunteered information. I wrote down: 'Orde – one thousand pounds. Halifax – eleven hundred pounds.' Things were looking up.

Orde was combing his hair at the mirror over the fireplace. He's six feet three inches, and the mirror is fixed for people of normal height, so he's developed a slight sideways roll from perpetual self-adoration. 'Hey, there's one and six on the mantelpiece! Write that down.'

We all ignored him and Ma shrieked, 'If you would spend one tenth of your hair time in brushing your shoes, digging the garden and doing your homework, you wouldn't get on my nerves so much!' But he knew that she was consumed with interest about buying the house, and accepted her remarks as a sort of habitual twitch that he'd got quite used to.

Ma added up the sum with me. 'Four thousand! Blimey. I didn't know we were so affluent! What have we got in the bank, Sam?'

'Enough to buy fish in Ridley Road and to pay the gas bill,' he growled.

'Put down a total of four thousand two hundred pounds,' said Ma.

'And one and six,' shouted Orde. He's such a bore sometimes.

'No building society, however cracked, will give a five-thousand-pound mortgage for that sum at our age, and on our combined wages, and no decent house costs less than twelve thousand pounds,' Dad croaked joyously. 'And what about furniture, carpets, builders, decorators, curtains? Or are your tenants going to live in bare rooms?'

'What,' I said, 'about squeezing a loan from Auntie Sarah? She's got my dowry stuck away in a teapot somewhere. Why don't we ask her?'

I'll have to tell you about my Auntie Sarah. She lives in Manchester and is married to an extremely wealthy and successful businessman; but Auntie Sarah thinks she's still poor, and has been hoarding up her housekeeping money for thirty-five years, unbeknownst to her husband, who is apparently generous in this respect, and I happen to know that she's got a tidy sum put by. She always buys cheap food and cheap clothes, to the chagrin and fury of my uncle. She is kindly, lovable, irritating and nervous. It's hard not to quarrel with Auntie Sarah but impossible not to be sorry for doing so.

The most maddening quirk in her character is her obsessive desire for every female relative of hers to get married, whatever the cost. Once her own children were married, the focus of her energies was diverted with terrifying strength on her nieces, and the ones who have given her the greatest anxiety are my sisters and I. Two of them got married, in spite of my terrible aunt, and she gave up trying with Trudi after superhuman effort. But when I passed my twenty-sixth birthday and my ring finger remained shamefully naked, Auntie Sarah went into a frenzy of activity. She rang up two Jewish marriage bureaux to tell them about me, and she hawked my name around Manchester as a plain poor spinster whom she would graciously endow with a thousand pounds, if anyone would take pity on me.

I have had screaming, anguished rows with her; I have fled her presence, telling her that I would never speak to her again and that I would never dream of touching a farthing of her lousy money; and then I have turned round to shout the final insult, and seen the dry, untidy grey hair, the chapped, swollen hands, the wrinkled stockings dotted with darns; seen her standing at the door of her magnificent mansion, where she has survived the icy brilliance of her husband. She should have married a simple peasant – she would have been thrifty, happy to have saved a shilling, and she would have found the frugal life rewarding and exciting.

I've often said to my Auntie Sarah, in between quarrels, that if she'd give me the thousand now, I'd really make an effort, and anyway, it would surely be easier to get hold of a husband if I had the money in hand.

'Not a penny!' she shouts, over and over again. 'Not a penny until you're married! Why are you so choosy? Who are you to be so choosy? You're no beauty and you haven't any money – you can't afford to pick and choose! What was wrong with that one you were going out with the end of last year? You didn't like him? Don't be so choosy. He was all right, wasn't he? He hadn't a bad position. You'd get to like him after you married him. Not a penny until you're married!'

But we knew that the only way to buy our house would be through my Auntie Sarah's housekeeping money. We'd have enough capital to get a mortgage.

'You know,' said Ma, 'I'll write to her. She's not a bad sort. Straight after supper, I'll write.'

'Don't be in such a hurry.' Old Happy Harry again, but Ma threw her knitting down and turned on him.

'So when do we buy our house? When the money we've put away is worth twopence halfpenny? Five minutes before we retire?' But we knew it was settled because Dad and Orde were exchanging little smiles, and he was turning the wireless up to hear the news.

'Find the house, then we'll see.'

'Look, if you think I'm tramping around London looking at hundreds of houses just so you can change your mind . . .'

Ma poked me, with the needle point this time, and made a daft face at me, which Dad saw but ignored, although he knew it meant, 'Take no notice of him – he'll come round,' and got up to bring in the supper. 'When you find something worth while, let us know. Leave all the rest to me!' Old Lady Macbeth herself.

Big Ben boomed and scraped and whistled into the living room, and so, on 14 February at nine p.m. precisely, we became People in search of Property, and twenty days and thirty houses later, I found it.

Chapter Two

The first time I saw the house was one hideous day – a cold, harsh, sub-possible day that had jabbed its frost-bitten fingers into March. Thick icy slush covered the pavements. I'd left my gloves at the agent's office, and my hands seemed to freeze to the two rusty keys. Despite the weather and the cold, sad trees, I saw at once what a lovely road it was. The main street, with its smart brash shops, the tube station and the buses, disappeared as you turned the corner, and I felt as if I was walking along a wide country lane, with the houses set back among the trees and gardens, shy of being noticed; but I looked at them all, wondering which was mine. We're in the 1960s back there, up the hill and round the bend, but along this road it's still 1910, and there's no traffic, and only one or two parked cars to tell me where I really am.

I found that I'd walked past number thirteen, because it didn't bear a number on the broken gate. The green paint was faded and dirty and the 'For Sale' sign hid modestly behind an elm tree. The brick path, all wet and weedy, wound strangely between two boggy isosceles triangles of overgrown lawn, but the mauve and orange crocuses peered impudently above the dirty snow like bits of brightly coloured toffee paper littering the grass. The gate banged behind me and the next-door curtain gave a nervous twitch. You'd never believe that such a big, rusty key could turn a lock, but they seemed like old friends, and there wasn't any grumbling or fighting to have the door open.

The air inside struck so cold that I caught my breath with the shock of it and wound my scarf over my ears. How dirty and drab and silent it was! I stamped around uneasily in the hall for a little while to tell the ghosts in friendly fashion that I was here, and perhaps they'd grant me the courtesy of a private visit. The parquet floor was thick with dust and the panelled walls were sombre and covered with cheap, cracked paper; but I could see the hall with that fire in the corner glowing on copper pots and on soft, mysterious panels and bright rugs lying on the glossy, honey-coloured floor. A dark red carpet had been left on the stairs, leading up into unknown regions, as if once used by a bygone royal person, long since dethroned and forgotten, but it was waiting for me to place my icy feet on its dusty face.

I pushed open the door to my left. The ghosts had nowhere to hide, so they lingered in the corners, hidden by the early darkness. Great ugly flowers, blue and faded pink, decorated the walls, the floorboards were broken and rough, but a beautiful window covered one wall and I knew right away that this room was going to be mine. It faced east, and if the sun ever shines again, it will stream through all morning. The other door off the hall led into a huge funereal room, the panelled walls covered in thick brown paper, but the magnificent French windows looked out on to rough green lawns and wild swaying trees. I examined the kitchen, the maid's bell still intact; the little cloakroom, the sordid scullery; then I ran up the lovely red stairs into the gloomy regions above. Darkness was falling and I wanted to know everything today. The four bedrooms were dreary, cold and grim but beautifully proportioned. Everything was brown and I wondered for a minute about the paranoid people who once lived here.

I had promised to drop the keys in at the agent's; he'd told me the office closed at five thirty. I shot down the stairs, took a second look at my room and closed the front door behind me. It felt warm and light outside, compared with the chill darkness within, and my frozen blood tingled and moved again. I started to run up the hill. Perhaps if I hurried, I'd get back to the office before someone pinched my gloves and my fingers dropped off. But if I hung on to the keys, no one else would see my house and get interested in buying it. They were bound to have duplicates though. I leaned against a hedge for a moment, wondering what to do, then I dashed back to the house, let myself in and went into my room. I wrote SOLD on the whitewashed window in huge mirror letters. Perhaps that would help to nonplus prospective buyers in spite of the 'For Sale' sign, and who knows – maybe we would be the only people to turn up for the auction on 15 March!

I could hardly wait to ring my folks. I flew up the road, across the main, homeward-bound traffic and into the phone booth on the concourse, where all the different bus routes wind up. So many bus routes – so handy for the tube and the Green Line buses too! Even a row of telephone boxes which don't seem to be vandalised.

'I've found the house, Ma!' I shouted down the phone; 'the very house; the one on the list that's due to be auctioned. I told the agent that you and Dad would come tomorrow afternoon, to see.' I described it to her, extravagantly sticking in another sixpence. I felt so excited.

Ma kept saying, 'Goody, goody! It sounds just right. We'll be there.'

'Listen. I sent those stories to Carol Smith. The ones you liked. If she sells them to America, we can buy carpets and furniture and we'll work on Auntie Sarah a bit more. Maybe we'll get that mortgage and it's such a good area, we can charge high rents!'

'Yes,' she said eagerly, 'we'll certainly do that!' There was something wrong; a note in her voice, false; off-key. I could hear the anxiety, the lost hopes, the lightly veiled pretence.

'Are you going out tonight?' she asked brightly.

'Yes.'

'Anyone nice?' Don't say that. Don't be like Auntie Sarah. Don't sling that rotten apple at me.

'Just to the pictures. Probably with Cassy and Rina. There's a season of Celia Johnson at the Classic. We're going to wallow in *Brief Encounter.*'

'Oh. Enjoy it. Have a good time.' I could hear the disappointment in her voice. The house didn't matter to her that much, and even though I was happy about it, she wanted me to be happy in the way she felt I should be.

'Don't shout; don't get cross, but you're not still thinking . . .'

'No, I'm not. Leave me alone, for God's sake. I'm not thinking about anybody. Just because I'm going to a flick with . . .'

'Don't get mad.'

'I'm not mad.'

'Have a lovely time. Enjoy yourself.'

I hadn't got anything to read for the bus journey back to Notting Hill Gate. The girl at the estate agent's denied any knowledge of my gloves and the circulation in my fingertips had come to a complete halt. I made a muff with my long scarf. I'd think about the house, how I'll arrange it; where we'll put the upstairs kitchen; but all I did was think about Joseph. He pushed his way into my thoughts, greedy for possession, suffocating me, stopping the flow of oxygen to my lungs, so that I had to gasp like an asthmatic in a thick fog.

'Let's be sensible,' he'd said. 'We've had wonderful times and been good friends, but I think we should stop seeing each other. You're getting too fond of me; you've put all your eggs in one basket.' He actually tittered at the double innuendo of his last words.

I was living with my parents at the time, teaching at a terrible school in Tottenham, cycling there every day, unable to keep discipline, ineffectual, immature; wondering why all the other members of staff were so much more capable than I, wishing I had that elusive talent. But I was gay, careless, because I'd be spending almost every evening with Joseph, and the daily drag hardly touched me.

It was the Easter holidays and the Passover, a word that meant at that time that all light and joy had passed over me. I'd be sensible; tough; look around. I didn't leave the house for that three weeks' holiday, in case he rang. Sometimes, in the early hours, I'd creep downstairs, my face blotched and swollen and my head throbbing with pain, ranting and praying. 'God, please make him phone. I'll count to a thousand, concentrating all the time, and when I've finished the telephone will ring.' But it didn't, and when I rang him, which I did with awful regularity, his flatmate Eugene would answer and say Joseph was out. I wrote, but he didn't get my letters.

Yankel, my uncle and friend, came to see us. We went to a party together and I got drunk and maudlin. He took me home and we walked together through the pitch-black, silent streets. The dustbins were standing out on the pavement, because tomorrow was dustbin day.

Yankel said, 'When I was a little boy, my mother used to wrap up fish-heads in newspaper, and all sorts of other horrible rubbish, and she'd give us these little parcels and make us go out and distribute them, because we only had a tiny bin; so we'd put a fish-head on a wall and potato peelings over a hedge, and then scurry away very quickly. If only I'd known then about people putting the bins out for the morning collection.'

I sat down on the nearest dustbin, laughing, holding my chest so as not to shake too much and make the lid rattle, and then I burst into tears and told him about Joseph and the letters and the phone calls, because I felt like an old fish-head left behind a wall. We sat there for hours, talking over everything, and I finally promised never to get in touch with Joseph again.

The next day I wrote to Joseph, and telephoned some seven times during the following week. I gave in my notice at school, collected my superannuation and went to New York. I sent him a funny card on the day of my arrival and he announced his engagement in the *Jewish Chronicle.*

His fiancée was a girl with whom I went to school; she was in the fifth form when I was in the second, and I got to know her because she was always late, like me, and we used to run down the drive together. It seems he liked provincial, unpunctual types. She was clever, dull, uninspired and a slow runner. My family didn't tell me but Eugene wrote a short letter to me and sent me the cutting from the paper.

I sat in the little room in Brooklyn and watched the people chatting to each other in canvas chairs on the street, and boys and girls sitting on the parked cars, laughing and calling to one another; the kids playing on the hot steps. I walked to Washington Square and read *Washington Square* and ate a jam sandwich, thinking of the jilted Miss Sloper and me.

I worked in an office in Fulton Street. I hated it and couldn't make friends.

I used to stare at the big, frosted glass doors leading out on to the street, waiting for his reflection to appear behind it. I found out that he was getting married on 10 July. On 4 July, Independence Day, we all had the day off, so I went to Coney Island to swim and read. I went on my own, although Henry, a sweet and good Hungarian, totally alone, had asked me to spend the day with him. A stranger came over to me as I lay on my towel on the beach; a rough, stupid man, whose name I knew afterwards. I think of that day with shame and horror.

I went to a five-dollar doctor because I had difficulty in swallowing and couldn't sleep. 'Nerves!' he shouted at me. 'That's what's the matter. Go home. You're not happy here. Go home to Europe!'

'Doctor Jacobson, give me some pills! Just to get me over the next few days. After, I'll save up and go back to England.'

'How long will it take you to get the money to go home?'

'I don't know. My wages aren't much and I have to pay the

rent and fares and food. But I'll try to save something every week if you'll give me some pills meanwhile.'

'I'll give you a prescription on condition you write home for your fare money. Your papa will send it to you. Come to me after a week when the pills are finished.'

I wrote to Ma and Dad to ask them to lend me the fare money. The pills worked. I don't know what they were, but a sponge, soft and thick, covered my agonising jealousy and at seven o'clock on 10 July I thought, 'It's midnight in England. Their wedding night.' The sponge dried up and slipped away; no buffer protected me and I panicked. I rang Henry, faithful, kind Henry. He was out. I poured myself half a beaker of gin from the bottle I had bought to offer to friends. I drowned it in ice cubes and water and it took me about half an hour to get it down my throat. I accompanied the final swallow with my last three pills, just to sleep for the next twelve hours or so. But I wasn't accustomed to such a cocktail. I woke up in the dark quiet heat, felt my way blindly to the toilet then had a drink of water and got back into bed. The next thing I saw was the sun streaming through the window and Gina, my landlady, standing over me fearfully, shrieking my name, shaking me, waving a telegram; thinking I was dead.

'Sweetie pie, what the hell! Where've you been, for God's sake? I had such a fright. The wire's been on the table for two days already. I thought you'd gone away!'

'What time is it?'

'Quarter after seven. Two days I haven't seen you! Two days the wire's been laying!'

'I've been sleeping,' I smiled. 'Gimme the telegram. I feel so good, so refreshed.'

'Henry's been calling you; I thought you were out or away!'

'Gina, what's the matter with you? I went to bed early, that's all. What's the crime in that? I'll be on time for work for a change.'

'It's a quarter after seven AT NIGHT!' she bawled. 'See the

sun? It's turning into the moon! You've gone crazy! Haven't you been at work?'

I fumbled with the telegram. 'What day is it? Monday?'

'I been hollering WEDNESDAY at you for the last hour. Wednesday NIGHT! Here, I've got the coffee on. I'll bring you a cup.'

I sat up and read the telegram as Gina came back with two steaming cups and sat on the bed. I felt like kissing her.

'My dad's sending off money for my ticket home. I'm not going back to that bloody job any more. I'm leaving, Gina. I'm going back home. I want to go home.' I swallowed the coffee. I felt wonderful, revived.

'I'll kind of miss you,' she said. I saw that she was crying. I jumped up on my knees and hugged her.

'Let's have Henry over for dinner; and look after him after I go. Everything'll turn out okay. You'll see.'

Everything did – for Gina and Henry, anyway! Gina's little daughter has a father now; Henry has a lovely wife and family; and the last time I heard from them, they were hoping for twins. I'm just about the world's best matchmaker. I'll swear that Joseph cottoned on to that pie-faced Marjorie because she came from my school, my town, and he had something to gab about in order to get to know her. It's two years already. Why do I still miss him? If he was dead it would finalise things; I'd make a clean start. And if she was dead, I'd probably don my hunting cap again and have another shot at dragging him back to my side.

The new telephone books came out last week and I checked up. He's alive and kicking all right, in some posh house in Totteridge, not giving a damn about me. I rang the number, and I let her say 'Hello' three times before I put the phone down. With enormous effort I wrenched my thoughts back to my house, and wondered whether Ma and Dad would like it as much as I did.

It turned out that they were very enthusiastic, especially Dad, amazingly enough, who fell in love with the vile brown wallpaper. He griped a bit about the garden, and how much it would cost to get it in order, but he was absolutely sold on the idea of bidding for it at the auction. Ma, of course, was delighted with it, and decided there and then to have Orde down every Sunday and holiday to weed and dig. Dad said he'd arrange for a surveyor and everything, and told the agent that he was interested.

I told the kids on Nightingale all about the house and what it was like inside. They all got busy drawing it with their coloured felt-tipped pens. I asked them what sort of furniture we were going to need, and we made a fairly comprehensive pictorial inventory. Bernadette was back in her cot.

Staff Nurse brought me a rubber square for my lap and carried Bernadette over to me wrapped in a warm, winceyette sheet. 'Oh, ooh, Teacher! Bernadette's ready for her long-division lesson! But I don't want her catching nits or bad language from you.' With great gentleness, she placed the child on my knee, then leaned over the kids to see what they were doing. 'Hey, how much do you pay the Education Authority for letting you come here?'

'Staff, would you kindly get back to the sluice where you belong!'

She gave Bernadette a little kiss and went over to Tara and Dawn. 'You'll have to excuse your two star pupils, Teacher. It's time for Sunshine. Look after Bern till I get back, will you?' She took the two children by the hand. The Sunshine Room is a euphemism for deep radium therapy, which makes them both vomit for several hours afterwards.

'Teacher,' Dawn called, 'will you let us come to see your house when it's got new paper and furniture? Will we come to tea, and I'll sit on the orange and yellow armchair I've drawn?' Tara giggled and sighed with pleasurable anticipation.

'You'll be my very first guests. We'll have Tizer and Walnut Whips and cream cakes in the room with the flowery wallpaper that has been designed here, and Dawn will be sitting on her beautiful chair. That's a promise.' The lie sticks in my throat. The radium treatment is a sick joke. They told me the other day that Tara only has a few months left and Dawn might last until the autumn if she's lucky. My two little girls. All the kids were happily engrossed with their drawings and Patrick's tongue was practically licking the paper in total concentration.

I cuddled Bernadette. She's a favourite with us all. Most of her hair has fallen out, but there are tufts of it growing in little patches on her otherwise bald head. Her few teeth are crumbled and discoloured and her nose is broken. Her arms and legs are skinny and wasted and her body is round and swollen. She can't speak or sit up. She's five, and was found three months ago in a small, dark cellar where she'd spent her life, starved and filthy; reviled by her middle-class parents, who lived on the ground and upper floors of the house in comfort and ease. Staff Nurse took the day off work to attend their trial and told me all about it. The nurses and children on the ward have taught Bernadette to like cuddles and kisses, smiles and kind words.

I was soon ready to leave, but Mr and Mrs Randall, Tara's parents, came into the ward, and I was forced to sit down again, and chat and face their unbearable grief. I showed them her books, and all the stories and poems she'd written, and the drawings she did today. 'Could we have the books when . . .'

'Of course. As soon as they're full.' I interrupted quickly. 'She's so clever, so promising . . .' I was saying the wrong things. I always do. I got away as fast as I could and nipped over to the plug-in phone to ring up old Violet at Beechwood to tell her I was too poorly to come in that afternoon. She knew I was lying, so I didn't try anything elaborate. I was going to have lunch with Cassy and Rina before meeting Dad at the auction room.

Cassy reminded me of Joyce Grenfell, one of my favourite

actresses. She's a marvellous mimic. Every time she sees me, she lapses into a Yorkshire accent and swears she can't help it. She changes physically when she takes someone off, and I got quite a shock, the first time I met her at a party, when she was doing her drama teacher that was, whom Cassy claims was a lesbian with a crush on Cassy. Cassy was hunch-backed, her legs spindly and strangely spaced, her voice deep and manly; it was incredible. I thought and still think she's one of the best comedy actresses I've ever seen. If she gets something on telly, it's an on and off job, like a maid or an old fogey, who pegs out in Part One of a soap opera.

Rina is tall and red-haired and strikingly attractive, and enviably experienced with men. Cassy and I have often spent hours listening to her exploits, amorous and otherwise. She maintains that ninety per cent of actors are camp, and it's virtually impossible to meet a prospective husband in the theatre. When Rina laughs, everyone turns round to stare or scream with fright. She's had two West End runs but they've never gone on for long. Quite recently she landed a part in a twenty-six-episode serial on ITV. She'll be able to buy a new blouse and give their flat a face lift, since Polly will never do it.

They both felt sad about me leaving Coventry Square, and I felt downcast too, because the closeness and quality of our friendship is bound to change. We're like inseparable chums of Miss Hamilton's School for Young Ladies, by Angela Brazil, being put into separate dorms. Love and loyalty win through, however. We drank too much and laughed too loudly and we talked about Kate with gusto and malice, topping each other's stories with something even more horrific. At last it was time to go to the agent's, where the auction was supposed to take place. Cassy suddenly reminded me that it was the Ides of March, and the three of us trampled off to the bus stop, doing *Julius Caesar*:

O! That a man might know
The end of this day's business, ere it come;
But it sufficeth that the day will end,
And then the end is known.

They screeched 'Beware' at me and the conductor as I sailed off to my rendezvous with Dad and the auctioneer. Strange things seemed to be happening to the weather this year. The snow was still ankle-deep and it was freezing cold. With luck, we'll be up to our waists in it in mid-August, and could be, we'll be sunbathing in our bikinis in November.

I was so petrified as I got off at the auction rooms, I didn't know whether I was shaking more with fear or with cold. Dad was standing in the porch, as if scared to go in by himself, and his ears were peeping purple from under his big black hat and his hands and wrists were blue, the fingertips dipped into his pockets. We went in together; into the large warm room. We both gasped with horror when we saw that the place was crowded to capacity. All these people wanted our house.

'Dad, it's hopeless. We'll never outbid this lot. Nine thousand's our limit. We might as well give up and go home.'

'Maybe there's a few houses to be auctioned today.'

I made enquiries at a desk at the top of the room and the girl said, no. Just number thirteen.

The auctioneer will be here in five minutes. I've got to go to the loo. Whenever I'm shocked, afraid or freezing, the first and most urgent thing I need before sweet tea, tranquillisers or a fire, is a ladies' convenience. I asked her.

'Over there, in the station.'

'I can't make it.'

'Sorry, there's no other place nearer.'

'Do you go over there?'

'We've got staff offices, of course.'

What a bitch; what a prize cow. I could last another thirty

seconds. She was probably scared she'd have to mop the floor. With extremely bad grace, she showed me up some dark narrow stairs, and stood outside in case I pinched the piece of soap on the sink.

By the time I had come downstairs, the auctioneer was standing at the table, and Dad was clamped between a couple of fat dames, but he'd managed to save a chair behind him for me. I slipped into it, and he turned round to give me a smile and to say, 'We'll never get it.' Obviously, he was back on his usual keel.

The auctioneer stood up and in a gabble told us about the property and the executors of the late Misses Maffin. Suddenly, I thought of something, and poked Dad in the back. 'Who's bidding, you or me?'

'Both of us. Don't go over nine. We'll take it in turns. Shush.'

The auctioneer started off at seven, and Dad shouted out before the other hundred people knew what'd hit them. 'Seven, five hundred!'

The auctioneer said, 'Seven, five offered.'

Before he finished, Dad bawled, 'Eight thousand!' I'm going to die. He's outbidding himself; he doesn't know what he's doing; he's gone mad. I'm sorry for all the wasted time, Mr Auctioneer. My father hasn't got fifty thousand pounds. The balance of his mind is disturbed. I'll get him to hospital at once.

He turned round to me. 'Bid!' he whispered, desperately, 'BID!'

'Dad, don't say a word. Just keep QUIET!' Everyone was staring at us.

A woman said, 'Eight, two.'

Before Dad could open his trap, I shouted 'Eight, three.'

Dad outbid me. 'Eight, five.' He's throwing his own money away. Not another soul except the woman and us has said a word, and she's obviously given up. If only he'll shut up, we've got it.

The auctioneer's talking, lifting his hammer, 'Going...'

A little chap in big glasses jumped off a table in the corner and squeaked, 'Nine thousand!' Everything seemed to sag inside me, a hush fell over the room and a strange tension gripped the atmosphere. We couldn't go beyond that figure.

But Dad was off his head. His voice cracked, sad, foreign, desperate. 'Nine, one.'

'Nine, three' trilled the goggly man.

'Nine thousand, four hundred pounds.' Dad spoke the words softly, precisely and with authority and finality.

'Let him have it,' sneered Goggles.

The hammer came down with a loud 'GONE. Mr Lazarus, would you like to come over to the office, please?'

I felt dreadfully ill, and had all the symptoms of an approaching seizure. But for that little man, and Dad outbidding me and himself, we could have saved hundreds of pounds. The woman next to me was talking to me, asking if I was with 'that gentleman', letting me know that we're a couple of fools, unused to the business of house-buying.

'Why is it that there are so many people here, and yet hardly anyone bid for the house?'

She smiled at me condescendingly. 'They're only here to watch! They come here for entertainment and to get out of the cold. Did you really think...?' I really disliked this woman and wished that I'd never allowed the conversation to develop.

'And the little man who bid against the gentleman you're with. He's here practically every time a property is auctioned.' She leaned against me, lowering her voice to a confidential whisper.

'They say he earns fifty pounds a time, to get the price up.'

Dad came over, smiling. 'Well, we've got the house, now we've got to get the money.' He was happy and confident, and I felt cheated and miserable. I could have shaken him for showing what a greenhorn he was. But it was nice to see him grinning. I won't tell him about Goggles.

'Mazeltov! Well done!' We shook hands. 'And now for Auntie Sarah!'

The next two months were spent in a frantic shopping spree, while three workmen – Arthur, Pat and Davis – put slates on the roof, moved sinks and baths and pipes, mended floors and plastered walls and painted and papered. We scoured Articles for Sale in the local papers, crossing items off our mammoth list as we bought them and watched them mounting up in the hallway of our new house. We bought the gas fires and fridges on HP and the stoves secondhand.

One boiling hot day, Ma and I went to Shoreditch together, to a warehouse owned by a man who knew my father. We oiled and oozed our way around the wardrobes, chests, bookcases, coffee tables and chairs, laughing loudly at his unwholesome jokes, making round eyes and mouths at his unabashed praise of himself as a self-made man and his shameless worship of his creator. We bought everything we needed there and sat listening as he totted up the figures, telling us how enormously generous he was and how cheaply we were coming out of the deal. We left, with smiles of adulation still pinned to our faces. It's amazing what depths one sinks to, for the sake of a few pounds, but by the time we'd walked to the bus stop at Shoreditch Church, the perspiration rolling down our necks, the contemptible Mr Frisby had disappeared into the heat mist. We had spent every penny of my new story money and most of Ma's savings.

With the little money left, we went to Manchester to visit an old friend who had plenty to do with divan beds, carpets and curtains, and we stayed over at my Auntie Sarah's, remembering that we had to pay Arthur and his mates. I hardly discussed my course of action with Ma, but we both knew what it must be and I tackled Auntie Sarah right away. It worked, and home we went with fifteen hundred pounds and a receipt for all the things we had ordered and paid for at Cyril's.

The fifteen hundred pounds were in exchange for my freedom. I had promised, solemnly, and with no hesitation, that if I was not at least engaged to be married within one year, I was bound to pay her every penny back, or meet and go out with any man she produced for me, marriage bureaux clients and others. Even if I disliked them on sight, I had to give each one a chance to see what might develop. I felt Auntie Sarah's contempt for me, as we made our pact, but there was too much at stake for me to make a proud gesture. Somehow, I would pay her that money back; write a best-selling novel; play roulette; make a fortune on the house. She would get her pounds, but not of flesh; not at the expense of my soul and dignity.

And yet, as Ma and I sat on the London-bound train, with the table between us and the money stuck down my tights in case of train robbers, making notes and adding up figures, I felt an immense burden come to rest on me. I put my head down on the table and huddled my shoulders, aching under its strangely physical weight. I despaired of us ever getting the house in order, let alone making a profit on it. Twenty years to pay. TWENTY YEARS. Me almost fifty, they eighty. Twenty years of non-stop payments and the non-stop weight on my back. I thought of a tortoise carrying his house along through his slow and ancient life – wherever he goes, whatever he does, he's got to drag it along, foundations and all. That's me. I've bought myself a bondage to last for years and years, and have played into my Auntie Sarah's hands.

Luckily, I had several cousins who were lawyers, all of whom had been obliged in the past to offer their services free to their impoverished relatives. Pity that a couple of them didn't take up painting and decorating, because we could have saved on that. Isaac, who lived round the corner from our new house, was the cousin selected for all the legal work involved. On one of our many visits to the house, he asked us to pop in and see him.

'Auntie, please God may it not be for one hundred and

twenty years, but at the end of that period, what . . .?'

For a moment, we didn't know what he was talking about, then Ma giggled and said briskly, 'When we're dead, the house will belong to all our five children – no, perhaps just the ones who are single when Uncle Sam and I go.'

That meant me. Why didn't Joseph marry me? I would have lived in a sandcastle on the edge of the ocean with him. One day I'd get over him and start looking around again, but by then I'd be a middle-aged woman with no hope of issue; and anyway, who'd want *me*? I'm no spring chicken as it is.

Each Sunday, and on most evenings during the week, we worked at the new house, cleaning the rooms, tidying the garden and setting down the carpets and furniture. The electricity, water and telephone box had all been laid on, and on the final Sunday, Rina and Cassy turned up at lunch-time with cider and sandwiches, and Mavis, my friend from Manchester College days, went to and fro in her van, bringing my stuff from Coventry Square. We drank toasts in each room, and in the evening when all was ready, we worked out our advertisement for the next day's *Evening Standard*. Anyone coming to see our rooms would find it difficult not to gasp with pleasure at the two doubles and three singles and the shining bathrooms and kitchens smelling of fresh paint and disinfectant.

Mave squashed Ma, Dad, Orde, Cassy and Rina into her van and I waved to them as they jerked along, up the road, away from me. I'd no curtains up at my windows yet, but they were whitewashed and no one could see through, yet I felt exposed, scared, strange. I took two sheets from the cupboard, and tied them to a couple of hooks, and then started to put away the mountains of books and clothes that filled all my floor space. This was my home from now on. I worked for two hours, stalked about the house for a bit, wishing that someone was here with me, set my alarm and took myself to bed with a big green apple and *Compulsion* by Meyer Levin, which I read compulsively until an hour before the alarm rang for me to rise.

No matter how horrible my day turns out to be, I reckon that the very worst moment is when my little clock jangles into my dreams, wrecking my nerves and causing my heart to lurch into an assault in my chest. When you've only had an hour's sleep, and you've got a grim day ahead, you don't feel all that healthy as you swim to the surface. I've been under the impression for quite a long time that I've got a weak heart, and every morning, that alarm bell makes it a little more delicate. I always feel lousy in the mornings, anyway; it's because I've got extremely low blood pressure which makes me shaky and weak for an hour and a half after rising. Not for me a refreshing cup of tea and a leisurely adjustment to the day. I can't see. Apart from the fact that my eyes are tight and stinging with weariness, I have to force them open to jab in my contact lenses, which always seem to contain dust and fluff, no matter how clean I keep them, and the pain and discomfort set my eyes pouring with water. I always look terrible in the morning. Terrible. I've never seen anyone who looks worse than me, either straight after I've stuck in my lenses, or when I'm wearing a swimming cap. When I managed to focus, I felt pleased at the sight of my lovely room and crawled out of bed to put the kettle on and turn on the bath tap. In thirty minutes I'd dressed, was slapping on my Oil of Ulay and drinking my third cup of coffee.

Arthur and Pat arrived as I was leaving, to finish the tiles on the roof. They just had time to tell me that Davis was in Moorfield's Eye Hospital, due to some plaster that flew into his eye and he may lose his sight. They tell me this dreadful news accusingly, as if it's my fault, because it's my house where it happened. My new telephone box is near the door and I stopped on my way out to ring up the hospital to ask how he was. If you open the front door, you can actually stand outside and chat, or sit on the steps and watch people going past.

As I waited to get through to the ward, Pat passed my door,

not horizontally, but vertically, head first, from the roof. He landed on the triangle of grass and lay there. I banged the phone down, screamed for Arthur and telephoned 999 for an ambulance. Pat is dead, I know he is. We should never have bought this house. It has a green door and is numbered thirteen. Davis blind and Pat dead.

Pat was conscious and groaning. His hair was soaked with perspiration and his arms were twisted into a curious angle. I brought out a cushion for his head and left him to Arthur while I prepared hot sweet tea. I remembered a miniature bottle of brandy too, and swilled the two drinks shakily down Pat's throat. Not a soul had passed by since the accident, but as soon as the ambulance stopped at the gate, the street filled up. A district nurse appeared at the door of number eleven, to give the lady there her insulin injection, just as the ambulance bore Pat away.

I told her everything that happened and how I wish she'd come ten minutes earlier. She told me that I shouldn't have given the patient tea or brandy, and that if he has to have an operation, he'll have to wait for five hours. I've never heard of such nonsense. Arthur told me that Pat would not be able to claim for his accident as he didn't have safety ropes on his ladder and he fell because the ladder slipped. I left him in the house, swigging the rest of the brandy to get over the shock, insinuating that I'd now got Pat on my conscience as well as Davis. He said he'd finish the roof on his own. Everything's going to be all right. Davis is in the best eye hospital in the world, and after all the plaster only went in one eye; Pat is alive, albeit his arms are probably broken. We've got the mortgage, after arranging one or two adjustments in our weekly earnings, and although we haven't got permission to let, no one's going to start prowling around to spy on us. No one, not even Arthur and the district nurse, can put the dampers on me.

I tottered off to the bus stop, late, still shaky, dreadfully depressed. It would take me twenty minutes longer to get to the hospital.

Sister called me into the office, looking obtrusively at her watch, to tell me that she's noticed how late I am. 'Tara has gone,' she said.

'Home already!' She must be very near the end. When there's nothing more to be done, the parents take the child home for the last six weeks or so. 'I must take her books over – I promised Mrs Randall and I'd like to see Tara again to say "goodbye".'

Sister looked at me queerly, almost gloatingly. She had a big white face and small dark eyes, and at that moment I could see little sparks of pleasure dancing in the centres. She stood up, dismissing me, so I stood too. 'By "gone", Miss Lazarus, I don't mean "gone home", I mean dead. Yesterday.'

'No, not Tara! Not yet! Oh, no, don't say that!'

'Come, come. Pull yourself together. You knew quite well that we expected it. There's no need for any sort of performance; it's unnecessary.' She's trying to tell me that I'm acting, that I'm going hot and cold for her benefit; that I'm affecting horror and grief and loss.

'You big, fat, smooth-tongued, lying bitch! I've seen how you carry on in this ward, bullying the nurses and not letting the parents in, when visiting is supposed to be unrestricted. I've seen you make the Randalls sit in the corridor, waiting and waiting, while you give rein to your power-mad aberrations. You scare the kids and smile at the big shots, and treat me as if I'm scum. I'm going to report you to the authorities!'

She came towards me, her face whiter than ever, and there was a muscle twitching at the corner of her eyelid. 'Leave this office. At once! You will not enter my ward. We can do without your so-called teaching in here. You ARE scum, and I am informing the Education Department of this, and of your impertinence. Get out.'

I sat down again in the chair, and stretched out my trembling legs, watching the hate on her stupid face. 'You have no authority to sack me; I am not your employee.'

She marched out, probably to call someone to remove me by force. I fumbled in my bag for the Randalls' number and called them on the office telephone, cool as a cucumber.

'Is that you, Mr Randall? Sister told me. I'm so sorry; so very, very sorry. May I come and see you both? I'll bring the books. Please convey my condolences to your wife. She was such an adorable little girl. I loved her very much.'

He was crying hard and loud from his throat. I put the phone down and ran out of the hospital before anyone could come to annoy me. I knew that I would never return to this hospital or see the children again. I wondered if I'd have to hand in my resignation, and decided to go to County Hall to explain myself to the Department.

I stopped on the curve of Westminster Bridge, as I always did when my journey took me there. Maybe I was trying to prove to Wordsworth that I'd got a shining soul, but it helped me to calm myself and I leaned over the side, gazing at the dear old, dirty river, listening to the birds and the traffic and the sad chimes of Big Ben, tolling a knell for Tara.

Miss Sanderson, who ran Home and Hospital Tuition, had already had a telephone report from Sister, and had obviously informed the rest of the Department, because an ominous stillness enveloped the huge office as I walked in. Yes, I did call her names. Yes, I did know Tara was dying. Yes, I do make a noise on the ward. Yes, I do agree that it would be unwise for me to continue at the hospital. Yes, I also think it would be quite unnecessary to apologise to Sister. Yes, I would like another job, but not with mortally ill children.

'There's Muriel Towey. Here's the file. Is Hackney okay for you? She's twelve, and five or six months pregnant. She's a very sweet child, but rather backward, and her home conditions are appalling, but you'll be able to cope. Her last school was

Quiller's and we'd like you to make a visit to her teacher and headmaster, who will be very helpful. Muriel says she was raped by a man who gave her a lift in a car, but medical evidence seems to denote that sexual relations have been going on long before she started menstruation. In fact, she's never had a period, and that's why it wasn't known she was pregnant until two weeks ago. The welfare officer thinks it's the father, Muriel's father, who's responsible. Perhaps you could gain her confidence and find out. The police would be very interested to know. Do you think you could manage to take her on?'

'Make it for a week's time. I've got a lot on my plate just now. Is there anything you want me to do about Nightingale Ward? I don't want Sister to get the needle for the next teacher, just because of me.'

'Don't worry about that! She doesn't sound a very charming character, and although we didn't think it wise to tell you before, she's been complaining continually about you. However, we don't take the slightest notice of her criticisms regarding your teaching. Our inspectors have always had the highest opinion of your work, and we prefer to listen to them. We value your services, but you must try not to take it too hard about Tara. Her parents have known for years that she couldn't live, and we gave you Nightingale because we know how much these children need a person like you.'

Antithenes recommended his children, 'never to regard with gratitude or favour the man who praised them', but I've always found that a very hard line to take. Miss Sanderson's a good old stick. I reminded her that Jack was due to be discharged from Beechwood fairly soon, and she promised me an 'easy' as soon as I was through with him, but I knew she'd sort out the most difficult teaching jobs possible, because you don't get flattered for nothing in this joint.

I didn't feel like work that afternoon, so I spun a good yarn to Violet about severe stabbing pains in my chest, then wended my new way homewards to flick a duster over the spotless furniture, arranged so sweetly in the shining, sunny rooms, check my advertisement in the paper and await the hour of four and the stream of calls which would surely follow.

Chapter Three

The telephone rang twice during the next four hours. The first caller was Pat, telling me that both his arms were fractured, but he was having to wait for his operation because of the tea and brandy I'd given him. If anyone came to ask whether he'd had safety ropes on the ladder I should say 'Yes'. Cassy and Rina called a few minutes later asking whether I'd let all the rooms. After that, I swallowed a dented Valium capsule that I'd stolen from Kate several months ago, and sat wringing my hands until the ringing of the telephone took over.

'No, I have no objection to coloured people. Yes, the rooms are rather expensive, but wait till you see them.' For three hours the phone rang almost non-stop and I oozed charm and gave out all the information like an old cracked gramophone record.

Mandy was the first to appear on the step. She'd come from Leicester and had started work in a local bowling alley. She seemed quiet and shy and thin and sad, despite the brave, brassy-blonde over-dressed hair, shouting garishly around her closed, secret face. She chose the cheapest room, the small bed-sitter upstairs, and gave me the deposit in exchange for the keys and a little green rent book wherein I entered all the details with excessive care and neatness. She told me that she was staying with friends, locally, and would be bringing her things tomorrow.

As I showed her out, a couple came up the path – a couple of outstanding beauty. She was small and almost white, wearing a cornflower-blue sari. Her eyes, dark and wonderful, took up half her perfect face. Her husband was tall, slim and immaculately dressed and the handsomest man I had ever seen. His teeth shone in a phosphorescent smile against his black face, and his hair lay long and blue-black against his magnificent head.

'Miss Lazarus? My name is Jayatissa. This is my wife. We telephoned a little while ago. We are interested in a double room.'

'Yes. I remember.' I couldn't stop goggling. 'Please look around and take your time. The two doubles are both vacant and the same price. Would you excuse me? There's someone at the door.'

By the following evening, all the rooms were taken. Upstairs was Mandy, and the other single was taken by Dinah, a medical student from a village in Yorkshire, who brought all her luggage in big white pillowcases, aided by an army of boyfriends and giggles, great wheezes and howls of mirth as they struggled up the stairs like a miniature exodus with the endless bundles.

The large room next to mine became occupied by my beautiful couple, Ranjini and Sarath, and the upstairs double was taken over by a remarkably plain, sour-looking, middle-aged German Jew. He drove up in a large white Citroën and spoke in an unpleasant clipped accent. He gave his name as Rosenfeld M., together with a very generous deposit. He never smiled or told me where he worked and I didn't have the nerve to ask him. That he said no one would be sharing with him, and that I had six weeks' rent in advance, was sufficient attraction. He then disappeared for two weeks during which time I used his room to park a few of my things. An ideal tenant, but I was glad he wasn't sharing my kitchen.

I rang Ma and Dad to tell them that we'd let all the rooms, and on Friday night I arrived at Bolsover Road with my old plastic handbag full of pound notes. Ma was the book-keeper and Dad the banker, and she bought two large maroon books, one for the

Truth and one for Income Tax Cookery. The Property was Let.

I never go to bed before one thirty and then I usually read for ages. I'm a very light sleeper too. On the following Monday, my first day with Muriel, I woke up an hour before my clock rang, due to the banging of the front door. Mad with fury, I wrote a nasty notice telling everyone to close the door QUIETLY, but I suddenly saw Rosenfeld M. reading it with an expression of scorn, when he eventually took up residence, so I tore it up in a rage, and decided to buy some earplugs from Boots, instead.

I walked up the road with Sarath, Ranjini's husband, who told me he was a United Kingdom representative for the Ceylon Tea Centre, and worked in the head office in Piccadilly, but that occasionally he had to be out of town for a few days. He carried my bag of books and touched my arm as we crossed over the main road. I could hardly take my eyes off him, and stared at his retreating figure as he went towards the tube station. It isn't right for people to look like that at half past eight in the morning. It makes me sick. His wife left for her work at Air Ceylon, an hour earlier, and probably looked too exquisite for words as well. I thought how bad it was going to be for my morale, and wondered what the hell I'd let myself in for, sharing with these two film stars.

I usually prepared my lessons in the bus, but a little girl of twelve, pregnant, probably petrified and dull-witted, wasn't going to be exactly in the mood for academic advancement. I decided to kill an hour by giving her an IQ test. I remembered giving a little boy I once taught the question about the old woman who made candles. She bought the wax, enough for a hundred candles, but being thrifty, out of every ten she made, she managed to scrape up an extra one out of the shavings. How many candles did she manage to knock up altogether? Most children answer one hundred and ten, and they make up sixty-four per cent of the population, so I'm told; some say twenty-three or one thousand or none, and they're just about on a par with me; but some little smarties hit bang on the right answer knowing that one hundred and ten is too easy and get the right number of one hundred and eleven, if you're still struggling. My little genius had 111.1 recurring, and at nine years old, having never been to school because of severe haemophilia, that's rather devastating.

As I walked down the long road, looking for the house where Muriel lived, I saw a post office parcels van delivering parcels to every single house, and when I came alongside the postman, I asked him where Number 87 was.

'About seven houses farther up, but there's no number on the door. Take this parcel with you.' He gave me a Littlewood's mail order catalogue which was what he was delivering all down the road, and I used to wonder who on earth took notice of leaflets coming through the letter box!

The whole street was very dreary, but I don't think a single house I passed came down to the standard of Number 87 for pure sordidness. I wondered what rent they charged down here. There was a basement area without a dustbin, and six months' unwrapped rubbish was thrown into it with moronic abandon. Obviously, the dustmen gave this house a miss, and I can't say I blamed them, because, after all, why should they pick it up by the armful? I must remember to mention dustbins to the Welfare Department.

The house was tall and unpainted and ragged net curtains hung at the cracked, begrimed windows. There was no bell and no knocker, and after banging repeatedly at the filthy glass panel, I heard the slupp slupp of an old woman in slippers dragging herself along the passage. The door was opened and the old woman stood unseen behind it. The smell from the passage overcame the rubbish dump and invaded the outside air with the most horrible fumes. I took a deep breath through my mouth and entered and the door was closed silently behind me. I turned to say hello and to hand over the parcel, but it wasn't an old woman.

It was a little girl with a red ribbon tied round her frizzy black hair. She wore women's furry slippers, too big for her, red three-quarter socks and a dirty pink dress, short, with smocking across the chest – a little girl's dress which no one with the beginnings of womanhood could decently wear. The child's face was right for the dress, for the dark, stained cheeks had the sweet roundness of childhood, and the big brown eyes looked shy and frightened and recently tearful.

I wanted to squeeze the fat cheeks between my hands and ask her what she'd been crying about, but instead I said, 'Hello! Are you Muriel? I'm Miss Lazarus and perhaps you and Mum were expecting me.'

Her breasts pushed huge and aggressive against the smocking, and her belly hung down as if a pillow had been stuffed up her dress, making it immodestly short at the front, only reaching the join of her thighs. The ragged grey petticoat covered her up, and yet she was a child, not knowing how to cover this load that had been thrust on to her. She shuffled along the stinking passage in front of me. Answer questions one to ten. How many candles could the old woman make? Change these fractions into decimals. Did he do it? Why? What is it like to live with a father who does that to you?

A door opened on our right and a face pushed through the crack, gazing without expression or curiosity at us. Muriel mounted the stairs, past two landings, and finally we reached the top one. There was a filthy cooker against the wall, jammed in by the bannister, and greasy pots and pans sat on a couple of broken chairs next to it.

The smell churned the air which I was forced to breathe and I retched into my handkerchief. You can actually get used to a terrible smell. It takes five minutes of concentration on other matters; but when I walked into the living room, the smell was different and I had to notice it. It was of unwashed bodies, sweat and urine. The room was packed with furniture. Photographs in ornate gold-lacquered frames garnished the damp walls, and an oil stove fumed away, dangerously squashed by a huge bed and a cot. Two tiny children lay on the far upper end of the bed.

A woman sat on the rag-laden, tattered sofa, writing in a notebook, beautifully dressed and coiffeured. I smiled and said, 'Good morning' but she didn't even look up. I stood there irresolutely, suffocating. No one had spoken a single word to me, let alone invited me to sit down. Muriel went and sat on the bed next to the children, picked up a torn piece of comic and pretended to read it.

I sat down, next to the woman, who immediately got up, tore the page out of the notebook, and pushed it into an envelope. She slipped on a coat, picked up her bag and umbrella and said to Muriel, 'I go now. Give them porridge.' She stepped past me as if I was another greasy pan, ignoring Muriel's 'Goodbye, Mummy,' and I heard her descending the bare staircase. The front door slammed and rattled.

I went over to the bed to take a peep at the kids lying there and as I looked at their yellow-brown faces and breathed in the scent of their unchanged clothes, I saw that they were both dead. I mustn't shout out and alarm the little girl sitting next to them. I felt the most dreadful, uncontrolled hysteria rise in my throat, which changed quite suddenly and without any warning into vomit, which I managed to land in the comic on Muriel's lap. She hardly stirred. I folded the comic and screwed it up, then dragged her to her feet. She looked at me fearfully.

'These kids! What's the matter with them?' I screamed at her and shook her.

'They my sisters. She Jocelyn and the little one's Hyacinth.'

'Get me a glass of water.'

She shuffled out and down to the sink on the lower landing. I leaned over the babies, the elder being no more than three. Their eyes stared, death-like, at the ceiling, and then to my tremendous relief I heard the bronchial breath of both of them, and saw their little chests rising and falling painfully. I touched their faces. Both were burning hot and their eyes still stared, unseeing and unmoving. They were alive, but blind. Muriel returned with the water in a cracked, filthy cup, and I drank it down, feeling much worse.

'What is the matter with your sisters?'

'They asleep.'

'Their eyes?'

'Always they sleep with eyes wide open. Daddy, Desta and the others, they all do. Mummy and me are the only ones who sleep with eyes closed. The new baby, she in hospital, but she sleep like that too.'

'Open a window. It's too hot in here.'

'Mummy say not to. They not well and mustn't have no draught.'

'Do as I say.'

'Mummy say . . .'

'I don't give a damn what Mummy say! She isn't here, suffocating to death. We'll close the window before she comes back, so she'll never know. Don't tell her, that's all. When will she get back?'

'She come an hour after Daddy, sometimes later. The babies will get sick from the cold.'

'I will put them under the blanket. They need some ventilation.'

She made no movement, but I felt her watching me as I banged at the rusty catch, and the top window slid down very fast with an awful crash, as the fraying, rotting sash cord snapped. We certainly weren't going to be able to shut the window before Madam returned. In fact, we weren't going to be able to shut it at all! When I turned around, her eyes were starting out of her head with terror, and she was making odd little animal noises in her throat.

Stark fear is more contagious than measles. 'What's the matter with you?' I quavered.

'The window . . . the window! Mummy will see when she come back!'

'It is my fault. I broke the sash. I will leave a note for Mummy to tell her I did it. The babies are ill, but they must have air as well as warmth. I was a nurse before I was a teacher so I know,' I babbled on. I shivered with cold. 'Has the doctor seen the children?'

'They go tomorrow. I must make the porridge, but there is no milk.'

'There is a milk cart in the street. Go down and buy two pints.' I gave her five bob and she waddled out of the room. I covered the babies with the top blanket, trying not to look at their eyes. Both of them had wet themselves six times over. I could feel the heat of their bodies through the thin blanket.

Muriel and I warmed up the milk on the putrid gas stove, and we each took a baby and a cup of warm milk and fed them. They didn't cry or make a fuss, but smiled and giggled, and their temperatures felt like one hundred and five degrees apiece. Jocelyn brought the milk up on my bosom and wee-weed on my knee.

'Are there any clean things for the children? Nappies? Towels? Nighties?' Muriel shook her head all the time.

'There ain't nothing else for them to wear. They dirties everything and them's all in the washing bag over there.' I took one whiff of it and decided against going to the launderette. Instead, I hit on Ridley Road Market.

'What food is there in the house?'

'Mummy will bring fish and chips for supper. There ain't no food nor no money.' I assumed that the double negative didn't mean that the cupboard was bulging with first-class protein.

'I'm going out shopping. Be a good girl and take off all the children's clothes and put the things in the washing bag. Heat up some water and wash them all over, then dry them with something from the sofa and put them between the blankets.'

She didn't nod or smile or change her expression in the slightest, but she took both children on her knee. I wiped my blouse and skirt with my hanky and ran down the stairs into the dirty street. I walked along Ball's Pond Road, thinking of the rabbi's advice to Mrs Cohen living in a small cottage with six children and a lazy husband. 'Rabbi! Help me! The children are under my feet all day; my husband won't move himself to get us a bigger place. I'm going mad from it all, Rabbi!'

'Do as I say, Mrs Cohen, and bring in the goats and the hens to your cottage, and come back to see me in a week.'

'Rabbi, I have done as you said. Do you want to kill me? My children, my no-good husband, now the animals! I'm at the end of my tether!'

'There are two poor students needing a place to stay for a few days. Give them the benefit of your hospitality. Come to see me next week.'

'Rabbi, I asked you for advice, not for a rope to hang myself. You want to kill me?'

'Send the animals out into the yard again. The students will be leaving tomorrow. Come and see me next week.'

'Rabbi, it's so marvellous at home. I have so much space. The cottage seems like a palace. The children are good and quiet, bless them, and my husband does his best to help me!'

It had never occurred to me before that Balls Pond Road compared so favourably to the Champs Élysées. I had always considered it a dingy, mean kind of thoroughfare! The atmosphere struck me like a fresh sweet breeze, blowing from the sea. I drank in the clear air and it tasted like wine, warm and racy. Who needs the drag of flying off to Majorca for health and relaxation; keep your Swiss Alps; your Dorset village; your lonely moor! Dalston and District are good enough for me!

I bought nighties and throw-away nappies with holiday abandon; then fruit, eggs, bread and butter with careless rapture, and scudded back to the muck heap with my heart beating excitedly. During a moment of inspiration and with mounting glee, I bought a bundle of lurid comics and bags of sweets for all three of them.

The door was ajar and I swam through the stink to the sanctum above. The little girls were washed and naked, covered by the blanket. I showed Muriel the things and her sad little face lit up into a lovely smile. She laughed out loud when she saw the comics, and we put the nappies and nighties on the sleepy children and made them comfortable. We put the horrendous pots and pans to soak in the sink and removed the washing bag out of reach of my nose. The room was fresher now, but shivery cold despite the stove, because of the great window gap, and Muriel and I boarded up part of the space with two dirty wooden trays and a flattened cardboard box. I wrote a note to the lady of the house, apologising for the damage, and then got ready to buzz off.

'Will you come again?' she asked.

'Tomorrow. Could be we might do a few lessons one of these days!' It was worth the dough, just to hear her asking a question. I checked up on the kids' eyes. They were asleep again, and I watched them for a few moments, fascinated; and then I left her, a little girl again, happily engrossed in the comics and digging into the Maltesers like nobody's business.

The words nose and nostalgia have the same root for me, albeit the Romans thought of one and the Greeks the other. Long ago, during my wretched teaching career in Tottenham, I would go for walks during the lunch-hour – past the assorted, stinking, porous-walled factories, where most of my pupils would end up – thinking black, smoking thoughts on how to rid myself of the necessity of earning my living. One day, walking along Philip Lane, I came upon an unusual, sweetish smell which gave me singular pleasure. I walked backwards and forwards, inhaling it, mesmerised by the poignancy of its associations which I could not grasp.

'Hello, Miss!' shouted Rosalind Carpenter, on her way to the saveloy-shop.

'Hey, Rosie, what's that smell coming from Sankey's factory?'

'Can't smell nothing. Doreen! Miss wants to know about the stink from out Sankey's!'

'Smells like bleedin' niggers' sweat,' sneered Doreen, who never seemed to wash or change her clothes. 'S'long, Miss!' They went on their way, giggling, and I leaned against the wall, languorous, intoxicated.

I realised at last that I had been surrounded by that lovely aura on my sixth birthday, when I had been given some thick, crumbly wax crayons, and had sniffed their delicious aroma, like a dog finding a treasured bone. Now, years later, I had dug it up, and I ran back to school through a blur of tears, impotently wishing for that too-bright happy day. The sense of smell affects me more deeply than any of our other, more developed ones, giving me that tinged pleasure, brief memos of joyful times which escape me the moment after recapture.

Muriel, what will your childhood memories be? May your senses be perpetually dulled, and your remembrance short-lived. The man opposite is mowing his lawn, sending me the free and fragrant message of another summer. My room is full of sunshine, spacious and comfortable. I have never known the ice-cold, evil stench of poverty, like the millions around me, coldly ignored by the smug middle class, invisible to the rich, patronised by the educated, despised by those one step above. You crouch, twelve years old, pregnant and unloved, a victim of your vile, contemptible surroundings. Your life is finished; neither you nor your child have any earthly chance. They pay me to teach you, because by law, you must be 'educated'. They will provide dustbins, give you clothes, deliver your baby and regurgitate you both back into horror and squalor.

Your headmaster and teachers give me a concise history of you, compiled with the help of the social workers. Born – twelve years ago in the West Indies. Lived with her maternal grandmother from the age of four until two years ago when she joined her parents in this green and pleasant democratic land of opportunity; but she alighted on a dung heap, from which the rest of us averted our noses. The parents meanwhile produced five other children, of which the one boy had lacked the required stamina, and died of asthma and bronchitis a few months ago.

They breed like flies, said the headmaster's eyes, waiting for a greasy acknowledgement from me, so that he could say it with his lips, but disappointed, slightly wary, when he found no sympathy.

'Muriel is probably not her father's child, but the police want him for this business, father or not!' snapped Mrs Lebor, child care officer for the borough. 'Mrs Towey has been on the game since she came here, her husband poncing for her.' I wonder when she finds time, then, to have babies. They're obviously her husband's if they all sleep with staring eyes.

Muriel, do you wish you were back on your sunny island, away from this dirty hole and these protectors of yours? There is a healed mark of a flat-iron on your back, from when your grandmother tortured you, and twenty lines written with a pea-stick on your behind, as a punishment for some long-forgotten misdemeanour.

Don't think about the past or the future. Stifle your senses. Cover your mouth and nose; blindfold your eyes; but if you want to peep, look only at the pictures in the comics and stumble through the words in the bubbles issuing from the villain's mouth. Taste only the Maltesers and the crisps I bring for you. Feel only the slacks and soft sweaters that I took from my cousin's children's unwanted wardrobes. Sniff the perfume and soap and bath oil I found in my cupboard. Hear the few friendly words we exchange. But stifle everything else. Ignore ninety-nine per cent of the present. Let me get away and forget about you for another twenty-two hours. Muriel, my unpromising pupil, with your bellyful of doom.

After the first few weeks, my nose became accustomed to the morning atmosphere. The afternoon clamour of barking and yelping still ground my nerves to powder, but I was no longer consumed by these episodes as I had been hitherto. The house took over; the occupants' lives became more to me than the twitch of my net curtains, more than giggles on the stairs, the slam of the front door or the sound of a car humming ominously to a halt outside.

Ranjini was the tenant I got to know first and most intimately. Her husband always came home from his work well after eight and usually much later, but she would arrive at half past four, laden with bags of shopping, and bathe and change into slacks. God forbid that I should ever see her legs she maintained were like a couple of burnt matchsticks. She'd then start her cooking, chopping vegetables in a frenzy, opening innumerable, strangely labelled, aromatic jars, seemingly at random, and throwing pinches and teaspoonsful and grains into this pot and that pan.

At first, I'd creep into the kitchen like a criminal to make a cup of coffee and rush out with it, so as not to be in her way, but quite soon we became less self-conscious with each other, and while she cooked her rice and prepared the gargantuan meal for herself and Sarath, I'd sit and chat to her. We'd exchange news of the day's events and after a few weeks we were friends.

Now that the warm weather was here, she'd taken to sticking the cardtable out in the back, pretending she was setting it out on some sun-drenched patio in Colombo or Kandy. A crossword and ice-cream addict, she was always at one or the other, but usually both, after she'd finished her massive preparations. During the waiting period, she'd sample ice cream and tea and pore over cryptic clues and anagrams, and if I came in at this time, she'd greet me like a prodigal son. 'Hello!' she'd shout, as soon as she heard me clomp down the passage. 'Come out for a while. Yours is in the glass bowl in the fridge. Bird's Eye have brought out a new one – Chocolate Chip Mint. Bring it with you. I've got fresh tea out here. What's "Newgate for instance was the very devil"? Three, four!' It still sounded strange to me when she spoke, especially with the remotest echo of blasphemy. I'd gorge down the ice cream and drink the iced tea, refreshed and alive again. 'How was Muriel today? What new words did you learn from Jack?'

'The sisters are both in hospital, and today I found her sitting all alone on the bed, with a grey, blood-sodden pillowcase on her lap. I thought, "Hurrah, she's had a miscarriage," but it turned out her nose had been bleeding!'

'Has she said anything about her father?'

'Nothing. She's got a story and she's sticking to it. I'm sure she's terrified to speak the truth.'

'You know,' mused Ranjini, 'I was thinking of the obvious hereditary factor regarding the other children. They all seem to carry the father's characteristic of sleeping with their eyes open. Muriel and her mother are the only members of the family who don't, so if he's the father of Muriel's child, then it will probably have the same quirk, as it seems to be a strong factor.'

'Listen to Whimsey! I can see the little foetus staring round Muriel's belly already. It's not the loveliest of visions. Give us another clue. I don't know anything about Newgate except knockers and executioners.'

'Sammoc? Nine, six.' I got that right away, and she filled in 'inverted commas' with shrieks of admiration. Certain clues are easy for me because I've no sense of direction, read Hebrew and am left-handed. Only those people with similar afflictions and a small dose of dyslexia would understand. We fill in a few more blanks.

'They told me at the office today that I can fly to Ceylon for ten per cent of the actual fare. I've worked there for a year now, and I'm due for the allowance.'

'You'll go, of course! Well, why aren't you jumping for joy?'

'I might. I worry about leaving Sarath, though.'

'Come off it. He's perfectly capable of surviving without you for a few weeks. Stop acting like the little woman. I'll get in shopping and stuff for him if it makes you feel better, and empty ashtrays when they start groaning. Why don't you go for your next leave?'

'Yes,' she said. 'Yes, why not!' But she didn't look particularly happy at the prospect.

'What's up?' I said.

'They cannot forgive me for marrying Sarath. They hate him for primitive, backward reasons. We do not understand one another any more. Back home we have servants to see to our every need. It's inconceivable that I should wait on myself at home or treat the servants as equals. I was brought up with that attitude, yet I always felt uneasy in the role of mistress.

'I remember a terrible row once, when the garden boy came round to the back door to ask for a drink of water. He gave me a coconut shell and I took it and filled it from the tap. Next to me was a row of shining glasses and iced pineapple juice. I tipped the water out of the shell and filled a glass with the cold juice and brought him into the kitchen to sit down and drink. My mother came in as he was sitting there. She was confounded by what I had done. After the boy had slipped out, she smashed the glass and threw it away, because for her it was tainted. She lectured me on keeping my distance and maintaining respect. To her, the boy was sub-human; of as much consequence as a fairly useful animal. I feel totally separate from my family. I am their daughter and sister, but a stranger. But I want to go home. I want to go home. I'll speak to Sarath and make arrangements.'

I shivered. 'What's the matter?'

'Someone just walked over my grave. Let's go in. Guinevere has a date with Lancelot, this eve. It takes me at least an hour of hard work to look presentable.'

We chased the newspaper and carried the things in. With all the strength of my intuition and rooted unreasonable psyche, I didn't want Ranjini to go home.

Apart from low blood pressure, rheumatism and frighteningly short sight, I suffer from a wide and varied range of ailments, most of them cunningly concealed from the doctor. The clear vision of my name inscribed on a simple tombstone haunts me during idle moments at night, when I occasionally receive the knowledge that my end is nigh, and that I will not live to see the sunrise or hear the eight o'clock news. I am awakened by my battering heart, my breath comes and goes in short, shallow, panic-stricken gasps, my throat constricts and I find that I cannot swallow. It all stems from when I was ten, said the psychiatrist I went to see after the doctor assured me, following a gasping, endless night, that he couldn't find anything amiss.

I remembered that day when, as a nervy, undersized, skinny little girl, I came running into the kitchen as usual after school, to find my cat Snooky, in a noose hanging from the knob of the oven. A young Polish refugee, Leon, who had been staying with us, used to boast that if he raised his hand above the cat, she would lie down flat on her belly, with her hair standing up stiff. I knew he must be cruel to Snooky when no one was around, but this was the first time I'd actually witnessed his warped intentions. I screamed and attacked him in a frenzy of rage and horror. I loved and spoilt my cat, and had invested her with human sensibilities. Leon lunged back at me, pushed me over the arm of the chair, and pulled my school tie tightly around my neck. He's going to hang me, like Snooky, or strangle me. I was screaming, in anticipation of a violent death. Someone was heard at the front door and Leon let go of me. There wasn't a mark on my neck.

Snooky, who had managed to wriggle free, seemed to suffer no ill effects, but I stayed in hospital for six months, shuddering and jerking, gasping and choking, dancing like a puppet along the macabre path of Saint Vitus, until I emerged, drugged and still. I spent a further six months playing by the sea and went back to school a year after the incident, tanned and strong and cured. The teachers were kind and patient with me; the children, too friendly and compromising, but everyone soon returned to normal and I grew up and my illness became an unpleasant memory. But like a criminal with a conscience, the past occasionally catches me around the throat with a hard, cruel hand. Nervous tension, a fishbone, a playful hand on my neck, can send me reeling into paroxysms of hysterical terror as my throat closes up, and all swallowing and breathing seem to cease for longer than the living body can stand.

'No, Doctor,' I persisted to my hack quack, 'I do assure you that it was never in my mind that Leon was a rapist. Not in the deepest recesses of the subconscious was I aware that this sort of attack could possibly take place. I knew about birds, bees, cats and rabbits but I didn't know about people. Doctor, I thought, quite simply and understandably, I would suggest, that he was going to strangle me. Isn't that obvious or bad enough? Why do you insist that I'm spending my lonely, choking nights locked in fear of being raped?' I'm protesting too much – I mustn't keep on villifying myself.

Perhaps it was due to all the anxiety of getting the house in order, trouble at work, and on top of everything, never having enough sleep, which brought on one of these attacks. I was drinking a cup of coffee in bed around two in the morning, which is the time I catch up on my light fiction, when without warning my throat closed. I spat out the coffee, my hands and feet became as cold and as wet as ice, my heart hammered unevenly and my breath came and went in short, progressively shallow, noisy gasps.

I've not felt like this for ages. Surely this was different; worse. Don't panic. Lie down, close your eyes and think of shady trees around a blue lagoon and see yourself completely relaxed; but all I could see was that space beyond the stars and the narrow slit in the cold, hard ground.

I must get to the door for air. My teeth were chattering uncontrollably, but I heard it as a death rattle which struck me stone cold with ominous terror. The street was dark and deserted, and I hung on to the door-jamb trying to swallow, trying to breathe, trying to loose the invisible bond around my neck.

There was a white car standing outside my house and a man was locking the door. I wanted to shout to him to help me, but I could barely utter a sound. He couldn't possibly have heard me, but he was running up the path and I recognised the grim, inscrutable face of Rosenfeld M. He didn't speak to me, but took off his coat and wrapped it round me and drove me like a matchbox car into my room, sitting me on the bed, crouching down next to me, chafing my icy hands.

'What is the matter?' I could not answer. I pointed to my throat. He looked at me, then, with very brief but immense concentration. 'Don't be afraid. You are not going to suffocate. I will be back in a moment.'

I clutched him around the neck. 'Don't go. Don't leave me alone. Please stay!' The words came out in a hoarse, cotton-wool-wrapped whisper. He put his hand under my chin, gentle and warm and not strangling; he stroked my neck and I felt the tension ease and my panic dissolve into an agony of embarrassment.

I didn't know how to stop clinging to his neck, but he managed temporarily to save the situation by untangling himself to run upstairs for his bottle of brandy. He was back again in a few moments, sitting down close to me, holding the glass, and I managed to swallow some of the contents. It roasted my intestines and snapped the iron strength of the ghostly hands around my throat, giving me life and oxygen.

'Tell me,' he said.

I told him. About Leon and the cat and how the fright seemed to follow me through the years. His arm was around me, his hand stroking my throat. However was I going to get out of this ridiculous situation? I took a great gulp of brandy to assist me in my dilemma; I felt perfectly well, my death throes were a full century away and quite suddenly and irrationally I was consumed by irritation and dislike of this strange, ugly man who was making such a mountain out of a case of mild hysteria. He peered at me intently as the thought encased my mind and I made very little pretence of how I felt. He immediately averted his gaze.

'I feel quite better, thank you. The brandy's done the trick.' I sneaked a quick swallow to make sure. 'I'll go to bed now. I hope that you find your room comfortable. I assure you that I won't impinge on your time and patience again. It must have been somewhat devastating to find a hysterical woman on your doorstep!' I simpered foolishly, wishing him in hell.

'Yes,' he said, 'I suppose you might call it that.'

How discomfiting and ungallant he is! He stood up, and I noticed with what unselfconscious grace he moved his bulk. But he didn't go. He just stood there in the middle of the room, still and silent, with his eyes fixed on a static point somewhere behind my head, and I wondered if he might be a little mad. Then his mind suddenly jumped to attention.

'The two young ladies upstairs – I have seen them but you have not told me their names.'

What a formal, ridiculous man! Why couldn't he ask them himself? I had more important matters to occupy my mind. He continued watching the dead invisible fly.

'Dinah is the Yorkshire girl and the blonde in the little room is Mandy. I don't know much about them; they're out working most of the day. I'm sure they won't be in your way.'

'I hope that will be the case. They are both single?'

'Yes.' I wondered which one he had designs on. I wouldn't

back him with a bad penny. Apart from all his other setbacks, he must be fifty, at least.

'In that case I want to mention to you that when Mandy has her baby, she will be welcome to my big room. I find it pleasant and extremely comfortable, but her need for a larger place will arise and her room would be quite adequate for me. I would not like her to worry unnecessarily about the future, so perhaps when you have the opportunity, you could say as much to her: that is, if you have no objection to the arrangement.'

I stared at him in amazement. The man had a warped imagination; a sort of manic, wishful thinking, unfulfilled sexual desire. I'd better be careful how I answered him.

'Mr Rosenfeld, whoever put that idea into your head? It's ridiculous! She's as skinny as the lead in my pencil! If she had so much as a pimple on her body it would look as if she was having quads. You are imagining things.'

'It is quite glaringly obvious that she's pregnant. Thin girls do not walk in the way she does when they are unburdened. She has a pronounced pregnancy mask and I hear her crying in the night.'

'Whatever you think, I don't believe it. I would have noticed. I'm certainly not going to approach her with your suggestion. You'll have to tell her yourself. I really don't want to get personally involved with the people living in the house and I advise you to follow my example. I've more than enough of my own problems to cope with. Anyway, the rent for your room is double that of hers. How will she . . .?'

'I shall continue to pay in the way we arranged, of course.'

'I must appear mercenary to you, Mr Rosenfeld, but really we can't afford . . .'

'But I can.' He smiled. He must be rolling in gelt. I wouldn't mind getting my fingers into his pay packet. I wonder what he does.

'But what if you decide to leave, what then?'

'And leave you holding the baby? No. I will not leave. I decided tonight that I would stay on. I will speak to Mandy myself about the matter and give you four months' rent in advance so that you will have no reason to distrust me on this issue.'

'Are you staying because of her?'

'I knew about her situation the first time I saw her. No.'

'And a crazy woman, gasping on your doorstep, grabbing you round the neck, doesn't send you rushing off hell for leather to find another place?' I giggled.

'On the contrary,' he said, 'it decided me to stay. Goodnight.' He bowed, almost clicked his heels and left the room.

He'd conveniently left the brandy behind so I poured myself a generous dose, drank it, and then staggered into the kitchen to see what I could find to mix with the next few nips. I felt extremely well, tipsy and not in the least sleepy. I stealthily sorted out a bottle of grapefruit juice from Ranjini's well-stocked fridge and sat down at the kitchen table with my booty; but Marks and Spencer's do an excellent job of ensuring that their bottles are airtight. I needed a special spanner to twist the lid; a knife to stab it through and let some of the air escape; near boiling water to expand it.

I was making yet another mighty effort, before having to make a choice, when a voice behind me said, 'Here. Let me!' I screamed and turned round. Sarath stood there, grinning with pleasure at seeing my fright.

'You bloody fool,' I shrieked. 'What do you creep about like that for?'

'To catch you in the act. It's after three, and naturally I don't expect other people want to hear my comings and goings at this time, but I'm delighted to hear yours! It is a pleasant surprise to have company.'

'I was just borrowing something to mix this brandy with.'

'Don't tell me you're going to murder it with that stuff?' He opened the larder and brought out a bottle of ginger. I liked the casual easy way he poured out the brandy for himself, without asking. He drowned mine in ginger and sipped his neat.

He offered me an unsmokable French cigarette in exchange. I started to totter down the hall to get my own. Sarath followed, uninvited, holding the drinks in one hand and pushing me with the other. We sat in my room, glugging and smoking.

'What are you doing up at this time of night, or is it routine?'

'I felt ill. I got this choking feeling, which is routine, and Mr Rosenfeld saw me and gave me this brandy. He left it downstairs by mistake, so you're boozing stolen goods.'

'In that case, we might as well hang for a sheep as a lamb.' He emptied the contents of the flask into our glasses. 'To mine host, our Rock and Salvation, the good Samaritan from Prussia!' We clinked glasses. I couldn't stop laughing. I sat on the floor, contorted with mirth.

'And what, may I ask, do you mean by coming home at this hour and leaving Ranjini alone all evening and half the night?' I loathe this kind of idle, coy stupidity, and when I hear myself in the act, I later turn my face to the wall and claw the paper in self-disgust, but now I felt witty and cute.

'She's asleep, isn't she? That's all she seems to do – sleep! Does it look as if she's missing me?' He downed his drink. 'Well, does it?'

'I cannot possibly concentrate on what you are saying, if you're going to get riled and defensive. Just you wait until she goes away, then you'll realise her true worth!' My nails hovered in the direction of the far corner, throbbing with my inanities, but curled comfortably back towards the brandy glass. 'Do you expect her to be waiting at the door for you with arms outstretched at this time of night? She works full time, cooks half the evening, cleans and sees to your needs. Isn't she allowed to sleep then? Poor, lonely, neglected fellow!' I would suffer a discomposure of mind tomorrow, rarely hitherto experienced.

'Anyway, I don't want to discuss your private life.' I had a muzzy feeling that I'd gone too far.

'Sees to my needs,' he sneered. 'And what do *you* know about my needs?'

'I am only interested in mine at the moment. Fill the cup!'

He laughed too long and complied. I liked him. I lay down on the floor, waving my cigarette above my head, looking at him from the top of my eyes. He looked arrogant and impossibly handsome, floating above me, upside down. I wondered if Ranjini ever felt jealous or mistrustful about his outlandish working hours. He smiled down at me, warm and friendly.

'And who sees to your needs?' he asked.

The brandy enhanced my loneliness. I wanted to cry, make drunkenness my excuse for touching the hand which was poised two inches above my waving palm. I would tell Ranjini about this chat, tomorrow evening. She knew me well enough. I stopped waving my hand around. His remark was impertinent; significantly crude. I held the balance. Sit up and stare at him coldly. But I didn't get up. My head spun in ever diminishing circles against the floor; the end of the filter slowly burnt itself out, and we both watched it. He removed it from my fingers and leaned, suspended over me, and I knew that I wouldn't tell Ranjini anything about tonight.

Chapter Four

What a burden! What a fatiguing and wearisome responsibility it is, being a landlady! If only this room belonged to some grasping, hardened rent-collector to whom I could give a moment's notice, then return to my sordid hole at Polly's. Perhaps I could do a swap with someone who needed a room in Golders Green, the way people did with council houses. I tried to think of some excuses for giving notice to Sarath and Ranjini. How could I tell them to go? I couldn't face either of them again. Sarath might blackmail me; he might tell Ranjini. The thought made my stomach somersault. I would tell them that my parents had been evicted from their house and that they needed the whole flat; that they and I would have to leave. I would set an example by packing my things immediately, to demonstrate the urgency of our departure. If Sarath turned nasty, I would deny everything; concoct a story about how he attacked me while drunk and threatened me. I would write my story down, learn it and swear to it in court. Everyone would believe me – they always take the woman's side. I would reject all the jurors who were male or black or under the age of forty and have a row of prejudiced, white, tight-lipped matrons who would hate Sarath on sight, because he was so un-English looking and so suspiciously handsome. He would probably be sent to prison for seven years. I wouldn't let on that I was Jewish. I would perjure myself on the Christian bible and let it be known that my father was a vicar. I would have to start concentrating on believing that he was an unbalanced monster, who attacked me viciously in the night. Anyway, a million married men were having extramarital relationships, and they managed to face their spouses with equanimity, sleep with them, weave a double life for themselves. I didn't have to answer to anyone. It was Sarath's problem, not mine.

I thought of Rina, dancing insolent and carefree through a series of intimate encounters, careless of whether the wife knew or not. 'Peter says she'd be positively grateful, anyway. At least he leaves Sheila alone now. She's never been remotely interested and Pete's so alarmingly randy. Apparently she used to pretend she liked it, just so he would marry her. She admitted it herself when they had this last row. Of course I don't want him to leave her; not on my behalf anyway. It isn't tense and terrible with us, we just happen temporarily to need each other.' And then she'd open her eyes wide and shriek with mirth at my serious view of it, and I would wonder if Rina herself wasn't pretending about the huge theatrical set she had built as a camouflage for reality.

I spent the next few days, after work, visiting my parents and friends, going to the pictures and not entering the house until well after the time I knew Ranjini would be in bed. I became a fearful intruder in my own house. I didn't want to see Rosenfeld either. The thought of him even, embarrassed me. He would wonder where the rest of his brandy was and I intended to return half a bottle to him when I could afford it, which wouldn't be until the end of the month. To avoid Ranjini was absolutely essential to the resurrection of my tattered nerves. I spent half the night listening for Sarath to come in, crouched in my dark room like a jealous wife, but I never heard him, and not feeling capable of facing anyone in the morning, I would wait until they had both left the house, my bladder bursting, then rush through my ablutions and leave for work, late, furious with them both, livid at my own coyness.

The years crawled by, but the universe had shifted its bulk

somehow, in space, because only four days had elapsed when I refused to be intimidated any longer. I bought a pint of 'sherry on the wood' at the discount off-licence, after walking up and down Golders Green Road for two and a half hours; ate my supper at the fish and chip shop; then stole silently into the house and consumed half the sherry in my room, like a lonely alcoholic. When I was eventually forced out to visit the toilet, I collided with Ranjini in the passage.

It was the easiest possible confrontation. I invited her in for a drink, and she sat on the floor, on the spot where Sarath and I had made love. I felt happy and relaxed, as if a heavy rock had rolled off my chest. She'd bought her ticket for Ceylon, and would be leaving in two weeks.

'I'll be away for a month. Sarath has been wonderful about it, urging me to go. Too wonderful. He won't miss me as much as I'll miss him!' It was the first hint I had ever heard from Ranjini that the relationship between her and Sarath was loaded and somehow unsatisfactory. 'Mr Rosenfeld is taking me to the airport. I met him this evening and he offered to give me a lift. Sarath won't be able to see me off, as he's working all hours this month.'

'Then I'll come too.'

'Would you? Oh, would you?'

I didn't know why I'd said I'd come or why she seemed so delighted, as if I'd just offered to pay her fare and give her a year's rent-free accommodation. It irritated me and I'd have to ride all the way home from London airport with that awful man.

'I know that you'll see that Sarath's okay. He won't need anything really, but if he's got any problems with the shopping or the cleaning, it'll be a comfort to me to know that you're around.'

'Don't worry about a thing. Just concentrate on enjoying yourself and I promise that Sarath won't die of hunger, or drown in dirt!' It was so easy, smiling, talking, making plans, wondering what would happen whilst she was away.

She invited Jack to a curry supper for his last evening before he returned to Wales and we arranged that I should bring him home, direct from hospital.

'I don't often have company; it'll be a celebration send-off for Jack and me.' She giggled, as if the prospect, which was grim to me, of entertaining the frantic Jack, was of some pleasure to her.

She sat there, idly stirring the contents of the ashtray with a match, loath to leave my presence; me paralysed with fear, aware that she was playing with a profusion of mucky and unique burnt-out Gauloises. I had to get rid of her.

'I've got to do some writing now, Ranjy. Push off!' She left, cheery and smiling. Her life seemed bleak; empty. She was a girl to whom solitude was a burden, an affliction. She had just admitted to herself that her marriage had grown rancid. To have supper with a disturbed boy of fifteen (when she was doing all the cooking) and a landlady was something for her to look forward to. She yearned for children, but none were forthcoming, and this seemed to enhance her pathos and vulnerability.

She was going to consult an astrologist in Ceylon, about her future. They had the reputation, there, of amazing powers. Sarath's mother had been advised by one in Jaffna. He had said, 'I see an accident concerning a motorbike. Your younger son will be killed within six months, if he rides during that period. All will be well, thereafter, and he may be allowed to use it in safety.' During the same horrifying session he had assured Ranjini's mother-in-law that Ranjini would be the mother of three children. Apparently, Sarath's father had promised his doomed son that he would not sell the bike, but lock it in the shed for the danger period, but one night the boy broke open the shed door to pillion his friend home, and he was killed on the way back to his house.

Ranjini intended visiting this Nostradamus to find out why the rest of his prophecy showed no signs of being realised. I could see him, sitting cross-legged and turbanned, his luminous, prophetic eyes sending invisible rays across Time and the Palk Straits, through Indian Deserts and London traffic, into my room. His face would harden. He would have no pity on either Ranjini or me. He would tell all. I felt afraid and uneasy again, about her forthcoming holiday, as if I, too, were invested with the power of the occult.

I took Jack back to the hospital after our supper with Ranjini and we said 'Goodbye'. We would never see each other again. He was so excited about going home to his family and had spent an entire lesson writing out his and my addresses so that we could correspond. I knew that by the time my letter arrived it would have to be forwarded to the mental hospital in Flintshire. If, in my travels, I passed by the gates of his 'home' I would not call in. I would write a letter, and Jack would reply. How long, I wondered, would it take him to write a hundred words? I'd answer and then that would be that.

I hugged him and held him close to me, and when I relinquished his exhausted, jerking little body, I sat on the hospital wall and wept with grief and relief. Tomorrow he would be on the train, proudly wearing the shirt that Ranjini had given him, and the expensive blue jeans which were a present from me, devastating his fellow passengers, who would all end up standing in the corridor; journeying back to Wales, to his father, mother and sisters all of whom must be dreading his arrival. I pictured the family, gathered around the table, shattered, horrified, sick with pity, disgust and guilt, eager to be rid of him, desperate to have him certified or 'looked after', longing for his death. Sitting on the bus, I wondered how long it would take for me to shift him from my thoughts.

Ranjini looked pale and tired. 'He was delighted with the shirt and the meal was delicious. He enjoyed himself so much.' She just shook her head, unable to speak. 'Come on!' I said, and we drank to Jack and his bitter future, that it would be short and end peacefully. Her mind lingered on his tragedy, but neither of us wished to discuss it.

'The other night,' I said, changing the subject, as if I was starting a new serial in a teenage love book, 'Rosenfeld told me that Mandy upstairs was pregnant. I wasn't too well, and he gave me that piece of information to make me feel better. I think he's riding on three wheels.'

'Is she pleased?'

'Who?'

'Mandy. You said she was pregnant. It will be nice to have a baby in the house.'

'*He* said she was pregnant. Because he'd heard her crying in the night. By his logic I'm expecting a litter of ten. He needs lessons in the facts of life.'

'Mr Rosenfeld wouldn't make a statement about anything unless he was sure. I don't see Mandy very often so I haven't really noticed any change in her. What will you do?'

'Nothing, because she isn't. I don't make statements either, unless I'm sure.' I must make a point of having a close look at her. Maybe Rosenfeld is a fraudulent abortionist by trade and makes his money persuading girls by fiendish psychological methods that they're pregnant, and then performing phantom operations.

'Mr Rosenfeld knows what he's talking about.' I felt affronted by her attitude. 'Have you noticed his arm?'

'Yes, it's thick, hairy and ugly like the other one and the rest of him.'

'You haven't noticed.' She sounded irritable and angry. The strain of an evening with Jack had overtaxed her. Well, it had overtaxed me, too. I wondered crazily if there was anything about his arm which showed that Sarath and I had been locked in an intimate embrace.

'What's special about his arms?' I asked carefully. I must try to see tomorrow. Thursday: ring about pupil replacement for Jack; look at Mandy's stomach and her pregnancy mask, whatever that is; look at Rosenfeld's arms.

'His hands too,' she said. 'I'm going to bed. I can't keep my eyes open.' New pupil, stomach, mask, arms, hands. Two hours later, Sarath tapped on my door. I lay in bed, stiff with terror, sure that Ranjini could hear. Speak to Sarath about leaving me alone. I tiptoed over to the door and he slipped into the room as silent, as confident and sure-footed as a panther. Try to have a nap some time tomorrow.

Miss Sanderson was much too friendly and flattering when I rang County Hall, so I knew that Susan Tiffin had not only been rejected by her parents and society, but by all the home and hospital tutors as well. 'I think you'll find her an interesting girl' meant that she was probably a maniac as well as backward, dirty and violent, and I would have to accept her because I needed the money. There must be a ratio of ten pupils to one teacher but Miss Sanderson got rid of the most difficult ones by ringing me.

'All right! All right! I'll take her. Just do me one favour. Don't insult my intelligence by your transparent flattery, or by expecting me to believe that Miss Tiffin is anything but disagreeable. Why don't you just come out into the open and say that no one else will have her?'

'Ring up Miss Gavenda and she'll tell you all about her. I've got a queue of people waiting on this line.'

'Just watch it! I might change my mind, then where will you and Tiffin be?'

'You won't. You can't afford to. The only other one I've got is Gbinje Okunmokumboka, a boy of fourteen who lives in Wandsworth. He's been expelled from school for burning it down and wrapping a girl round a lamp-post because she failed to pronounce his name correctly.' I could tell she was lying. 'Anyway, Susan might be grist for the mill!' She was referring to a novel that I kept telling her I had almost completed about my lousy job, and hadn't got past Chapter Four.

I rang Miss Gavenda and went to see her that afternoon at the Child Guidance Centre, a shabby office mouldering under North Thames Gas down a turning off Hornsey Road. I do nothing but tramp from one vile place to another. She pretended she liked Susan, but I could tell she didn't. She took me to the flat, three floors up concrete stairs, decorated with misspelt words in yellow chalk.

There was that sickening stink again, attacking my cardiac sphincter muscles, as soon as Susan opened the door; a pretty, sullen girl with a mouth like a bow, and strange blue eyes – the white completely encircling the irises – giving her an amazed, unpleasant appearance.

While she made us coffee, Miss Gavenda started whispering to me. I always find it dreadfully embarrassing to be whispered at, when the subject under discussion might quite easily be able to hear us. After all, Miss Gavenda didn't know the flat *that* well. The thickness of the wall might be totally deceptive, and Susan might possibly have her ear to it right now, squeezing into it the hurtful warnings of her shortcomings.

'Psst!' hissed Miss Gavenda; she really *did* say 'psst'; she must have read *The Beano* when she was a kid. 'Psst' as, quite plainly, I heard Susan pottering about in the adjacent little kitchen. 'Whatever you do, don't leave your bag unattended; not for a minute. She takes anything and everything, then she'll swear she hasn't, and you'll believe her! She'll help you to look for something she's pinched – she'll search for hours!'

I could hear Susan stirring the coffee. I wished Gavenda would shut up. I moved away from her, in order to indulge myself with a few sexy thoughts about Sarath and to stop the whispering. I fiddled with the clutter on the mantelpiece, which was covered with knobs of yellow chalk, cigarette ends and a couple of watches, and a little steel sword that I'd seen somewhere before, innumerable times.

Susan came in with three cracked mugs, spilling the pale coffee on to the greasy carpet. 'Heeyah, Miss Teacher!' she giggled, and handed me the anaemic mess, made from warmish unboiled water, Camp coffee, condensed milk and a tablespoon of sugar.

'How are you getting on with your mother these days?' asked Miss Gavenda.

'Her! That old slag! Biggest pro in the flats. I don't talk to her. She started on at me about some old watch, didn't she? Said I'd took it from 'er, didn't she? What do I want her stoopid watch for? Fuckin' old cow. She started on at Micky an' all. I won't have her startin' on Micky. You know she won't let us get married, don't you? I hate her, and the others. They're all bloody on at me. I wish I could marry Micky and get out of here. He sleeps here every night, doesn't he? I don't want no bloody schoolteacher. She can't learn me anything. I'm too old for school. I just want to be with Micky!'

'You're just going to bloody well lump having a teacher, aren't you then?' Give it back to her in her own style. That'll stop her in her mucky tracks. 'It's the law. You're only fifteen. You can't leave school or get married for another year. You've got two things to look forward to – a long way ahead. Get used to the idea. Be ready at twelve thirty tomorrow. I'll want to see all your school books.'

'You can't come tomorrer. I got to be with Micky.'

'Micky can be here! He can have lessons as well.' Howls of mirth from Miss Tiffin. 'I want to start work as soon as possible. I get paid for every session and if you do me out of a single penny by not being ready, I'll have no hesitation in letting on about that sword on the mantelpiece. Do you understand?' I knew it had been stolen from an exhibition on advertising. I couldn't bear the girl. A shameful, bourgeois, primitive antipathy swept through me. There was something crude, unwholesome, rotten and cruel about her that sickened me.

'She ain't like the other teacher is she, Miss Gavenda?'

'You don't resemble my other pupils who are waiting for me,' I lied. 'See you tomorrow.'

I reached for my sunglasses as we got into the courtyard, but I'd left them on the coffee table upstairs. Susan answered the bell after a short wait. 'Sorry, I left my sunglasses.'

'Oh, come through, Miss. Where'd you put them?'

'Just here, on this table. They are new and expensive. Where did you put them? Up your knicker leg? I'll give you one minute to produce them!'

She grinned. She wasn't offended. 'Look, see Miss, there they are over on the *Daily Mirror*s. They were hooked on your blouse and must of dropped off when you leaned over to get the ashtray.'

I smiled but did not apologise. We understood each other.

'Get some Nescafé tomorrow – and fresh milk.'

I stuck the glasses on my nose and saw Miss Gavenda's dark blue Polaroid face turn static with surprise as she saw my retrieved possession. 'Tell me, Miss Gavenda, with your vast experience as a social worker, why I always get the rottenest little sods.'

We hopped into her nasty little pale blue Mini and she told me, with all the embellishments, a list of the girl's misdemeanours, details of her precocious sex-life and sordid background.

What evil doings lay in the trail of this girl of fifteen? Is there such a thing as a bad seed? Could her environment be so influential? If she had been given, as a babe in arms, to people who cared for her, talked to her and gave her a loving and responsive background, she would have been different, more civilised in her behaviour. But would the mischievous undercurrent have lain there, waiting for the time when it could break away from the clear water, to find its own level in the dark and polluted tributaries of life? I would find out. I would try to feel the true texture of her personality and examine the fabric of her mind. I would try to like her, and give her chance after chance of proving that environment, not the formation of her chromosomes, was her curse.

I decided to have yet another go at paying off my Auntie Sarah by getting on with my novel, since I had quite a lot of afternoon and evening left. The sun was streaming into the kitchen, so I settled myself down at the table with a pen and school notebook, and proceeded to print my name and address in a variety of fancy styles all over the first page. Where was my inspiration? Why couldn't I write any more? I thought back to the time when I could knock up a story a week.

New York, misery and poverty. Arriving home from work with the two pens and the poor-quality yellow scratch pad which I stole from the office. I'd make a jam sandwich and a cup of tea and shut myself in the little bedroom in Brooklyn. I'd draw the curtains to keep out the sun, pull the dressing table towards the bed, and sit and write; and then, for a few hours, I would run back to a little village in Yorkshire, and be seven years old again, carefree, happy and secure. On Monday nights I'd appear at the Creative Writing Class and hand in my story.

Miss Zeigler, our teacher, would come in with a bunch of papers, iced with my yellow ones, which I'd given in the week before. 'A quality story is coming up!' she'd say, 'and after you've heard it, I want you all to tell me why. Sit back and enjoy it!'

Dear Miss Zeigler; benevolent and generous classmates; how you praised and encouraged me! Miss Zeigler sent my stories to her agent and they were sold to an expensive magazine, one after the other.

I was back in England when I heard that the first story had been bought. O, God! The joy! No one can go through that experience twice, and live. It was the second day of the Festival of Pentecost and I had been visiting Shool* for a chat and a nosh. I turned to walk up the road with my friend Lara, when I saw and heard my mother calling from the doorway.

'There's a letter for you from the American agent! Shall I open it?'

The reason for this peculiar request was that we don't tear letters open on Sabbaths and Festivals, being orthodox, but my mother and I were both somewhat sluttish about these matters and she was telling me that she'd steam it open under the kettle lid for me before Dad came in.

I shouted, 'Yes, okay!' and walked along, gossiping to my friend, not in the least excited. I thought the letter was just to say she'd received my stories, as I imagined that agents took at least six months to do anything of import. Suddenly I was aware of a faraway high-pitched noise and a boy running behind me. I turned round to see Orde, his face red, his eyes mad, calling my name and my mother, waving from the gate and screeching unintelligibly.

'You've sold a story for seventy dollars!' Orde yelled.

Thereupon I must have created some kind of disturbance for all the people leaving Shool came rushing towards me, windows were opened and a wall appeared for me to sit down upon. I was then helped back to my parents' house, a bottle of kosher wine was poured and the Shool-goers received a bonus that day.

My mother was yelling, 'Seventy pounds! Seventy pounds! *Redbook* is a very high-class magazine!' Never, until five minutes ago, had she ever heard of that now much-beloved name.

The rabbi's wife was reading out the letter. '$700. It says it in words too. Seven hundred dollars!'

The room went silent. The earth trembled. No, this was too

* 'Shool'. A word always used by Jews for 'Synagogue'.

much. Half a dollar a word was beyond comprehension. Under no circumstances would I have changed place with any other living soul that day.

Give me an echo, a morsel, a glimpse of that Pentecostal bliss! Perhaps I can only write when I'm miserable or exiled. But I'm not exactly happy just now, sitting in my kitchen, impotent and anguished, because pleasure and excitement and love for writing have vanished. God, let me find the secret again; I won't think about Auntie Sarah and the debt. If you let me get on with the writing, I'll give half the royalties to charity, so it would be worth your while to give me inspiration. I'll pray and concentrate for a full five minutes. The noise upstairs irritated and maddened me; yet it was nothing to the kids shouting and screaming in Sterling Street, Brooklyn. I turned on my radio loudly, so as to drown the merriment, but my curiosity gained mastery, and I turned it off again, in order to hear what it was all about.

I could endure Dinah's laughter, her music and dancing; I'd got used to it and was not disturbed by it, or by the smiling affable Walter, her boyfriend, who had become part of the household in the evenings. When I saw them walking towards me in the street, from fifty yards away I heard Dinah's giggle, and saw Walter's grin and the brightness of their eyes. By the time their steps reached me, the gaiety had risen to its crescendo, and I found that I was laughing too.

I wished they'd shut up when I was trying to write. How would they like it if I started whooping when they were studying for exams! What had Rosenfeld got to be merry about? When I see him, he's never anything but dour and silent. There he goes again, loud and deep and rolling, probably leaning back on one of my chairs, breaking it with his enormous weight. What had he got in common with those two? Whatever his past, it was certainly remote from theirs. I felt a strange, unwanted tinge of something akin to jealousy and of total exclusion. Wasn't it through me that Dinah and Walter had banded together so happily with Rosenfeld? I'd even seen them sitting on the back lawn as if three was perfect company, studying. Dinah and Walter were in their fourth year at medical school and I'd heard them calling up to his window, asking a question, familiar, friendly – then he'd come down, patronising, explaining a point, drawing a diagram and they'd listen and take notes, venerating him. Then he, too, would sit down and lose himself in one of their immense books.

I sat in the kitchen, fuming, looking out on the lovely soft early June evening. I heard Dinah and Walter come crashing down the stairs and the front door slam behind them. Now, I thought, I'll have a little peace. Then I saw him, walking in the garden, unaware that I was watching him, his head bent as if in extreme sorrow. It was as if his elation had to be paid for by woe, which followed, too soon, on the echo of his laughter. I watched him bend towards a little rose bush next to the kitchen window, and gently free it from the weeds. I flattened myself ridiculously against the kitchen wall so that I could observe him secretly. I could see nothing special about his hands, or either of his arms, though the sleeves were rolled to the elbow, except that they were unusually hairy and muscular. I saw tears in his eyes, and a few rain mournfully on to his busy hands. I heard Ranjini come in and got her to peer through the kitchen window with me, and confided my observations to her. 'The merrymaking is a front with him. He's in love with Dinah and distraught with jealousy.'

'Why don't you wash the window so that you can see better and polish your contact lenses, or alternatively get on with that novel?'

She wouldn't gossip, so I carried on with my solitary Peeping-Tom vigil, and in spite of myself, I felt sorry for this strange, lonely man with the gentle hands. I remembered how he had stroked my throat, and wished painfully that I could go out and ask him why he was sad, but I was afraid of the coldness within him, and closed the pristine pages of my notebook and left him to his isolation.

Ranjini said goodbye to Sarath the day before she left for Ceylon. He'd had to go to Birmingham and would not be back until later in the week. Her flight was due to leave at eight thirty and when I arrived home that evening, I found her and Rosenfeld drinking tea in my kitchen. I could tell that they had been talking confidentially and that neither of them welcomed the interruption. I felt angry. If they wanted to exchange secrets, surely they could do it in her room or his. I wondered if he'd swapped with Mandy and determined to ask him on the way back from the airport. This, however, was my kitchen. And why had Ranjini been so delighted at the prospect of my coming to the airport? I was obviously in the way.

'Hello, Ranjini! Hello, Mr Rosenfeld!' He stood up but did not draw a chair for me. 'I didn't realise you were chatting here. I've got one or two things to do in my room. Call me when you're ready to go.'

They didn't ask me to join them for tea. They were glad to get rid of me. 'Take a cup of tea with you, and cut yourself a piece of love cake.'

Love cake, shmuv cake. I was too hungry to refuse, since I'd had nothing to eat all day, and wasn't likely to get another chance. It was thoughtless and selfish of them to sit there, knowing that I wouldn't fancy poking about in my cupboard in front of them. The cake was chewy and delicious. I walked apologetically out and into my room. I'd put myself out to go with her to the airport and she seemed so off-hand now. She looked so lovely in a blue and white sari. I felt clumsy and ugly.

I washed my face and put on my brown skirt and matching battle-dress jacket. I had always liked this suit, but now it looked dull and dowdy, mannish and unflattering. My hair, coarse and shaggy, fell untidily over my heavy brows. My round Russian face did not improve with make-up, and my eyes looked small and narrow. I saw in the mirror that I was unbelievably plain. What a contrast Ranjini and I must seem! Beauty and the Beasts if you took Rosenfeld into account. My spirits drooped as she tripped gaily into the room.

'We're ready to leave. Come on!'

Rosenfeld was effortlessly and competently piling the luggage into the back seat and I felt like an old brown suitcase, stuck in the front with Ranjini sitting between us; like Cinderella and her ugly sisters. I wished it was after midnight. How many more fairy stories would I be telling myself before we put her on the plane? She chattered all the way there, cocking her head towards each of us alternately, like a little bird, excited and nervous, and Rosenfeld asked questions about her family and her plans, concerned, anxious to know – yet I knew that his mind was elsewhere; that he was showing interest merely to keep her happy and occupied, and I found the deception patronising and repellent. I wished I was going too, instead of having to ride back with him along the North Circular. The silence of the return journey would be embarrassing and obvious in contrast to Ranjini's cheery yet tedious chatter, and for a moment I let myself think of me and Sarath, alone in the flat, unhampered by her presence.

We had time for a quick drink, after she checked in. She was silent now; afraid, insecure. She hugged me tightly, but it was Rosenfeld whose hand she took last, and he pressed hers between both his own, reassuring and kind. I watched and waved until she turned the corner and disappeared.

'She is an unhappy girl, your friend.' We were walking across the road to the car park. I wished he would fall down and hurt himself. I wondered what he had said about me behind my back, to the unquestioning Ranjini. I would ask her as soon as she got back.

'I thought she seemed very gay this evening. What makes

you think she's eaten up with misery?' His idiotic way of saying things annoyed me.

'Her gaiety.'

'I was never clever at riddles, Mr Rosenfeld,' I said sourly. 'People aren't necessarily always double-dealing in their emotions.'

'In my experience, they are.'

'In that case, you and I are secretly brimming over with joy, and someone like Dinah is in despair because she's always happy and smiling.'

'Yes.'

'I am glad to hear that you are a happy man. A shame about Dinah though.'

'She has much courage, but she is not as you think.' He was purposely ignoring my last remark. 'Her future is short – or terrible.'

I felt afraid of him. Perhaps he was planning to murder her because of unrequited love. I looked out of the window. This was nothing like the North Circular Road or the M4. He was right off the beaten track. Twilight was turning to darkness. Perhaps he was going to practise first on me, down this country lane. I fumbled for a cigarette, and looked at his hands on the wheel. They were enormous, the fingers strong and slender, the hands of an artist or a strangler. Ranjini had commented on them. Perhaps she was trying to warn me. Why had I come? I felt my throat begin to close and put out my trembling cigarette after three puffs.

'You are afraid of me,' he said. 'Why? I am not a monster.'

'Of you! I most certainly am not! I don't know where we are, that's all, but I presume you're taking the short cut via Southampton.' He can't do anything to me until he stops the car. As soon as he slows down, I'll leap out and make a dash for it. He slowed down and stopped.

'I know you had no opportunity to have supper. We were in

the way, preventing you from preparing it. I had every intention then of asking you to eat with me, but I knew you would refuse.'

'Is it a habit of yours to kidnap people?' I felt so relieved that I started to laugh.

'You are my first victim and the ransom I exact is the pleasure of your company. Come. It is just two miles further on.'

He smiled at me and started the engine. His face seemed less unpleasant.

I eat a vegetarian diet and the meal befitted my principles and palate exactly. I ate sufficient for the rest of the week, and drank just enough to set my thoughts floating into the realms of articulation.

'You shouldn't make comments about Dinah as you did in the car. Nor about Ranjini and Mandy,' I added prissily, 'Dinah is the happiest girl I've met. You mix with her and know that too.' I took a great cowardly swig of wine and resumed my lecture bravely. 'Do you resent her gaiety? Does it irritate you? Why do you say such things? Why?'

He looked at me for a few moments, his eyes bleak. 'I am sorry that I spoke as I did. You told me that you did not wish to be involved with your tenants and I should have respected that wish.' He calmly continued to sip his drink as if the subject were closed.

I wasn't having it. I decided to be brisk. 'Come, come! That's no answer.'

'You cannot be curious and disinterested simultaneously.'

'I can. It won't affect me whatever you say. I haven't the time to worry about people simply because I rent them rooms, believe me. I've quite enough to cope with, but if Dinah's in some difficulty, perhaps I can help without putting myself out too much.'

'No one can help her.'

'That lets me out then.' O Christ, maybe she's dying, she's in the last stages of leukaemia. But that's impossible. She's too lively and energetic. It's this Jonah here who's sick, doing his best to impress, cause a stir, because that's the only way he can get the attention he craves. 'You shouldn't pass incomplete remarks either. It's the worst form of gossip. I find it maddening. Do you do it on purpose?'

He leaned forward as if about to speak, then sighed, emptied his glass and called the waiter, ignoring everything I'd said.

I sat in the car, vexed and silent. I wouldn't give him the satisfaction of asking questions which he refused to answer.

'What a houseful I've got,' I sneered as we rolled home. 'Mandy crying all night and pregnant; Ranjini having her heart eaten out. Dinah mysteriously afflicted and futureless; you . . .' I faded out.

'Well?'

'Knowing everything.' I made it sound like an insult, but he seemed unmoved.

'And what about the remaining two? Sarath and you?'

'Did you change rooms with Mandy?' I asked quickly and foolishly. He made me frightened, ill.

'Yes. She is very happy with the arrangement. She is going to speak to you to find out whether she may stay after the baby is born.'

'So it's true. You were right.' He didn't answer; the man didn't even get any pleasure out of gloating. I felt relieved when we drew up near the house. I wanted to get away from him. I disliked him overwhelmingly.

I could see Dinah and Walter at the open door, kissing each other. 'Let's just wait till she's gone inside. I hate butting in on bitter-sweet scenes.'

'But of course.' He wasn't a Peeping Tom. He didn't look in the mirror or crane his neck to watch.

'What's the matter with her? Please tell me. I am sure I could help, whatever you say.'

'It is possible, yes. Indirectly. But I do not think you will thank me for speaking. You have heard of an illness called chorea?'

'Of course. I told you. I had it as a child. St Vitus Dance is another name for it.'

'That was Sydenham's chorea. I mean Huntington's.'

He must be poking into their medical books non-stop. 'No, I never heard of it. It can't be more frightful than the thing I had, and look at me now. The picture of health! Adults don't get it – only kids who are particularly highly strung.'

'This disease is hereditary, dominant and remorseless. Her mother, grandmother, aunt and uncle became demented and succumbed before they were forty years old. Dinah helped to nurse her mother. She was insane for the last ten years of her life.'

I could hear Dinah and Walter talking and laughing in the still night. I thought of her bright eyes, her lilting step, her total allegiance to the joy of living. I would not answer him. I would not believe him. He's lying. She is young and happy and he is jealous. I remembered Oswald in Ibsen's play; his vacant eyes and lolling tongue.

'No,' I said. 'No. I never heard of such an illness. Only males suffer from those kinds of hereditary diseases. Muscular distrophy; haemophilia. They're always boys. I've taught them. It's something to do with the Y chromosomes. Females are carriers but they escape the suffering. I read about it. I know that it's so.'

'Dinah has made a practical and theoretical study of the malady. She is an expert on the subject. I have read the paper she has written. The diseased branches of her family tree are the main characters. Thousands of studies have been made of victims in the USA through several generations. All of them have been traced as the issue of two brothers who came to Boston in the eighteenth century. It is unfortunate, it is terrible that both branches of her family stem from that root: "I visit the sins of the fathers upon the children unto the third and fourth generation." Her blood is tainted. Both her parents were sufferers and carriers.'

I could not stand it. 'They ended up like Oswald? They ended up like THAT!'

He shrugged, knowing what I was talking about.

'But the signs are plentiful in this case. Jerky, irregular movements, lapses of memory and incoherence. Dinah will never go beyond that. She will laugh all her life. She has no fear of death. She has lived with it for too long. Her only terror was to end like her parents but she won't.'

'You said . . .'

'I have little respect for a life without hope. Walter loves her and may be unable to keep his word. She knows she can trust me.'

I could hear someone walking quickly along the other side of the road. I wondered where he was going. The night was so cool and fragrant; so beautiful. Walter had gone off long ago. Mr Rosenfeld's hands rested on the sides of the driving wheel. They were the strongest, most beautifully shaped hands I had ever seen. He was gazing ahead looking at his thoughts, and I looked too, and saw pity, grief and loneliness.

I leaned over and kissed the back of his hand and left him alone in the empty street. I sat on my bed, numb, amazed that this man should trust me. I dreamed of the soothsayer, turbanned and cross-legged, telling Ranjini all she should know, staring at me through Rosenfeld's eyes, and I awoke in shame and fear. I felt Sarath's delicious body next to me, dispelling all unpleasantness, and eventually fell asleep in careless bliss.

Chapter Five

Some of us – the lucky ones – look forward to the summer holidays with pleasurable anticipation. The rush in Marks and Spencer's for the new line in bikinis; the anguished preparations for wearing them involving uncomfortable hours lying on the weeds in the back garden, ending up pink as a pig, raw with burns and lumpy with gnat bites. The two weeks in Benidorm or Cattolica. The heat and boredom; the over-indulgence, the overspending; the easy lessons in learning to loathe your loved ones. The quick bunk-up for the romantic who nevertheless can be practical when it comes to packing their birth control pills, and who, during any other fortnight of the year, would turn away derisively from the crude approaches they now encourage and accept. The unspoken longing for the holiday to come to an end. Preparations for departure two days before it's due; lying to workmates about the wonderful time they've had; booking up defiantly for next year – same place – same time.

I never go on holidays like that, hence the rancid, poorly hidden envy and spite that I feel towards all those who do. I watch others looking through brochures, hear them planning all sorts of jolly trips once they're 'over there'. Sneeringly, I join the tail of bikini buying. They are sold in three sizes; small, medium and large, and the final size bites greedily into my flesh and my confidence, so that I have to wobble shamefully back to Wood Green for a refund. 'Oh no, dear, there's nothing wrong with it; I just prefer the one-piece I bought at the same time!' I buy a packet of three custard tarts from the food department, and consume them before I leave the store and glare balefully at the size twelve dresses, tops and trousers, my mouth crammed with carbohydrate, determined to diet. I ignore the capacious size sixteens and scuttle into Boots next door for a large spray can of Quick Tan, Q-T or Cutie for short, and apply it secretively and single-mindedly, following the directions minutely. I end up with dark brown heels, hands and elbows, legs and arms and a curious matt make-up with gathering darkness around the eyebrows and lips.

That incurable, impotent longing to be lovely! The secret hours ineffectually trying to emulate a style, a face, to be met with, 'If you'd spend just fifteen minutes a day on your appearance, you'd be amazed at the difference!' Little do they know, these cool, assured, smooth-skinned, casual competents, that I spend far more time and money than they on diet books and foods, hairdressers, different cosmetics, squeezing, covering, brushing, washing, dabbing. The mascara runs, the hair is either very dry or very greasy, but always messy; the eyes small and watery, the nose broad and porous, the lips wide and cracked, the moustache apparent, the skin blotchy.

The money for holidays and clothes is not available, yet I own nothing expensive except for a plastic shopping bag bulging with make-up and an exquisite Armenian dress split down the zip because it no longer fits. No savings, no prospects and no risk of a holiday.

It is July; the school term is ending, but not for me. I teach right through those six weeks. I don't get paid for breaks, and Susan and Muriel have no plans for getting away from it all. Perhaps as compensation I'll treat myself to a new hair style, the casual, unkempt look, so that no one will guess my awful secret – not that of failing to look stylish and attractive, but that of trying.

My affair with Sarath did more towards crushing my ego than a concentrated session with an anti-Semitic physchoanalyst. He showed me that I was fettered with hang-ups. Why couldn't I be like Rina, careless and magnificent, or like Cassy, afraid, but honest about not being able to overcome her fears? I flapped around with Sarath whenever he appeared. I was never too busy or too tired. I always maintained I was in the mood when, frighteningly, I never was. I floundered like a fish on the shingle getting sustenance from the weak and regular little waves which unavailingly tried to carry it off into the great swell. Eddies of disgust washed over me constantly. I'd looked forward to Ranjini going away and this was my reward for all the guilt and trouble I'd been through. Here I had this polished, handsome, experienced man – too polished to trust, too handsome for any mutual sympathy, too experienced to arouse passion, too invulnerable to love. I continued to persevere as if an unpleasant task had to be accomplished. I hoped that Joseph had suffered the same kind of searing disappointment with his wife and that it would continue for the rest of their lives together. I made a firm decision to talk to Sarath about bringing things to an end, or better still perhaps, fading out our affair to its natural conclusion, timed for now; and then, faced with a choice, disintegrated immediately. Ranjini's return would decide matters for me.

Sometimes, during our periods of intimate desperation, we would hear Rosenfeld's car draw up and I would listen for minutes afterwards, wondering if he was listening too, in the hallway. To the dubious thrill of Sarath's irritation, I would wrench open my door in order to surprise him, but the hall was dark and silent; he had already crept quietly up the stairs and was, perhaps, crouched on the landing, observing me, knowing, disapproving. He lived in the small front room now, having made the exchange with Mandy who had inexplicably become very obviously pregnant.

She knew about me and Sarath too. She'd knocked on my door to speak about future arrangements yesterday, and I know she'd seen him through the crack when I'd stuck my nose out to tell her I'd see her in the week. Everyone knew. Ranjini would find out. I would end it the next time I saw him.

In the meantime, I had Susan and Micky to face. On Mondays, Wednesdays and Fridays I arranged to go to her flat for my first call and then on to Muriel's. On Tuesdays and Thursdays I swapped the times in order to give each girl some extra time in bed. Really, it was to try to vary and sweeten my own routine by this totally inconsequential behaviour.

No one opened the door to me at Susan's although I beat with my fist on the cracked glass and shouted through the letter box. I could hear laughter, certainly not girlish, and Radio One playing at full blast, and in my rage and impatience, rattled and twisted the door handle, which to my amazement responded. I marched into the living room where two girls wearing nighties and love-bites and two shirtless young men were sitting round the table, playing cards and drinking tea. The room was indescribably untidy and dirty and stank of stale tobacco and unwashed morning bodies. It was like a third-rate poolroom bar.

'She's in the bedroom,' said one of the girls, a fat, plain-looking creature of thirteen or maybe thirty, and they continued to play as if there had been no interruption.

I peered into three rooms before I arrived at my pupil's boudoir. One was a toilet which decided me never to use it; one was a vile bedroom with two single beds stuck together, the bedding raw and grimy, uncovered by pillowcases or sheets. The third room had a double bed within, the sheets and blankets chaotically disarrayed. A used french letter on the floor completed the picture.

I knew from Miss Gavenda that the two girls must be Susan's older and younger sisters. Joan had lost her unwanted baby a few weeks ago from gastroenteritis. She must have gained wisdom.

The fourth door exposed Susan and Micky lying on a single bed, covered roughly by a thin grey sheet, the corner of which was pushed into Susan's mouth to muffle her girlish giggles at being found out by teacher, namely Miss Coitus Interruptus. I was not disconcerted.

'Didn't you hear me knocking before?'

'I didn't know it was you.'

'Get up!'

She snuggled up to Micky who was lying on his back watching me warily, scratching his balls through the sheet. I changed my tactics. 'Come on, Susan! Show Micky how strong-minded you are! I'll put the kettle on for you both while you get dressed. We'll have lessons in the park,' I trilled, 'I'll buy you both an ice cream.'

'Will you come, Micky?' she said, wiping her nose erotically on his shoulder. He nodded, and I backed out hastily as they disengaged themselves from the sheet.

I retrieved the cups, all of which contained mixtures of wet sugar and cigarette butts, from the card players, who looked at their hands with dead eyes, not moving an elbow or a foot out of the way, so that I had to weave around them like a cat. Susan and Micky appeared when they heard the kettle whistling and sipped their coffee in sullen silence.

I couldn't face the park. 'It's going to rain,' I said, frowning at the blue, sunny sky. 'In which room are we supposed to have lessons?'

She slipped off the edge of the sink, opened the kitchen door and screeched into the poolroom, 'Gerrout of here, yer fucking layabouts! She wants to come in here! We got lessons wiv 'er and we mustn't be disturbed!'

That girl has a big personality problem. It's impossible to like her or even pity her. What have I let myself in for with this pile of trouble!

One of the young men stood up and stretched, exposing his

underarms and a powerful odour of sweat. He mumbled to the other one and they made off, the two girls hanging out of the window as they passed below, shouting goodbyes.

Without any warning whatsoever, a fight broke out between the two girls. The fat Sharon snatched a pile of Kensitas cigarette coupons from the littered table and began crushing and tearing them, flinging the pieces into the muddy yard below. Horrible screams rent the air. As Joan rushed into the kitchen for a weapon, Sharon grabbed the remaining coupons, fled into one of the bedrooms and locked herself in to complete the destruction. Susan and Micky watched, laughing, while Joan beat hysterically on the door.

We now had the room to ourselves. Susan locked the door from the inside and turned on the telly. 'Electric's gone. Got any money?' I meekly produced a coin. 'There's them education programmes on now. That's school. I learn a lot from them.' She sat on Micky's knee, smoking, and we watched *Read, Look and Learn for the Under Sixes* and listened to the high shrieks from the passage. I felt overwhelming distaste and dislike for them, and smiled.

'Are either of you able to read?' I enquired brightly. Sighs, uplifted eyes, slight movements of the head convinced me of their undisguised impatience and irritation. How I hated them! I gave them each a ballpoint pen and a new exercise book. 'Write your name on the cover.' Susan slipped on to the floor and rested her book on Micky's lap and he leaned his arm on the chair. 'Write today's date. Micky, "Susan" is the title of your essay, and "Micky" is the title of Susan's. If you know anything about paragraphs and punctuation then use your knowledge.'

I picked up yesterday's *Daily Mirror* which was spread out on the floor on the racing page. 'You have twenty minutes. Start now.' I ignored their conversation with each other and busied myself with 'The Old Codgers' and 'Your Prayers are Asked . . .' I was well on my way to finishing the crossword when I bethought to look at the students. Susan was crouched down with her back to Micky, writing busily. He was lolling in the chair, the pen hanging loosely from his mouth, a few scrawls covering an inch of paper. I sneaked back to the crossword. The noise in the passage had diminished, for Joan had decided to stall the attack and retrieve as many torn bits of coupon as possible. They were all by now out of the window. Sharon had the radio on at full blast in the locked bedroom but it in no way seemed to disturb Susan who was fully immersed in her writing.

I went over to Micky and leaned familiarly over his shoulder to look at his work; blotchy, unintelligible scribble. 'Come over to the table because I'm going to teach you to read. What do you say?'

Susan had stopped writing and broke in. 'Go on, Micky! She's a teacher, ain't she? You're always saying you wished you could read.' He slouched over to the greasy table while I tore up paper into squares and then produced my coloured pens. The 'Look and Say' method, I thought, would be the quickest, and he wouldn't have to admit he didn't know his letters. The Private Education of Tiffin and Co. began. Twenty minutes later, he had learnt to recognise thirty words of his choice. He looked less brutish; less hostile.

I sent him back to the armchair to copy out the words he could read and called Susan over. Her handwriting was childish and ill-formed, her spelling poor, her punctuation non-existent. She had written three pages, trying, with her limited vocabulary, to set down her feelings about Micky. I would never have recognised him from her physical description. 'One man's meat . . .' I thought with a shudder. She watched me anxiously as I read what she had written. It was less than mediocre.

I turned to her and said, 'This is most beautifully written! You express yourself so well, but you need to develop your style with practice. Will you finish this and then we'll go over it carefully together?' She nodded, reading over her work eagerly, and then continued writing, with enthusiasm.

I finished off the crossword, jotted down a few words that I would introduce to Micky tomorrow and made an essay plan for Susan. I leaned back, watching them. They were really quite a nice couple of kids.

I had to admit to myself that I seemed to have a unique way with the wayward; an intuitive style of behaviour with the aggressive, the unhappy and the so-called incorrigible. I would change the lives of these two pathetic creatures. I would teach them self-respect and self-love, by trusting, liking and developing them. I thought of Dibs' teacher. I'd read the book, listened to its serialisation on *Woman's Hour* with filling eyes. She'd turned an autistic, half-mad child into a loving, talented teenager. All it needed was dedication and flair. I had both. I tossed my head at all challenges. Here I come, Muriel. Your saviour from degradation and misery.

My aplomb plummeted when I saw Muriel's dad lying on the double bed, conveniently vacated by the little girls who had gone to hospital. He looked worse than Bela Lugosi, with his wide-open eyelids showing double blanks, and open mouth emitting base noises and the odour of stale beer. I hoped he wouldn't sleep it off until my two hours were up. This was the first time I'd seen him.

'We mustn't wake Daddy,' whispered Muriel. I heartily agreed, and we sat hunched together on the rag-laden couch reading the new issue of *True Confessions* which I now ordered every week. Special Education had promised to reimburse me. They thought I was buying *Teacher's World.* Muriel was becoming a fluent reader with the help of this thoroughly enjoyable magazine. She had a much sterner moral sense than I.

'I believe Kathy was right in going off with Dominic. Bill's so dreary.'

'Yeh, but he was kind to her. He gave her all his wages, didn't he?'

I had to concede. Muriel, wise twelve-year-old, understood what was important. She didn't waste her sympathy on Kath and the sterility of her life. Compared to her, Kath had had a life of bliss on earth with Bill. Sex was unexciting, but at least Bill was her husband and not her father. Dominic was a snappy dresser, quick, witty, lantern-jawed and passionate. 'He knew what a woman wanted and made her want and want. She became a frail, trembling, writhing, helpless thing under his searching kisses, exquisitely gentle hands and sinewy body. She became a WOMAN!' Poor old Bill. He must have made her feel like a man. He didn't stand a chance. After all, he was only the hard-working owner of a garage, bringing in a paltry weekly wage, no doubt. Honest and struggling; whereas Dominic was a high-powered executive with clean fingernails and lots of time for champagne and sex during the day. Bill was a fumbler, humble, needing her. Frankly, I hated the whole lousy trio and told Muriel so, before we turned the page.

I had forgotten to whisper. The man on the bed growled, 'Come here, you!' in his sleep, apparently, and rolled over, snoring in a different tune. Muriel pressed herself, not against me, but into the corner of the couch, her arms crossed in front of her, her body bent over.

I said, 'He means you, doesn't he? You two were busy together before I came up here. You've never done it with anyone else. You spun that yarn because he told you to. He's always messing about with you when no one's around. That's why you're pregnant, isn't it? Isn't it?' I yelled, shaking her. 'Tell me the truth and he'll go away. You won't ever have to be frightened of him again, and no one will be angry with you. You won't ever have to see him again, ever!' I pulled at her rigid arms which were wrapped round her body, so that I could hold her hands and plead with her.

There was a movement over on the bed. He was sitting on the edge, quite naked, his hands hanging providentially between his knees. His eyes were back in focus and he was glowering at me. Oh Bill, what I wouldn't give for your presence here; reliable, sensible, no-nonsense blunderer that you are! Dominic, you would take command of the situation without a shake of your lantern jaw. Muriel moved herself closer to me.

'What you say just now, eh? What you say?' I would swap this scene any time for a tango with Carl armed to the teeth in the Beechwood Hospital gym. How do you deal with an offended grizzly bear? 'You say something I don't like, woman!' He stood up, his arms at his sides. Muriel had squeezed behind me on the couch.

I grabbed the only weapon to hand, my plastic bag containing a few hard-backed books and a glass bottle of Oil of Ulay, jumped up and turned to face him. 'How *dare* you,' I screamed, stamping my foot and sending an excruciating pain through my ankle. 'How *dare* you interfere with my lessons! I am here to teach Muriel, and you are obstructing me in my work! I will send for the Education Officer if you have any complaints to make! Muriel, sit up at once! We have a lot of work to get through. We will do some geometry now.'

He was standing two strides away from me. I sat down again, pulled my pencil-case out of the bag, and extracted my metal compass, which I adjusted to an angle of 180 degrees. His set of instruments were at eye level, the adjacent angle increasing and the hypotenuse decreasing at every second.

I jabbed the compass point into a fresh page in the notebook and inscribed a large black circle. I gave Muriel the pencil and ruler and told her to draw a diameter, a word she had never heard of. The man retreated and I heard him growling obscenities and then lighting a cigarette.

I realised that Muriel was clawing at me frantically. Her fear was horrible. She was sopping wet and to my shame, I discovered that I was too. How could it have happened without my knowing? Water was streaming on to the floor. It wasn't me at all; it was all her. The waters had broken and she was going to give birth in this sty with the pig over there for company. She would have puerperal fever and on no account was I going to be the midwife.

I pushed her roughly away from me and flew down the stairs before he could stop me, my sodden skirt clinging to my legs. Leaving the front door open, I ran across to the junk shop and told the owner to telephone for an ambulance immediately for number eighty-seven. Back in the house, I saw that he had put his trousers on and was making himself a cup of coffee on the landing while Muriel crouched in the wet. If only someone would torture him to death, I would watch, knitting, with a smile on my face, until he expired. She was crying. I pulled her awkwardly on to my lap, wiping her nose and eyes, telling her that the ambulance was coming in a minute and that everything was going to be all right. I wasn't sure whether she realised she was about to give birth and hadn't the strength of character to enlighten her.

Why was the ambulance taking so long? One could always hear the bell ringing ten minutes before it appeared. That devil in the shop had not done as I asked because I hadn't left him money. Maybe he didn't know that a 999 call was free. If a fortune-teller told you to watch your health next year, you should rush out of the tent and phone for an ambulance and then your life might be saved in the nick of time. The man was blocking the doorway, slurping his coffee and poking his ear, not looking at us. I dared not move for fear of jolting Muriel and encouraging the unborn infant to think it was time to make the great leap forward. Also, I didn't relish the idea of saying, 'Excuse me, I'd like to get past', to the abominable hulk.

I felt dizzy and faint with anxiety; there was a ringing in my ears and then the regular sound of footsteps running up the stairway and voices calling. 'Up here!' I yelled. 'The patient is up here!' Two uniformed men entered the room, slipping past

Muriel's father without having to push him aside and without his moving an inch. They looked spruce and pleasant and had obviously washed and shaved and put on clean shirts this morning. They had come from another planet.

'Muriel is having her baby now, I think. She's booked in at St Ann's. I would like to come with you, please. I'm her teacher.'

They wrapped Muriel efficiently but tenderly in a fluffy red blanket and joked and smiled. I felt myself falling in love with them. He was back on the bed, busy with his other ear. I hoped there was something in there, which would drive him mad; female, if possible, laying thousands of eggs. I followed my heroes down the mucky stairs, feeling ashamed at the state of the place, as if I were responsible for its neglect. I marvelled at their amazing calm and speed and competence. One of them drove, while the other sat next to us talking, telling us about all the babies he'd delivered. I watched Muriel nervously. Her face was expressionless, untroubled, but her hand gripped mine, painfully.

While she was being examined by the doctor, I sat with the medical social worker in her office. She'd lent me a hospital dressing gown to wear, while my skirt hung over the radiator, steaming gently. She'd been reading Mrs Lebor's notes, but I told her, in case it had slipped her notice, that Dad and Grandad were one and the same; that I'd promised the child that she didn't have ever to mix with her father again, and suggested, also, that she should be kept out of her mother's way, too, because she was a nasty piece of work and Muriel was frightened of her. 'I hope we'll be able to find her a good foster home and then get the rest of the kids away from their terrible parents.'

'Now, now,' she said. I prefer abuse, obscenities and personal invective howled at me, than to tolerate the utterance of those two neat little words. 'You can't go making rash promises. We're not able to give any such assurances or back you up in what you've told Muriel. We have dozens of other, more pressing cases. We're not unsympathetic, but we have no proof that her father has been sexually assaulting her. We're trying to get in touch with Mrs Towey to interview her about the position at home and to discover whether her husband is, in fact, Muriel's father. If he is, and we find out from the girl that he was responsible for her pregnancy, the baby may be defective, and of course he'll be arrested whether he's Muriel's father or not. But suspicion, and the medical evidence we have, isn't enough to convict him. Look, would you like to pop over to see her? She's in the isolation ward. She's got German measles. She's lucky she didn't catch it a few months earlier, otherwise we'd have even more trouble on our hands.' Lucky old Muriel! How the gods do smile on thee! 'She isn't in labour yet.'

'When I see her, I'll squeeze the truth out of her, but I can't now.' Suddenly, I was sick to death of them all. 'I've got to go home. I will visit her this evening. When that kid's born, you'll see that it sleeps with its eyes wide open and all the whites showing. No one else does that except that pig of a father and his offspring. I know he's continually messing about with her when the mother is out. He was at it this morning when I came in.'

'Really now?' She was showing me a little more respect. 'You actually witnessed . . .'

'Of course!' I lied. 'Do you think I'd make such a statement when I may have to swear to it in a court of law?' I really did have to get home very quickly. She might be about to ask who let me in this morning. I needed time; and my skirt. I whisked it off the radiator and squeezed myself into it, hearing the zip go. It must have shrunk. 'I really must rush off. I'll probably see you tomorrow. Goodbye.'

I walked along St Ann's Road miserably aware of my stained, torn skirt. I should jump on a bus, phone a friend, go to the pictures, think about Chapter Five, then hurry home in a taxi to write it. This time next year my novel would be published. I would enter a private clinic with a fraction of the royalties and have plastic surgery on my nose and mouth. Then I'd enter a health and beauty farm, and emerge, slim and lovely, into TV and radio interviews, belittling my talents modestly, answering all fan letters personally.

I'd buy houses, holidays and luxuries for my parents and sisters, give Orde a huge allowance, help my impoverished friends, pay back Auntie Sarah, give generously to charities, learn to drive, and then escape for a while from all the publicity and adulation, motoring off to lonely places that I'd always wanted to explore thoroughly; Brontë country; Hardy country. Visit old friends, old haunts, my childhood environment. I'd want to be alone and travel as a private person, but occasionally I'd be recognised by people anxious to interview me and unwillingly allow myself to be drawn into the limelight again. Then I'd return to the bosom of my friends and family, my second novel miraculously completed, and the round would start again. I'd probably have to advise on the filming; I'd make sure that Cassy and Rina were offered major roles. I'd have to tell Kate she was unsuitable for the singing part...

But I am still walking along the drab road, the depression taking over from decision and infantile fantasy which would have helped to waylay it on its doleful approach. I'd go and see my mother, talk to her, let her try to pull me out of it, be a child again. Instead, I succumbed to its black, beckoning hand. I emerged from a newsagent's with four women's magazines under my arm, and two family packs of Revels to consume alone and at speed – an acknowledgement of the onset of the dead weight setting itself heavily on my spirits. The last time I had a spell of this was when I was living in Coventry Square.

The bus journey home passed drearily, the walk down the hill was totally without cheer. The house was silent and empty and chill. I should turn on the radio – and listen to *Woman's Hour* – put the fire on, and the kettle; take off my outdoor jacket and scarf, have a hot bath, change my dirty clothes at least.

I did none of these things. The depression has taken hold, and like a full-blown migraine it was too late to do anything to relieve it. I opened my second packet of Revels, having finished the first one on the bus, sat at the window with my *Woman's Own,* and turned to Mary Grant's Problem Page for Men, paltry compared to mine. They're all so frantic about themselves, just because they are impotent or four feet eight or homosexual. All is vanity. The women's problems did nothing to cheer me. The advice was good and sensible, but I reckoned they were all too far gone to take any notice. I gazed out of the window, composing a letter to send to her, begging for help in my distress.

Mr Rosenfeld drove up to the house, locked his car and walked up the path. He seemed to be staring directly at me, but I knew he couldn't really see me through the net curtains. Like riding in an ambulance. I'd discovered that morning that people inside were able to see what was going on in the street, yet those on the outside, however much they peered and strained, curious of the drama within, remained unenlightened. I gave him a mocking wave, a rude sign, in fact. I had no idea why, since I had never used the gesture before, and immediately afterwards I felt frightened and peculiar, wondering whether I'd gone quite mad. Perhaps I was turning into someone like Jack, who couldn't help himself. The ringing of the door bell startled me. He must have forgotten his key.

'Good afternoon.'

'Good afternoon, Mr Rosenfeld.' Goodness me, how awkward he makes me feel! Why doesn't he say thank you; I'm sorry to have disturbed you. I've forgotten my key. He acts as if he doesn't live here and behaves like someone from Jehovah's Witnesses. It's on the tip of my tongue to say, 'I believe in blood transfusions,' because he's still standing on the doorstep. I can't very well just walk away from the open door and on the other hand it would be absurd to say, 'Won't you come in?'

'Won't you come in?' I smiled, 'I'm making coffee.' I realised that I was behaving oddly and unpredictably and wondered rather fearfully what I was going to do or say next. He beamed at me and followed me into my chilly room. I lit the gas fire and went into the kitchen to put the kettle on. Now he would be looking at my new magazines, knowing that I was lowbrow. I wished I'd been reading *Homage to Catalonia* or *The Works of Josephus* and that I'd changed my clothes. He had a doubtful talent for dispelling every vestige of dignity that I possessed, and I wondered if he had the same effect on other people.

I handed him the cup and offered him the last few sweets. I never keep biscuits in the house because I'm always slimming. I felt as if I was still at school, my blazer held together with a safety pin, my blouse crumpled and scruffy, entertaining the headmaster to afternoon tea; the only difference was that I'd had a complicated crush on him.

He'd left his key in Grantchester, having taken a violin there to be repaired. I said that I'd give him a spare set.

'Thank you, but I must go back.'

Well, if you're going, GO already, and whatever happens, don't presume to explain yourself to me. Return to Grantchester; regulate the sun and make the rose official!

'When I leave things behind,' I said, 'it's usually on buses going to Wandsworth or Whitechapel, never to be found. I've never been to Grantchester:

> Stands the church clock at ten to three?
> And is there honey still for tea?

That would show him that *Woman's Own* and *My Weekly* weren't my staple diet! He's probably never heard of Rupert Brooke and Grantchester was just a village where he left his keys and bought strings for his bow.

'Yes. The chestnuts and the tulips are there, too, and we will barely be an hour late. *Come* with me, please.'

Not 'Come with me *please*!' An order, almost; certainly not a charming request, which I would have refused anyway. I followed him to the car and saw Sarath hurrying hopefully down the hill towards us and Mr Rosenfeld and I recited 'The Old Vicarage' all the way up the A 10.

Chapter Six

I'd never known a depression lift so quickly and completely. It was as if this time I'd been cleansed by it and I felt well and confident and on the brink of some hitherto undiscovered joy. Even looking in the mirror and thinking of Dinah, or knowing that Ranjini would be back in a few days, did nothing to eliminate this lightness of heart. Sarath and I caroused nightly and Rosenfeld was away so there was no presence to discompose me. I wondered if I might be in love with Sarath. Our affair blossomed; my spirits soared. We learnt about each other; I no longer felt inadequate, competitive or dutiful. I knew that we must 'do something about us' when his wife returned, but I could not make it matter to me.

Susan and Micky were industrious pupils. Sometimes we would abandon lessons and sit drinking coffee while they told me of their horrifying exploits. When I took her to the local dentist, he took me aside to tell me that the three girls terrorised the neighbourhood. Their mother was never in when I was there and Lil, the woman next door, told me that she was living elsewhere with a boyfriend and only came in occasionally during the evenings.

Lil also told me that Susan had snatched her baby from the pram and held him over the stairwell until she had given Susan five pounds. She'd had to bash open the gas meter in order to pay up and had then retrieved the baby.

I asked Susan and Micky about the incident. They rolled about, laughing.

'You wouldn't really have dropped the baby, would you, Susan?' I queried cautiously.

'Course not! She gave me the money, didn't she? I didn't 'ave to arst 'er twice. She doesn't like the kid, anyway. I often hear 'er yelling at it when it screams. It gets on everyone's nerves.' She made me shudder. She must be a psychopath. One day I would speak to her and Micky about their moral standpoint, but not just yet. They needed patience and kindness whatever they did or said. With me, they behaved themselves and treated me as a friend. The dentist and the neighbour marvelled at my tenacity and my optimism for their future development. Miss Gavenda left me to it, saying she thought I was doing an excellent job. Inner London Education Authority sent me my cheque regularly and asked no questions.

Every day I visited Muriel in hospital and was once allowed to peer through the incubator glass at the tiny baby girl, who was unfortunately wide awake. 'Does she always sleep with her eyes closed?' I asked the nurses, who exchanged glances. Muriel, ill with measles and exhausted after the birth, had never looked better. The staff fussed and babied her. Her mother visited her once, empty-handed, and stayed only briefly. Her father did not appear and remained at liberty. I avoided the social workers and continued to be paid for 'teaching'.

I felt in holiday mood. Ranjini was due to arrive, so I packed a small suitcase and went to stay with my parents for three days. Sarath was away, so she'd have to return to an empty flat. However, she was not my responsibility. I spent the few days overeating, guiltless and serene. I returned to my house on rent day and sat in the pictures until I knew that Ranjini had gone to bed. I noticed the white Citroën was parked outside.

I endured a dream that night of superlative horror. Someone was wailing and sobbing at a graveside and tearing at the earth. I saw that the face was Ranjini's and that the person beneath the earth was me, and not dead. I knew that she would never release me in time and the best thing for me to do would be to die quickly. I turned over in the coffin and tried to pretend that it was a bed and that I must go to sleep, and thus hope to die. I couldn't hear the sobbing any more; she had left me alone. I made a tremendous physical effort to get up and free myself. The blankets covered my face. Reason whispered that it was only a nightmare: some strange, supernatural fear and dread swept into my very soul, infinitely superior to reason. I turned on the lamp and reached over to put on the fire, but remained numb with fear. There was no sound anywhere. No one moved upstairs; no cars passed by. My watch had stopped and I was incapable of getting out of bed to look at the clock. A menacing force, inexplicable and terrifying, clogged the air. I screamed, and banged on the wall with my fists for Ranjini to come to me but there was no answer, no sound.

I managed to crawl on all fours to her door; I beat at it with my elbows and scratched and clawed like a dog. I raised myself, using the door-jamb as a support, and rattled and twisted the knob to no avail. I struggled back to my room and removed the key from my door, which opened hers too, and after interminable fumbling, I got it open. She wouldn't mind if I got into bed with her.

She was lying on the floor, one hand spread out against the bed in supplication. I took the hand in my own icy fingers, but hers were frozen beyond feeling. Her toes were stiff and contorted and her breath came feeble and shallow through her open mouth. I lay on top of her, shaking her, calling her name. It was as if I lay at her graveside, struggling to release her from the coffin.

'Ranjini,' I yelled, 'don't go to sleep! Wait for me! I'll get you out! Help! Help! Mr Rosenfeld! Help!'

'I am here.' He lifted me to my feet. 'Do exactly as I say. Ring for an ambulance. Turn on the fire. Fill a hot-water bottle. Come back here and look for a pill bottle – an empty one.' His voice was low and calm. It gave me strength.

'Yes,' I said, 'Yes.'

When I re-entered the room with the hot-water bottle, after obeying Rosenfeld M. to the letter, I found Ranjini lying on the rug in front of the fire, covered by his dressing gown. He was kneeling next to her in maroon pyjama trousers, his great naked torso stretched over her tiny frame, his hands pressed on her chest beneath her nightgown and his mouth against hers. The grotesque embrace continued as I placed the bottle under her feet, which were now limp and less icy. I found an empty, uncapped, small plastic bottle on the floor, unlabelled, anonymous, murderer unknown.

Mr Rosenfeld raised his head and felt her pulse. I could hear her breath rasping in and out. His hairy chest glistened with sweat and veins stood out on his temples. His face told me nothing. I fetched a towel and wiped his head and neck, then with one slow, incredible movement, he raised himself and Ranjini, simultaneously, to a standing position. 'Take her arm. We must walk her up and down until they come for her.'

I did as he said, like a robot. We dragged her backwards and forwards across the room, her legs trailing after her uselessly like pieces of string. He took nearly all the weight on himself, and we tramped back and forth, back and forth, up and down the long room.

'What is the matter with her?'

'An overdose.'

'Why?' I quavered. 'Why?'

'I thought perhaps you might know.' He looked at me over her head, grim and severe. I hated him.

'What do you mean?'

'You were close to her. You offered her the hand of friendship. You perhaps knew what troubled her heart.' His look accused me and I was afraid.

'You talk in the past,' I said. 'She's not dead. She won't die!'

'If she wants it so, then she will die. She has the right to choose. She reached the pitch of despair. Some of us manage to bear it. Others succumb.' I loathed his short, clipped, stupid remarks and the way he spoke about Ranjini while he slapped her face and dragged her across the room with me, as if she wasn't human; wasn't there. His hair stood up like an angel of death. Any moment he'd be off to Samara to keep another appointment.

I left Ranjini in his arms as I heard the ambulance approach. I rushed outside in my nightie as the men came towards me. Rosenfeld was at the front door, almost immediately behind me, and handed Ranjini over to the man. He gave the other ambulance man the little pill bottle and murmured a few words to him. I pulled on my coat and Rosenfeld his dressing gown and we climbed into the ambulance which immediately sped off. He and the man were doing something to Ranjini with a machine. I heard her retch and closed my eyes and put my hands over my ears. It seemed to me that I spent my entire life riding in ambulances, sitting in hospitals, talking to, listening to, and hearing about ill people. No more!

We sat in the little waiting room. He brought me tea from a machine on the wall. It had a pound of sugar in it.

'I don't take sugar.'

'Drink it, please.'

'I can't. I don't like sweet tea.'

'It is good for shock. Drink it.'

'No.' He was sitting across the room from me. He stood up. He's going to hit me. He's going to pour the tea down my throat by force. 'Keep away from me! Don't you dare come near me! I'll drink it!' I was spilling it all over the place, but I swallowed most of it. He sat down again without a word, his shoulders slumped over. This was the man who had come to my aid when I stood choking on the step; who had probably saved Ranjini; who had given his room to Mandy; who had shown me Rupert

Brooke's Grantchester. Why was I behaving like this?

'You think I am responsible for Ranjini's despair,' I cried. 'If she dies you will think I killed her.'

'You are too honest to deceive yourself.'

I shivered. 'What do you mean by that?'

'I am talking of her husband. You were one of many. She knows only of the many. She did not know of you. She respects and loves and trusts you.'

The many? I only knew of me! There was something I wanted to ask Rosenfeld about tonight... something important. I couldn't think of it. All I could recall was Sarath, his arms enclosing me, his face in my hair, his lips on my neck, his hands roving my body, his careless yet accurate knowledge of passion, which in him was like the bush that burned, yet was perpetually unconsumed. Incapable of love: insatiable because of it. His eyes, his beautiful polished eyes looking stealthily at his watch behind my neck, working out his next appointment, juggling with the minutes, considering whether there would be time for one more frenzied effort. Timing Ranjini's homecoming...

Ranjini, penetrating my dreams, rousing me by her terrible silence: counting out the capsules like so many of his lies and women; dying in frozen isolation. Ranjini, trusting me; caring about me – this cheap slut; this shallow, self-pitying fool; this less than nothing.

He knew. This silent, hard, repulsive man knew and comprehended everything. I couldn't bear it. The tea rallied me. I turned on him with scorn and hate.

'What do you know of me?' I shouted. 'Nothing! Nothing at all! You sit there with your overripe imagination, working things out in your crazy mind, thinking that you're God, trying to make me feel like rubbish, pretending you know everything, prying into matters that are no concern of yours. How dare you! Do I investigate your life? Let the rest of the household indulge you: I tell you, *I* won't tolerate a bloodhound sniffing around me. Your presence is distasteful to me. Just leave me alone!'

'Do not assume that because you are rubbish in your own eyes, you are necessarily so in the eyes of others. We all see and hear subjectively – the piece of glass or the jewel: a mass of daubs or a work of art: a noise or a symphony.'

'The wisdom of Solomon follows close on the heels of the miracle performed by Elijah,' I sneered.

He got up slowly, like an old, old man, oppressed and sad, and with his face turned away from me, left the little waiting room and closed the door quietly behind him. I sat there for yet another hour, half mad with worry, dying for a cigarette; for someone to talk to. I got up to find a ladies'. The early morning light shone through the little window. Everyone had forgotten about me – no one had come to tell me whether Ranjini lived or died. Rosenfeld stood in the corridor talking to a doctor, but I couldn't hear what was being said. Then I saw him walk over to the reception desk and ask them to phone for a taxi.

We sat in silence all the way home. I went straight into my room and sat on the bed, wringing my hands while he ran upstairs for money to pay the driver. A few moments later there was a gentle tap at the door.

'What is it?'

'Rosenfeld. May I come in for a moment?' I didn't even bother to answer. His unshaven face glowered at me. 'Give me your coat, get into bed and drink this. It has no sugar in it.' He thrust a glass into my hand, full of hot, spicy, delicious alcohol. He actually covered me up and fixed a pillow behind me while I sipped it. 'I will tell you as soon as there is news and endeavour to contact her husband. Perhaps you would like me to telephone your place of work later, to inform them that you will be absent. You are not fit.'

He was managing me again, but I couldn't be bothered to fight against it. I gave him the County Hall number, then with great difficulty I clawed up some tiny dregs of humanity for him. 'I am very sorry I was rude to you, Mr Rosenfeld. Try to get some rest yourself and thank you for all you've done.' I held out my hand. He took it in his massive one which shook with a strange tremor, then raised it to his lips, and no doubt feeling me recoil, released me and left the room without another word.

On the brink of sleep, the question that I had wanted to ask him came to me. 'Mr Rosenfeld, how did you know that Ranjini had taken pills?' The answer followed it, without a pause, bright and clear, in that moment of inspiration before unconsciousness. I heard myself gasp with amazement and fell immediately asleep.

I awoke to one of those horrible cold days when eleven o'clock looks the same as five and succeeds in oppressing you to the verge of suicide. Hail was drumming against the window. I needed a cup of tea, two slices of toast spread with Silver Shred and Ranjini knocking on the door to tell me she'd got it all ready. But she was dying; maybe dead. The knocking on my door was only Rosenfeld waiting to tell me something terrible. Please, God, let him give me good news; let him tell me that Ranjy is going to be well. If he does, I'll be nice to him, I promise. My nightie was open down the front. I jostled everything back into place and hooked up the collar.

I should have scrambled out of bed, slipped on a dressing gown and opened the door for him in a decent, normal manner, but I could not make my legs move properly. 'Come in, please.' My voice wobbled oddly and my eyes felt terrible: I'd fallen asleep with my contact lenses in, and my heart seemed to be banging in my head, dull, heavy and sickening, and there was a foul-tasting rock in my throat. I saw that his eyes were wet with tears.

'She's dead!' I screamed. 'Ranjini's dead!' I clawed at him like a madwoman, deafened by the ugly noise of my hysteria. I felt my arms clamped to my sides and his own binding and encircling me in the most effective straitjacket possible. So this is what Doctor Feber meant that I should have done to Carl when he became aggressive and mad – this strange combination of great gentleness and physical power.

'She is better and waiting to see you.' I could hear him through my own clamour and stopped yelling on the instant. 'When you are quiet and calm I will let you go.' But he held me still, as if forgetful of what he was saying. 'Come! Wash your face and get dressed!'

I was willing and ready to comply if he would give me a sporting chance and allow me to bend my elbows, which seemed to me to take an irritatingly long time. I crawled about stiffly, like a tortoise in its dotage. When I emerged from the bathroom I saw tea and toast on a tray outside my door. He was some sort of wizard: a nasty, rather frightening, interfering old wizard.

It took me ages and ages to get ready. I should have been dancing on air, knowing Ranjini was better, but I didn't feel like facing her. Rosenfeld and I drove through Hampstead to the New End Hospital. 'Did you find . . .?'

'No. His colleagues do not know where he is. It does not matter. She would not care to see him, but she will be happy to see you. I will wait for you here.'

'You mean you're not coming in too?'

'No, it is better that I don't.'

I thought so too. His presence would only confuse and embarrass her – and me!

She was in a small room just off the entrance to a long ward, and curtains were pulled around the bed. The nurse told me not to stay for more than a few minutes. She looked so thin and sad and pathetic. I kissed her cold forehead and held her hand which hung lifelessly in mine. I could see the clock on the wall above the curtain. Twelve hours exactly since we had brought her here. On the locker was a bowl crammed with blue and white hyacinths. 'From Leah and Rosenfeld,' the card said. He had written my name. Leah. Odd sounding, strange and too familiar coming from his pen. He remained remote, impersonal. Rosenfeld.

'Hello, you silly cow.'

'I do not care that he is not in office.' She always said 'office' without a 'the'. 'I know where he is; what he has been doing. He has time for so many and not five minutes to spare for me. I gave up my family, my friends, my status and dowry for him. I loved him. They had a servant to follow me to school to prevent me from meeting him. I thought they did not like him because he is Tamil. I used to bribe the servant so that he would leave us together for a little time. My entire family were against him and therefore against me too. In that society this means a life of hell, but I was strong because we loved each other. I am discredited, unacceptable, alone. I have nobody. I do not care. All I know is that I do not want him. Do not let him near me. Promise me, promise me not to tell him where I am!'

'I promise.' Guilt and rage and pity conspired to drive me directly to purgatory. She seemed to relax a little. 'Why didn't you come to me, darling? What are friends for? You could have trusted me to understand!'

'My best friend at school was forced to marry a man she didn't love. She had two children by him, but she could not love him, although he adored her, so she burned herself to death. I understood that; you don't. She felt degraded, and so do I. You cannot comprehend what it is like to live with a man whom you once loved and whom you now loathe and despise, and who is indifferent to you. I know you are my friend but I am an outcast with my people. All of them in Ceylon know what he is like. Last night he came in and he was drunk as usual. He mocked and insulted me. When he left, I poured all my sleeping capsules into my hand, and crammed them in my mouth all at once, like raisins. I drank some water and I remember putting the glass on the chest and not caring, not feeling anything, and that's all. I don't care now. Don't let him near me! Promise me!' She was shouting and shaking with sobs; pulling my hand.

The nurse came and I kissed Ranjini and was ushered out of the curtain, promising over and over that I would see her again, tomorrow. I ran down the corridor to where Rosenfeld was waiting, folding his paper as I came up.

'She seems very depressed, but she's talking a lot. I promised her we wouldn't tell Sarath where she was and she doesn't want to see him. What shall I do?'

'I will speak to him when he returns home. Do you want him to leave the house? It would be advisable for him to do so, so that when she is discharged from hospital, she will be able to have some time on her own to decide what she wants to do.'

'I don't know. I can't think! What if he refuses to leave? What if he gets difficult? What if he threatens to tell...?'

'Would you allow me to take on this responsibility? You have had too much to contend with and it will be easier for me to deal with him.'

'I am so grateful to you, Mr Rosenfeld; you're everyone's kind, dependable uncle. And thank you for sending the flowers to Ranjini and including my name. You think of everything!'

'You are mistaken. I think only of one thing.'

Heigh-ho, I thought; here we go again! The variation on a theme by Elgar. I didn't know what he was talking about, and he was embarrassingly aware of my complete indifference.

He pulled up outside the Indian restaurant in Belsize Road. 'Come,' he said, 'you have had nothing to eat all day.'

'I'm not dressed for eating out and I've got something in the house.'

'It's dark in here and no one is going to look at you. Also you have nothing to eat in the house.'

I felt like telling him to go to hell, but he was out of the car and opening my door for me, and I lost my nerve.

I was so hungry suddenly, I ate like one starving, swilling it down with two glasses of cider, and as always the alcohol seemed to soften not only my head, but my heart. They were playing Mahler's *Fifth* on a hidden gramophone, and it blended gloriously with the Indian atmosphere and the smell of curry. The music made me strangely happy, aware of the sad man opposite, and I remembered the last time we had dined together. It took the edge off my dislike.

His hand surrounded his glass, and the other rested on his temple; the fingers were long, beautiful and supple, oddly at variance with the rest of him. You didn't have to be Scarlett O'Hara for his hands to meet round your waist, but probably his preference was for the neck. Two almost identical stripes of scarred tissue drove along the lengths of both wrists and disappeared up the sleeves of his jacket. I struggled to repress a squeamish shudder.

'You play the violin, don't you, Mr Rosenfeld?'

'Occasionally, yes. You like music too, I see.' I nodded, wondering what I had let myself in for. He felt in his pocket and handed me a yellow ticket. It was for a concert at the Festival Hall, Row C., Complimentary, 14th February; months ahead. 'I hope you will come. You will enjoy it, I think.'

'Of course I'll come! I've never had such a marvellous seat!' There were a hundred excuses I could invent for not turning up and plenty of time to find them. I stretched my mouth at him and it managed to turn into a smile. I was being nice to him – keeping my promise with God. 'It's the anniversary of a special day for me, too, so it will be a kind of celebration.'

'A birthday?'

'No, I don't have any more of those; the anniversary of a decision.' I told him about the day when I'd made up my mind to buy the house, and then about everything else – my family, my job, my trip to New York. He was the Almighty's gift to intoxicated verbosity, freely opening all the doors of conversation through which I willingly and joyously pattered. It was singularly flattering. Too late, I realised that I had asked him nothing about himself and that he had volunteered no kind of exchange.

When I arrived home from work, the following day, Sarath was in the kitchen, reading the paper and swigging a can of Truman's Light Ale, taken from my fridge. I tried to creep into my room without his seeing me, but his ears were sharpened from perpetual wariness. He was standing next to me as I opened my door, and his arms were around me before I could put down my bag of shopping to stave him off.

'All's clear!' he whispered in my ear, 'and I haven't seen you for ages. Come, we'll have a drink in your room.' He walked over to the window and pulled the curtains to.

His carelessness of my reaction and his cool arrogance made me wild. I thought of Ranjini and wielded my plastic shopping bag over my shoulder, and heard the satisfactory sound of my Heinz tin of tomato soup smack the side of his head. He gaped at me, stunned and incredulous, until the expression in his eyes changed suddenly, to dark rage. A spoilt and indulged child, about to have a tantrum, ready to smash his toys, once cherished, in order to show his displeasure. He gripped my hand, squashing and grinding the knuckles together, calculatingly using his knowledge of me to cause pain and wreak revenge. I kicked him, and punched him ineffectually with my free hand, shouting abuse at him for all the neighbours to hear, but no one came to investigate. Rosenfeld had left me to deal with this creature, whom I so suddenly and easily hated; as quickly and as easily as I had fallen prey to him.

I managed to tear the curtain half open, knowing how Sarath dreaded the possibility of being observed – and there it was, the white Citroën, and the Wizard of Oz himself, striding towards the front door. He must have seen or heard me, for the next instant he was in my room, without so much as a gentlemanly tap at the door. I think he said 'Good afternoon' to us, as Sarath exchanged the golden handshake with me for one with

Rosenfeld; then hand in hand they left the room, Sarath first, ushered out backwards, irresistibly and obediently complying to the will of his master, and my door was gently but firmly closed in my face. I did not dare to open it; Rosenfeld's authority was too absolute. I crept over to the wall and stuck my best ear against it, but not the tiniest sound of voice or movement came through.

I gave up the thankless task and got myself ready to visit Ranjini, but I wanted to give her some reassuring news, like the sudden and ignominious demise of Sarath, which I was beginning to believe to be true.

Ten minutes later, Rosenfeld appeared, his face devoid of all expression, ready to verify my evil hopes. He's killed him; choked him with those amazing hands: or perhaps broken his neck with a neat, swift karate chop.

'He will be gone with his personal possessions by the time you get back. He will be leaving everything of any value here. I will be supervising his departure and the financial arrangements. He is not prepared to dispute with me any further, and neither you nor Ranjini need have any cause for anxiety on his account.'

How German you are; how charmless! How the burden of gratitude to such as you weighs me down! Can't you tell me what you said to Sarath or what you did to him? How did you bewitch him? What devilish acts have you been up to in there?

'What would we do without you, Mr Rosenfeld, I wonder!' My voice sounded so false and off key that I felt embarrassed for us both.

'You seemed to manage quite well without the good uncle. Sarath has a lump on his head which grew as I spoke to him.' Somewhere, there was a sour, bitter note which I had never heard before. Perhaps the one thing with which he was unable to cope was the idea that he was not an absolute requisite to the lives of those around him.

'I hit him with the soup, but the soup was in a can!' His face softened and he only smiled; yet it was as if the sun had quite suddenly and inexplicably swooped through the darkest cloud. It enveloped me with its warmth and radiance, and I raised my stiffened hand automatically towards its lovely light. 'He squashed my fingers. Look!'

He enclosed them in his own, smoothing out the stiffness and relieving the pain. 'Go now, to see your friend. I will meanwhile attend to his exodus. He will be out of the house before I go away myself. Please convey my regards.'

I ran off to the bus stop without a shred of regret for Sarath. Ranjini was sitting in a chair, looking much better, but there was a dullness in her eyes. Although she managed to smile at me, I sensed the supreme effort she was making to overcome her apathy and deep depression.

I told her that Sarath was on his way out, under Rosenfeld's supervision, and that there was absolutely nothing for her to worry about on that score.

'He wrote to me,' she said. 'What a comfort and support he has been! I will never allow myself to forget again what friends I have!'

'What do you make of Rosenfeld, Ranjy?' I felt ashamed for her to go on about friendship, assuming that I was included. 'You know, I've never been able to stand him. He always seems to be prying creepily into people's private lives, yet I must say that recently he's had his uses.' I stopped, horrified at my appalling lack of tact.

'Tell me,' she begged. 'Please. I want to hear how he saved me. I am better, I promise you that. I must know; it will do me good.'

I told her a little of what had happened that night, playing down my own crucial part, but she wasn't impressed or even interested anyway. Only in his miracles. 'He knew you had taken pills, and yet it never occurred to me. Later, I did have a clear idea about it, but it's gone. He knows every bloody thing, though; he's there with the answer even before you know you've got a question. He's as steady and as boring and as ugly as a great lumpy rock.' It was quite monstrous, the way she casually disregarded my actions. She must be obsessed with this man! 'In spite of all his do-gooding, there isn't a grain of softness in him; he hasn't the remotest genuine feeling for anyone. He's so supercilious, so contemptuous for others' weaknesses, because he's invulnerable, and therefore he assumes he's got none of his own. It's as if he does favours automatically in order to feed his ego, and there's no virtue in that. I get most unpleasant vibes from him; I've always been extremely psychic and instinctively aware of the subconscious in the people I mix with. He makes me feel like a scuttling, stupid, ineffectual vacuum. He tries his best to act in a way he thinks human beings should act, but he can't pull it off. He doesn't fool me, anyway. So he's got time and money to throw around those who are in the vicinity to worship him. We're doing him the favour, allowing him to indulge his craving for gratitude and adulation.' I knew that I was flagrantly misrepresenting him, but I felt compelled to indulge and gratify *myself*.

I was aware that Ranjini was looking at me with a singularly odd expression. She seemed to be shrinking from my presence. It was as if she hated me, and my whole inside contracted painfully.

'Is that all you have to say?' I was unprepared for such coldness. 'Let me tell you a few things now.'

She knows everything about Sarath and me. She's been pretending ignorance all along. No, she found out today. Rosenfeld has betrayed me; he has written everything in that damned letter she keeps fiddling with. I shall poison him with toadstool soup when I get home. I shall watch him die an agonising death, dragging him back to life just long enough to let him know how and why I loathe him.

'Have you no conception of goodness? We have all leaned

against that ugly rock. Do you ever spend a minute or two thinking of anyone but yourself? Getting rid of Sarath can't have been exactly fun, and he has done more for me than merely save my life. He knows about suffering and despair. That hard, stony robot has more compassion and feeling and love for others, than all the do-gooders put together, you included. It is you who are callous and shallow, full of self-interest, gorging on your own petty problems, too crushed by your house and your rejected love to think beyond the surface of the pain of others. You never really understood how I felt, because you have never known the total eclipse of hope. There has been no tragedy in your life to enable you to see it in the lives of those around you. What do you know of him? He understands more in five minutes than you ever would in your lifetime!'

She's gone mad. The pills she took have affected her brain and turned her personality upside down. I must get a message to her psychiatrist immediately. Whatever happens, I mustn't show that I'm wounded by what she's said, or that I know she's crazy.

'Ranjini, don't you know that I care about you? Just because I dislike Rosenfeld shouldn't mean that I'm hard and selfish. Don't turn against me like this.' I could hardly get the words out; my voice was as trembly as a late autumn leaf, hanging on to a dead branch, and tears were stinging my eyes. 'I shouldn't have spoken to you as I did. You're still feeling frail and shocked and depressed.' For answer, the nurse rang the bell to announce the end of the visit, and I managed to sway to my feet.

She thrust the bulky envelope into my hand. 'This came for me today, but it belongs to you. Whatever you think of the contents, remember that it has given me courage for tonight, and hope for tomorrow.'

It was probably some excruciatingly dreary tract from a guru on divine right. I could not bring myself to look at her, and I walked all the way home. The air was clear and frosty and the moon full and bright. She must be suffering from moon madness. I'd heard about women going quite insane at these times. I'd go to the library and look it up. I couldn't stop thinking of all the cruel and unjust words she had used against me.

I arrived home, exhausted, and barged into Dinah and Walter, standing in the hallway, enveloped in each other's arms, hardly conscious of my brief presence. My God, their constant public shmoozing got on my nerves. I heard Mandy singing upstairs, and wondered what she had to trill about, with a baby due in a few weeks. Everyone seemed involve in something or someone, except me.

I lay in the bath, weeping into the water, until chilled and shivering, I got myself into bed, opening up Agatha Christie's *Five Little Pigs* to turn me off all the pigs living around me. It was almost three before I found out that it was Elsa Greer who'd done it. She'd poisoned Amyas in quite a cunning way and they never found out until sixteen years later, Hercule Poirot being then one hundred and five, and all the grey matter still intact. If he'd checked out at a hundred, Elsa would still be sitting pretty. I thought again of indestructible Hercules the Second, up the stairs, and wished him a similar fate to Amyas'.

I had to rise in four hours' time, but first I'd plough through Ranjini's letter which I'd only just remembered. I pulled out the bundle of papers in my usual messy way, and began to read.

The birds were chorusing the arrival of the dawn before I lay down to sleep, and light filled the room, but the words in the letter burned clear, without its help, and the memory of his smile battled with the sunrise, churning my soul with pity and love, and my dreams denied sleep. I stood at the window, calling his name. He would come, the way he always did, when I needed him. But the white Citroën wasn't there. I remembered that he had told me he was going away, and there was no answer.

Chapter Seven

There are very few people who are aware of the activities of the Filthy Squad. Those of us who are helped by them and owe good health, decent, clean living and a fresh start to these giants of the community do not divulge its secrets.

The Filthy Squad, then, is a secret society and its official name is rarely used. Its members do not wear a uniform when travelling to work; no badge, no sign distinguishes them from ordinary travellers on the bus. They arrive at the appointed place separately, each Squad consisting of three women and one man. They meet at eight forty-five. A van arrives a few minutes beforehand, occasionally driven by the man in the team; a small, shabby, anonymous van, filled with large and small appliances. The front doors of the van are opened and the ladies remove their coats and place them neatly on the front seats. We may observe that they are now wearing clean print sleeveless overalls and flat, wide, comfortable-looking soft shoes. The man wears thick dungarees and gloves. A mask protrudes from one of his capacious pockets. He opens the back doors of the van and removes the heavier equipment, and each lady takes a pail crammed with an assortment of cleaning materials of various fragrances, dusters, dishclothes, a roll of muslin, brooms and mops.

Splendid Hearts! Bringers of Glad Tidings, Hope and Ecstasy! You, with your clean pinafores and cotton turbans! Your plump, pink arms send a sensuous thrill through me; your virile scrubbing brushes compare favourably to the bristly jaw of the most ardent lover. O, that lemon perfume of Ajax; that bosky, herbal freshness of Flash; the lavender of Mansion Polish, the pine of the disinfectant, the earthy smell of new dishcloths revives my soul and lightens my heart! Do not talk of new-mown hay, roses, lilac, or eau de toilette Chanel Number 5; for number 87 Eastgate Road is where I am sitting in thrall, at the broken window, watching the Filthy Squad preparing for battle.

Muriel was returned to her stately home minus the baby who was still in hospital. Her father had obligingly vacated the premises when cigarette burns had been discovered on her four sisters. He had apparently used their ears for ashtrays and various other parts of the body for his dog-ends. The girls were temporarily in care until more satisfactory accommodation could be found. Mrs Towey and Muriel were now the only two occupants of the third floor of the Eastgate Bug Hotel. They had been informed that it was to be professionally cleaned that day, and if Mrs Towey had made any protestations, they had been ignored. One cannot argue with a hurricane. I had been told to take Muriel out somewhere for several hours, but I delayed going, out of curiosity and respect for the Filthy Squad.

I could hear them now, chatting cheerfully and clanking up the stairs. They beamed at us and quipped with each other as they set down their utensils. The man, Jeff, took out a little box and went on to the landing, and caught a few bugs of varying species from the mouldering cupboard, which he then asked me to hand in for analysis at the Public Health Department, which was on our route.

I gave the box at once to Muriel, since I had the sandwiches and flask to carry. We were thus driven out of the squalid flat and were never destined to see it thus again. After we had delivered our unpleasant parcel, we turned northwards towards Clissold Park. It was a beautiful autumn day, and we sauntered along, looking into shop windows, not talking much.

It was barely morning coffee time when we arrived. I knew a grassy bank there, near the stream, and we lay down on it and watched the ducks and wildfowl, and the spotted deer, chickens and rabbits following their fussy pursuits in the large hummocky enclosure beyond, and devoured the egg and cheese sandwiches which I had prepared. I had brought along a few of Muriel's favourite comics, but she seemed dreamy and uninterested and threw little bits of bread to a blind duck who was given the crumbs of charity by all the park regulars, and thus thrived and waxed fatter than any of his fellows.

'Is this a picnic, Miss?'

'A sort of picnic, but not a real one.'

'Have you ever been on a real picnic?' I nodded. 'What's it like, a real picnic?'

A hot day in August when no one I knew went on holiday. Playing skipping outside the open front door with my sisters and friends, and then Mam, usually so busy and often cross, coming out of the house to shout at us for not washing the pots or wanting someone to run an errand, spoiling our game.

But not today! She stands for a few moments looking out at the sunshine and then she says, 'This is not a day for doing the blinking housework or cooking – let's go to Ferriby Foreshore for a picnic!'

The heart pauses, hovering between disbelief and ecstasy, and then jerking into action, we run into our respective houses to prepare. Two large glass bottles of cocoa; bread, hard-boiled eggs, perhaps a little soft in the yolks still because of the rush; tomatoes, a muslin bag of cream cheese and some empty jam jars for blackberries.

The joyous march up the street to the meeting place – the bus stop – for the three-mile ride to Ferriby Foreshore.

We played on the mud flats and threw driftwood into the river. We paddled in our vests and knickers, popping seaweed, making watery pathways in the sand; screaming with pleasure as the tide came in and Mam's dress got wet! Lying on the warm shingle, eating our soft tomatoes and eggs, and drinking our cold cocoa, and after that, running over the stones on to the grass beyond, to make buttercup and daisy chains, and to fill the jars with wild raspberries and blackberries and hips. Climbing trees and swinging dangerously on the branches; watching a busy ant-hill, and listening to Mam tell us the story of 'The Ant and the Grasshopper' and that day we were all grasshoppers. Oh, how many picnics studded my childhood! Walking back along the street in the cool evening, with our drooping bunches of daisies, harebells, foxgloves and weeds, wearing necklaces of seaweed and carrying our now half-empty jam jars; unkempt and dirty. Scratched legs and sandals caked with mud. That unforgettable after-a-picnic sweetness and quietness!

When was the last time I went on a real picnic? With Rosenfeld. Walking through the narrow pathways amongst the nettles and old man's beard behind the Old Vicarage. Strolling through the churchyard and reading the gravestones. We bought apples and cider from the village shop and a big bag of buttered scones from the Orchard and we lay down on the rough grass near the river and he read the entire poem to me from the book we bought at the church.

> I only know that you may lie
> Day long and watch the Cambridge sky,
> And, flower-lulled in sleepy grass,
> Hear the cool lapse of hours pass,
> Until the centuries blend and blur
> In Grantchester, in Grantchester . . .

A real picnic is nothing to do with duty or necessity, which is why I am in the park with Muriel. It is to do with warmth and love. 'I don't know, Muriel, but one day you'll go on one, I promise,' I lied, 'and then you'll know.' Yesterday, Tomorrow,

Sometime, Never. 'We'd better be getting back to see how they're managing at the flat, and you want to see Baby this afternoon, don't you?'

She did not respond. Obviously she didn't want to see Baby; but I was longing to see how the Filthy Squad was progressing.

The Temple of Diana, The Transformation of Eighty-Seven Eastgate Road, The Hanging Gardens of Babylon, The Colossus of Rome are separated only by commas and by Time. All converge into the category of Wondrous Sights, rendering Man stupefied, faint and speechless with shock and awe. The humble Filthy Squad had performed a miracle. The place shouted with cleanliness from the dustbin area to the front door; thence up the glassy lino of the staircase for further delights! The windows had been made whole again and dazzled mine eyes; whiter than white nets hung there. Each room had been totally stripped of every single article; not a stick, not a rag remained: the naked floorboards creaked uneasily, the layers of filth having been removed by a ferocious machine. The walls had been scrubbed with merciless abrasives and Jeff was in the middle of painting the ceiling. Brawny gnomes had visited in my absence and fumigated every inch of the flat, and carpets and furniture, bedding and crockery provided by the council lay in a huge van in the street. It was all to be moved in that afternoon once the first and second coats of paint had been applied. Apologetically, Jeff said that he would be busy here for another two days.

I sent Muriel off to see her child. Even she had gaped. Then I blessed them all, having finally recovered my speech, and left with a full heart.

Mrs Towey, feckless and irresponsible as she undoubtedly was, had been given a chance. Muriel and her baby would learn to avoid squalor, strive for an acceptable standard. Kindness and love may be denied them, but cruelty, muck and disease no longer threatened to swamp and destroy them.

O, Filthy Squad, I who have witnessed your Miracle and have

Faith, come to me! Cancel my mistakes, discount my lies, pay my debts, clear my conscience, erase my pimples, make me immediately and effortlessly slim, remove my addiction to nicotine, grant me a fresh, clean start! How the personality would blossom; the soul breathe pure air; the mind relinquish all turmoil and dread and guilt and discard its useless, time-wasting mess! Ministering Angels, your duties and talents lie elsewhere! And Rosenfeld has deserted me.

Three weeks had passed since Sarath's eviction. A cheque was left in an envelope from him, with a note telling me briefly that the enclosed was for the continued rental of the room, for the sole occupation of Mrs R. Jayatissa, and I could expect to receive the sum due every four weeks.

I detected a Fine Italian Hand behind it all. Rosenfeld's rent was not due for another three months and there was no reason, no excuse for me to try to discover his whereabouts or when he would return. Ah! But wait! He had, after all, promised to be responsible for Sarath's absence, and what would I do if he tried to come back to the house, or if he betrayed me to Ranjini! How could Rosenfeld be so sure of him? And then, what if Dinah started to become ill and he wasn't here to watch over her? Ranjini might make a second suicide attempt once she was released from hospital. Mandy was expecting her baby in a few weeks; it was his doing – not the baby, but the fact that I was lumbered with it. If it hadn't been for his generosity towards her, she would most probably have left. Who would look after her; take her to hospital when the time came? Not me! I was finished with sickness and other people's crises. It was imperative that I trace him as quickly as possible.

Ranjini would know where he was. Her colleagues from work arrived at visiting times, laden with flowers and gifts, and she revived and flourished. I thought that she had always been lonely and almost friendless, but I was mistaken. It was Sarath who had isolated her and cramped her personality, yet during this time, she quite deliberately drove a wedge between herself and me. She must have had news from the astrologist in Ceylon. I wondered apprehensively when she was planning to discuss the subject with me, and made sure that when I went to see her, others were present. On one of these occasions I asked her casually if she knew of Rosenfeld's whereabouts, since letters had arrived for him and he had forgotten to leave a forwarding address.

'I had a couple of cards from him, posted in Manchester and Edinburgh. I wouldn't worry about his mail; he obviously didn't forget.'

I felt like slapping her. When she came home and her friends were less attentive, she would be grateful for the opportunity of passing the time of day with me.

She was sent to a convalescent home in Dorset. I brought her suitcase to her and returned home with all the paraphernalia she had collected while in hospital. I felt discarded, like her get-well cards, which I sorted through, eagerly, but none were from him. She must have stuck to those.

I went upstairs to his room, after first ensuring that the house was empty. It was crammed with baby furniture – a cot, a pram and a bath. The wardrobe and chest contained tiny clothes, nappies and powders. Nothing of his remained. He had gone, taking all his possessions. Maybe he had said farewell and I had not heard; not listened. So he had told Mandy she could use his room as a nursery. She would know when he was coming back.

I heard her busy with the key at the front door and barely had time to run down the stairs. She staggered in with an enormous box. 'You shouldn't lift things,' I scolded her, 'in your condition.'

'Oh, for Christ's sake, shut up and close the door. It's only Brillo pads. They're lighter than my fingers. By "lift" I reckon you mean "carry". In my line it means something else! Here, you can have a hundred. Clean all your mucky pans. It's okay.

The bowling alley won't miss them.' I took them from her, asking no questions, and hid them carefully in an extremely greasy cubbyhole under the gas stove.

Mandy sat in my kitchen waiting for the tea I had offered her. 'My God, this place is a dump since Ranjy went into hospital. Honestly, you don't set your tenants a very good example.'

I had spent the last hour scrubbing, mopping and wiping all the surfaces which showed. She just happened to have seen the place where I'd put the Brillo pads. If anyone was sloppy, she was.

'I hope you don't mind me asking, but is it the Queen's garden party today? I've never seen you in such a lovely hat and coat!' I was wearing a torn overall and shapeless blue tam to protect my face from the cobwebs I'd been jabbing at with a broom. If Mandy ever told me I looked nice, I would have felt deflated and uneasy.

'Is all this flattery leading up to anything?' I had once thought her shy and reserved. I couldn't help marvelling at my incredible lack of judgement with regard to all my tenants. She took a cigarette from my packet and sipped her tea, pulling a face.

'Is your sugar rationed?' I handed the bag over. 'Actually, I do want to ask you a favour. George is willing to leave his wife and come down to London to live. That's if he can stay with me. He's been offered a job as a driver for Tesco's. Think of all those groceries falling off his lorry and coming your way!'

'First of all, just because you and George are low-lives don't assume that I'm one.' Her eyes slid over to the bottom of my cooker. 'And as to your request, how can both of you and the baby manage in one room? I'd be had up for overcrowding, and maybe Dinah and Rosenfeld would object. After all, only the three of you have been using the kitchen and bathroom, and Rosenfeld may want his big room back. He might think you're taking liberties. I want to avoid bad feeling amongst the tenants.

Don't you think I've got a point?'

'My God, you're such a crook; don't tell me you haven't poked around upstairs to see what's going on! You know bloody well that I'm using the two rooms while Rosenfeld's on tour, and by the time he comes back George will have found us a flat to move in to, so don't lose sleep over bad feelings or overcrowding. Now I'll come clean. George has been living with me for the last six weeks. When he rings the door bell it's just so that he can keep up the visiting myth with you. I've felt bad about not letting on to you all along. There must be an honest streak in me somewhere. He's sick of creeping about like a burglar – I can't tell you the number of times he's had to shin down the pipe via the bathroom window – and no one's voiced any objections up to now. I need him with me for when the baby comes. We won't be any trouble to you.'

'What do you mean about Mr Rosenfeld being "on tour"?'

'He's a musician. He's lived in this house for months and you don't even know about him! He's a professional fiddler – me and George have a lot in common with him!' She giggled.

'When is he coming back?'

'February. As soon as we hear from him about the exact day, we'll be off. Don't get neurotic about it. I wouldn't let him down. I never knew anyone like him before – so kind and generous, and a Jew and a foreigner at that!'

She was trying to rile me, and succeeded. I swore and screamed at her.

'You know that I said that on purpose. Why are you so edgy these days? Is it because that bugger you took a shine to has left? It's the best thing that could have happened. Ranjy's well rid of him and so are you. He tried it on with me and Dinah, but he got short-changed. You see, she's got Walter and I've got George; you didn't have anybody.'

'That's no excuse; no reason. How did you find out about us? Who told you?'

'No one, you dope. You don't have to be highbrow to know these things. And if it's crossing your stupid mind that I'm going to get out my box, bell and book and tell on you, then you should be on the phone to the police to split on me about the Brillo pads. You've got to be able to trust your friends. If they came knocking at this door, I wouldn't expect you to tell them the story of my life. Likewise, if Ranjy asked uncomfortable questions, I'd take her on a circular tour leading nowhere, and George and a few of his mates would meanwhile put Sarath in a cold sweat if he ever threatened to open his ugly mouth or tried to come here. Mr Rosenfeld trusts George to keep him nice and frightened while he's not here to take care of him.'

'Why did he ask George to keep Sarath away from here?'

'That's what you want, isn't it?'

'Yes, but why should he take the trouble?' I longed for her to be serious and say something reassuring and delightful; something I could chew over and relish for the eight weeks I would have to wait until his return.

'Sometimes you act so thick, I wonder why I bother; and you're supposed to be able to write stories and teach kids who have problems. I bet they end up a right mess after knocking their heads against yours. Honestly, you give me period pains, and the way I am, that's worse than bad. Let me get upstairs and make myself a decent cup of tea. I've got a family to think of.' She seemed so exasperated that I felt quite timid.

'Please, Mandy, be solemn for a minute. I only want to know...'

'Yes. Mr Rosenfeld will turn somersaults for everyone and never act as if he's put out, but we notice; he'll turn double ones for you, and all you've done is cock your snook and hang about with that horrible man. So why should he want him around? Don't kid yourself that he kicked him out of the house just for your sake, or Ranjy's. Men are selfish buggers; they've always got their own interests first foot forward. Mind you, it's possible he's the exception. After all, he swapped rooms with me and he didn't have an ulterior motive. But that's different. If you're asking me if he's said anything nice about you to me, the answer is "No". So why don't you bury yourself in your work until he gets back; then you can cross-question him. I've got to go and do my disgusting exercises. I don't want this baby coming out arse over elbow.'

I didn't ask her how the exercises could prevent such an event – it might appear argumentative. With Mandy you had to watch your step if you were feeling frail. I felt hurt that she had deceived me about George, and that Rosenfeld had connived, as if against me.

I wished that my relationship with adults and my knowledge and perception of their behaviour and personalities could match my style with the children I taught: I knew that I was making a breakthrough with Susan which no other person had succeeded in doing. I was not only her teacher and friend – I possessed a mastering influence over her and was directing her behaviour from the dangerous and amoral on to a plane that she had hitherto never known existed. She belonged to that strange, afflicted group of people who are unable to differentiate between the normal and the terrible; between humour and horror. No one knows the proportion of humanity who walk amongst us, hiding their iniquity by intelligence and guile; psychopathic; criminally insane. Psychoanalysis, kindness, punishment and discussion are as oil on water and it seems that incarceration is society's ultimate protection against these doomed people. Susan talked easily to me of her past escapades, treating them lightly, boasting of her crimes. I never ceased to be dismayed by the numerous tales with which the neighbours regaled me, and which she gleefully verified and embellished. I was possessed by some marvellous inspirational power which led me unfalteringly towards her salvation.

I managed to arrange an informal and private interview with

her mother, one evening. She disliked her daughter, and was repelled by her behaviour which, she assured me, had been bizarre from the age of four, when she had overturned prams holding babies; cut down neigbours' washing-lines or thrown filth at their clean laundry. She had toddled around locally parked cars with her fork and knife and scratched carefully through the paintwork, and as she grew older, learnt to use broken milk bottles and jagged tins, to make a more thorough job. She flung pans of boiling water down the stairwell at the occupants of the ground floor when they ventured out of their flats, causing pain, shock and injury. When she was eleven, she had thrust her sister, Sharon, on to the outside window ledge, a drop of certain death, and kept her there, screaming, while she joyfully jabbed at her with a broom. The superintendent of the centre which had remanded her had been unwilling to be responsible for her, after she had viciously attacked a fellow offender and vandalised the recreation room. She was too young for prison.

The diversions which had most recently excited her, and which caused her uncontrollable mirth when we talked about them, included a false tip-off regarding the whereabouts of a sought-after criminal. Police had invaded the home of a family of petty criminals, found a few stolen goods and arrested the father and son. She had called out the fire brigade uselessly, pretending to be the mother of a friend of hers, and sent them to the flat of an elderly crippled woman, who had irresponsibly and fearlessly abused Susan for her malice. She had followed the old woman and snatched her walking frame, causing her to fall and break her pelvis.

Each day we talked and talked. Micky had a temporary job on a nearby building site and we usually spent our time alone in the living room. She told me happily of his reading progress and how she helped him in the evenings. Her love for him was touching. I had abandoned formal lessons for the time being with Susan; after all, the Christmas holidays were almost upon us and I knew that our exchanges of confidences were of the utmost importance. For this was the core of my remarkable progress with her. *I* confided in *her*! For two hours each day we were equals. I told her about my work in the hospital; my final battle with Sister and how I despised her. And I told her about Muriel. When she chatted to me about Micky, I told her about Joseph and how much I had loved him, and how I felt when he left me. I imagined that psychiatrists in Broadmoor did not reveal anything of themselves to the prisoners they claimed to help and understand; the social workers did not tell their clients of their family rows and problems. We sat at the slimy table, smoking, and drinking our murky coffee, enjoying each other's company; helping each other. She refused to see the psychiatric social worker or to attend the Tavistock Clinic. She insisted that the only person she could trust to understand her, and to whom she could talk openly, was me. Unwillingly, I had to agree. Some innate sense of timing, of the absolute correctness of our flourishing relationship, made me confident and secure.

Two learned child psychiatrists interviewed me. I gave them a progress report. They listened to me with respect and admiration, and asked me to send in written reports and keep in touch by telephone if I needed their help and guidance. No one, they verified, seemed to have come so close to Susan. They were less despairing of her future. Micky was an unstable villain and would probably discard her, they thought. I didn't see it like that at all! They were both inadequate children, who needed each other to lean on and together they felt strong and secure. They would be constant and faithful.

'Has she,' asked Doctor Pritchard, suddenly rather cold and distant, 'ever shown disquiet at the pain and distress she has caused? Do you think she is capable of pity and remorse?'

'Yes. She is on the brink of it. She expressed something of the kind when I told her about the children I used to teach. And I sensed considerable sympathy emanating from her, when I told her about my being jilted.'

'Really.' It was actually quite chilly in this room and I felt like going home. 'I would, however, be more impressed if she was able to show remorse for her actions. I would like you to let us know when you honestly think that she can feel that.'

I acknowledged the rebuff. Nevertheless, I knew that Susan would not let me down. Remorse was on the timetable. I would concentrate on that for the next three days left before the end of term.

I'd been invited to three parties over the holidays – two of them masquerading as Chanukah celebrations. I dug out my Armenian gown and squeezed myself into it. I'd been on a diet for two years and during the last three weeks had lost ten pounds. This was partly because Ranjini's huge rice snacks had not been available, nor her deliciously rich and heavy home-made cakes; but the real reason for my sudden weight loss was anxiety and self-control. All I needed was a firm-control bra and a pair of ferociously restrictive elastic panties. I could wear my beautiful dress again. Susan would replace the broken zip for me. She'd assured me that she liked sewing and was good at small repair jobs. I bought a replacement zip and took the parcel to her the next day, together with scissors, a packet of needles and a bobbin of dark red cotton. Maybe she could fix it for me while we talked, as a sort of sewing lesson mixed carefully with The Rudiments of Remorse.

I had a psychological block about sewing which left me totally incompetent, not to say panic-stricken, when handed a needle and thread. A cruel and stupid teacher from my infants' school was at the root of my problem. I often wonder how many people there must be, talented, dignified, outwardly confident men and women, who carry an awful, secret ineptitude. Maybe Claire Bloom is unable to do purl knitting: it is possible Henry Kissinger has difficulty remembering the names of the enzymes aiding digestion in the small intestine: Her Majesty may carefully hide a tremor of disquiet when confronted with fractions that she has to convert to decimals. All these minor disabilities can be laid at the door of unimaginative, quick-tempered primary-school teachers. I knew that I had never given any of my pupils such a 'limp', always keeping in mind the effects of Miss Grundy on my ability to sew. The damage she caused did not stop at that.

Susan promised to work on my dress that evening as she didn't fancy doing it during the lesson. I assured her I would pay her for the job. I knew she wanted to buy Micky a gold ring for Christmas, bearing a couple of intertwined hearts, and she was expecting a diamond engagement ring from him. They were going, she said, to a hotel for Christmas, with two friends who had a car. She didn't know who the friends were, or which hotel they were heading for. It was obviously invention; wishful thinking. I cautiously asked her if she'd heard any news about Miss Cole and whether she'd be out of hospital for Christmas.

'Oo's she, then?'

'You know. The lady who fell down when you . . . when she lost her walking frame.'

'Elephant legs! 'Ow should I know if she's comin' out or not? She's seventy or eighty, ain't she? They don't heal so easy when they're old. She's pegged out for all I know!'

'Don't you care, dear, what happens to her?'

'Why should I? She don't mean nothin' to me. Nobody needs her. She's an old maid. She 'asn't got any kids or anything. She's all on her own, takin' up one of the flats, when people wiv kids are on the waiting list. She should be in some old people's home, out of the way. Look at Micky an' me, 'avin' to stay in this dump when we want a place of our own.'

I could hear a whine in her voice. It made me sick to listen to her. What had come over me? I tried to follow Dr Pritchard's guidance. I must be ready to expect anything – not merely the reaction that I wanted. Just because Susan and I trusted each other and had been on intimate terms didn't necessarily mean that she wouldn't disappoint me occasionally. She was, after all, an individual with a mind of her own, despite the fact that my influence was considerable.

I said, 'You seemed to be really sorry for and interested in those children I told you about who had illnesses they were dying from. Why can't you be sorry for Miss Cole? You caused her injury; she never hurt you – she only spoke to you sharply. Don't you feel anything for her? She must have suffered so much pain and shock because you snatched her frame.'

'Serves the old bag right. She shouldn't 'ave said them things, should she? Ugly old cow! All dried up inside!'

'But the kids! You seemed sad about them! You asked me questions and you were interested. And upset!'

'What you on about? I was interested because I didn't know kids caught cancer, did I? I thought it was just old people. It worn't my fault. How am I supposed to be sorry for them? They didn't catch it from me, did they?'

'Listen, I've got to leave early today. Don't forget to mend my dress.' I had quite a bad headache, and needed to get home and take some of my nerve pills. I was quite overwhelmed by revulsion, and even my stomach felt queasy. The coffee she had given me had had an oily layer on top, but I had drunk it, anxious not to risk giving Susan offence now that our talks had become so important.

'I'll 'ave your dress ready for you first thing tomorrer. You feeling all right, Miss? 'Ave you got a belly ache?'

I was quite touched by her concern. I bought two ounces of double-strength mints to help clear my system. I hoped I wasn't going to be ill. By the following morning, after an evening and night of severe diarrhoea, I felt tired but slim.

I met Susan on the stairs, wearing her coat and scarf. She seemed to be in a great hurry. I had never seen her moving at speed before; something odd was going on. 'Just gerrin' some milk, Miss! We run out. See you in a minute!' She pushed past me and disappeared out of the entrance.

Her front door was locked. It was so cold on the landing. I put my finger on the bell and kept it there. Was it possible that Joan or Sharon would bring themselves to admit me? Sharon opened up at last, grey-faced, wearing a black nightie, a filthy cardigan and a pair of high-heeled shoes.

'You seen 'er?' I nodded. 'I'm gonna get my feller to smash 'er!' she yelled. 'I'm gonna 'ave 'er put away! She should be hung for murder! She put some paraffin in my tea. Our Joan can't get out of 'er bed. She's real bad. She even done it all over the carpet and the mattress because that fuckin' cow locked 'erself in the toilet!'

I was still standing in the doorway when I heard the click. Not loud, but clear and extraordinarily frightening, because it emanated from within my head. Something must have been dislodged there, because immediately afterwards, a hollow wind blew through my right ear. I pressed my hand against it, expecting the gust of air to meet it, but there was nothing – yet the wind remained.

'Where is my dress?'

'That red 'un? She said you give it to 'er to make 'erself a blouse. She cut it in 'arf. It's in 'er cupboard.'

I followed her along the unspeakable passage, holding my glove against my ear. The top of my dress was suspended on a wire hanger hooked on the wardrobe door, and the frayed lower part lay on the floor, split and torn.

I knew that I had reached the end of my life. No one could experience that click and that wind without acknowledging the onset of eternity. I did not care. I calmly picked up the piece of dress and took the hanger with the rest of it. 'Where is she?'

''Ow should I know?'

'You had better tell me quickly where you THINK SHE IS

THEN.' I would kill her too, if necessary. She must have recognised her dreadful danger.

'She might of gone down 'arrington, or mebbe she's in the playground.'

The playground was a large square of mud, covered with dog-dirt and paper, tins and bits of glass. The only remaining apparatus was an iron 'spider's web' that no one ever used. The square was adjacent to the block of flats. I cannot recall my journey down the stairs, but I remember, at some time, releasing my ear and immediately clamping it again with my glove. I found her sitting on the spider's web circling slowly, her foot poking lazily at the mucky ground, keeping up the movement. She was grinning.

'Did you see our Joan? She's been shittin' all over the place! 'Ow've you been then, Miss? I thought you worn't comin' today, what with 'avin' the runs and that.'

The grin turned into a giggle. My gloves and bits of dress dropped in the mud. The gale in my ear had not diminished. Then she saw what I was going to do. I could see her slow-witted, squalid mind trying to move itself, but there were too many notches missing. Her foot stirred frantically, trying to get the spider's web to speed up, so that I couldn't get at her. She then scrambled towards the centre of it, but I already had the two ends of her scarf in my hands, like Hopalong Cassidy breaking in a horse. I brought her to the ground and she rolled away from me, beneath the iron mesh of the roundabout. Young, strong and vicious as she was, she might as well have been a tiny kitten in the inexorable grip of King Kong. I pushed her face into the mud, raised it with the scarf and pushed it down again, to the rhythm of:

'Why Did You Cut My Dress In Half?'
Up Down Up Down Up Down

I pulled her over on to her side. 'Now!' I screamed, 'I'm going to cut YOU in half!' She knew that I meant to strangle her.

Then a dreadful thing happened. I had to go to the toilet that minute. There was a tiny one at the corner of the playground, for children under the age of five. I rushed towards it, pushing past a large group of men, women and children, who were standing by quietly, watching. I had been totally unaware of their presence. Susan's liquid paraffin curdled within me, impatient; remorseless.

The dash of twenty-five yards was only equalled in horror by the following five minutes. The narrow, horizontal plank door, which flapped devilishly, hid only what was absolutely necessary. The crowd must be watching my hands and feet shuffling about on the floor, grovelling for bits of dirty newspaper. My respect for humanity reached its lowest ebb. Humiliation and despair overwhelmed me. I emerged, wishing for death.

The knot of people had their backs to me. As I walked towards the spider's web, they turned. Susan's neighbours had granted me the privacy which I assumed would be denied, with totally natural delicacy and sensitivity. Frank, the foul-mouthed layabout from number twelve, held my dress and gloves; Beryl, from the same address, ran towards me in her flopping bedroom slippers, and wiped my streaming eyes and nose; fat Maria put her arm around me. A young truant shouted, 'Good Old Miss! Good Old Miss!'

They had pulled her clear of the mud, and someone had put a pinny under her head, which was oozing blood. Lil, the mother of the baby Susan had threatened to drop down the stairwell, was stemming another flow from her nose. I could hear her screaming; then she saw me. She shrilly and obscenely abused me, defiling our confidential chats.

Lil stuck the pinny wickedly over her mouth and nose. 'Shut your gob. Do you want a drink of blood?'

'Tek Miss indoors, Beryl,' said Frank, Beryl's boyfriend. 'She don't need to be around when the ambulance comes. She's had enough trouble.' He turned towards the onlookers. 'She fell off the roundabout, didn't she? It weren't Miss's fault!'

Noble Anthony! Eloquent Defender of Caesar! An awesome stillness enveloped us, and I realised in that moment that my ear had ceased its clamour.

'What they call you, Miss?' asked Beryl. I told her. 'Lena and me's goin' upstairs for a Christmas drink. Frankie! See you later!'

She hurried me off. I heard my old friend, the ambulance bell, as we ran into Beryl's cosy flat. The design of it was identical to Susan's but it was beautiful – clean and gay with tinsel and plastic flowers, paper chains and a silvery Christmas tree, garlanded with red and blue lights that tick-tocked on and off. She led me into the bathroom, turned on the bath taps and told me to take off my muddy things. She handed me a fresh towel and flannel, a plastic bag for my clothing and a yellow quilted dressing gown.

'All right then, Lena?'

'Yes, Beryl. Thank you.'

She smiled. 'Get a move on. I'll have a nice drink ready for you!'

I heard people coming into the flat while I was drying myself but Harry Belafonte pervaded the air and made all other messages inaudible.

'Lena!' I opened the bathroom door to the knock and the voice. Maria, a Greek woman, handed me a tiny porcelain cup of something. 'You drink this down while it's hot. It's good for the tummy. She told everyone last night what she did to your tummy.'

I sat on the side of the bath. It was very sweet, hot, strong, Turkish coffee and tasted delicious. Maria put a pair of men's slippers on my feet and finished buttoning up the dressing gown, then took the cup from me and pushed me gently towards the living room where an array of bottles, shining glasses and biscuits were set. It was crowded with people, all talking to me at once; smiling; kindly; welcoming me. I felt so pretty. We all had a drink and wished each other a Merry Christmas.

'About time somebody walloped her.'

'She 'ad it comin' to 'er.'

'She ain't that badly hurt; got no more 'n she deserved.'

'If it hadn't been you, Lena, it would of been someone else. Just corse you're a teacher don't mean to say you're not 'uman!'

Gratitude and affection filled my heart and eyes. I would change my name by deed poll rather than hurt their feelings. I heard the doorbell being rung downstairs and then voices spiralling upwards.

'The Bogies!' said Lil's husband. 'Okay Frank?'

'Yeh.' Everyone knew it was the police, except me. In the following few moments of intense silence within the flat, we heard footsteps on the stairs and then loud knocking without. Frank marched sturdily down the passage. The volume of the record player was reduced and we listened to the conversation at the doorway.

... 'No, she worn't even there when it happened,' said Mark Antony. 'My Beryl was looking after her here. She'd been took very, very bad and I went out to fetch a taxi for her. That Susan was acting the fool on the roundabout. I seed her fall off. She must of split her 'ead on a stone or a bit of glass. You coppers know what she did to old Miss Cole? The Law didn't get 'er, but she tripped herself up, didn't she? She got away wiv murder, but it catches up wiv you in the end, don't it? She was in a bloody mess when we got to 'er, so we called an ambulance and Lil downstairs did some first aid.'

'She said her teacher attacked her with a broken bottle.'

'She said WHAT?'

'Is the teacher here now?'

'Yeh.'

'I'd like to see her?'

My glass was deftly removed from my hands and I found myself lying on the settee with a cushion behind my head.

'Come on in, then, but she's still very bad.' My hero spoke these last words mournfully, but loudly, and preceded the policeman into the room. I had the opportunity of seeing the expression on his face. His eloquence did not merely rest at the verbal level. He gave me my cue without uttering a word.

'Are you Susan Tiffin's teacher, Madam?' asked the officer.

'Yes.'

'Brandy, Lena? You goin' to pass out again?' Beryl poured out a tot, and put the glass to my lips, her features contorted with concern.

'I'm sorry to bother you, Miss. She has made an allegation against you. We know her, of course.'

'How is she?'

'Head and face cuts and a badly bruised nose. They're stitching her up and treating her for shock. She said you attacked her with a broken bottle.'

The outrage, shock and horror on Lil's face dissolved every vestige of my self-control. I was a schoolgirl again, with all the insane agony of suppressed mirth, avoiding the eye of my friend, stuffing my hanky into my mouth to quieten the paroxysms; forcing my crazed mind to concentrate on leper colonies, Germans; anything to do with suffering and iniquity. My body shook, as if in the throes of a dreadful fever.

Beryl turned swiftly, spilling the brandy over my neck, hiding my contorted face with her ample backside, knowing everything that was happening to me. 'That little bugger's the one who's been doing the carving up, Officer! Frank, show 'im Lena's dress! You know she put a fatal dose of liquid paraffin in Lena's coffee yesterday? We all seed 'er fall off the spider's web. She's not right – she should be locked up in the booby hatch. You should know by now what a liar she is, what with all them false alarms she's given you coppers! 'Ere, 'ow about a drop afore you go? It's Christmas, ain't it? We won't grass on you!'

'Come on, you know better than that!' He was smiling. 'Hope you feel better soon, Madam. Merry Christmas, everyone!'

'Merry Christmas!' The door closed behind him. 'Bleedin' Fuzz! Sodding Law!'

O, my new faithful, generous friends, worn and unemployed; ill-educated and often hostile; I was a stranger and you took me in: I was alone and you comforted and protected me. You honoured me in my degradation: you banded together with me against my enemies: my feet and form were dainty in the large slippers and the bulky dressing gown. But tomorrow I must speak the truth to Miss Gavenda and Miss Sanderson at County Hall. I will be banned for ever from the teaching profession; I will have to acknowledge my personal failure and I will care; and you, my comrades, will not.

In the dim afternoon, thus clad, I emerged from a taxi and swayed into my house with two more party invitations. I carefully prepared a cold flannel for my head and a hot bottle for my toes, and lay down on the bed to think calmly about my future.

Chapter Eight

Even the Muriels of the world are expected to celebrate Christmas. Even the Jews are given the option to rejoice, for Chanukah collides conveniently with the Festival of Good Will, and our overflowing cup lasts for eight days. I would use my holiday profitably and finish my novel; and if I was unable to dislodge myself from the sticking place, I would reel off three up-market short stories. Miss Sanderson could say what she liked: I would return her comments with well-flavoured language. I hated my job anyway. It would be easy for me to secure employment as a file clerk or a check-out assistant at the new Sainsbury's, what with my maths O level and former experience as an arithmetic teacher, until the cheques for my writing arrived. I had things to do; decisions to make; Muriel to visit for the last time; Miss Sanderson to telephone.

I made an appointment to see her later on in the day, and arrived at Muriel's laden with second-hand baby clothes, and a sweater for her. There was no denying it – that awful smell was back in the flat. The valiant Filthy Squad had lost, as surely as the Light Brigade. The twelve-year-old mother sat on the unmade bed, stony-faced, half dead from lack of sleep, her child sucking at a disposable, firmly sterile bottle. The maternal instinct is a terrible lot of nonsense which we learn to believe in only after we have reached our late teens. Mother and child were both babies with terrifying prospects.

'You've got to talk to the baby and cuddle her a lot and smile at her,' I said. 'That's almost as important as keeping her warm and clean and well fed.'

'She cry all the night. She don't let me go to sleep.'

I finished feeding the baby, changed her and laid her down on the bed, then took Muriel on my knee, and rocked her and sang a few of my favourite Yiddish lullabies.

'Do like this, even when I asleep.'

'Close your eyes. I won't stop, I promise.' The baby stared unseeingly at the ceiling while Muriel slept, a child for the first and last time in her life. Subjects recorded on my timetable today would be Child Development, Music and French.

I bought three custard tarts and a Crunchie Bar for my lunch and armed myself to see Miss Sanderson with the maximum of self-disgust. I would hand in my notice before she had a chance to tell me about myself, and demand reimbursement for my dress. Then take it from there.

I was shocked by the lack of decorum in the huge office. People were sitting on each other's desks, and most of the staff had drinks in their hands Miss Sanderson advanced towards me and shoved a sherry at me. I accepted with grace.

'You look as if you need topping up. I hope you've not come here to tell me that you want to stop teaching Tiffin – that wouldn't be at all sensible. Chopping and changing all the time isn't good for the pupils.'

I told her what had occurred. She giggled tipsily, and in a very loud voice told me not to shout as the chief education officer was standing a few yards away from us. 'You'll have a much easier time with her next term. She'll have a healthy respect for you and if you don't blab, neither will she. I've told you often enough that you're one of our best teachers, but frankly it would be much simpler for us all if you could learn to show some self-control and not cause trouble.' I wished she would lower her voice. 'Just get on with your work quietly like the other members of our teaching staff. Here, have another drink!' She must be really sozzled; I mustn't miss my chance.

'She cut my best frock in half after she'd promised to mend the zip.'

'If you're asking me for damages, take a form and fill it out. When did you buy it?'

'I bought it in Israel on my last visit.'

'Which was six years ago – I remember you telling me. The zip of the dress was broken. Make a claim by all means, but don't get greedy; you'll be disappointed anyway. I've got a real challenge for you to start the New Year with; you'll be able to finish your novel with a flourish. How many more of our exercise books do you need for your private use? Here's a little Christmas present for you.'

She handed me half a dozen nice thick ones which I stuffed into my carrier. I could tell she was sobering up, so I took my leave. Two hours ago I had felt quite ill: now I throbbed with pride and glowed with good health. One of her best teachers! How about that! I remembered she'd complimented me just before she'd given Muriel over to me and wondered what I was in for. Susan plus 'a real challenge' for next term. Crafty old soak!

I was walking towards Waterloo station when quite without warning I found myself thinking about peas and beans and barley. I backtracked slowly and gingerly so as not to break the connecting thread; for the life of me I could not think why a mixture of dried pulses was filling my mind, but I knew it to be of the greatest importance. It was as if I had travelled from London to Hull, emerged at Paragon station with a sense of urgency and a suitcase bulging with second-class protein, with no idea why I had made the journey, or why I was thus laden. I knew, however, that my family were involved, so I changed to the Victoria Line and travelled to Walthamstow Central, to ask what it was all about. I knocked at the house in Bolsover Road, banning the intrusive apple pie from my mind. My diet had already been badly disturbed during the last two days.

Orde opened the door, leaning forward into the gloomy evening, peering at me, saying:

Such eyes the widows in Corioli wear
And mothers that lack sons.

'That's all you know,' I snapped, 'and your mock O levels a few weeks away.'

'Really, I mean it; you don't look so good. I do know that bit starting "Chaste as an icicle" but I thought it might not apply.' He's all by himself in thinking he's one of the three Ronnies.

I felt stronger by the time I was settled with my tea and pie, and had recounted my experiences with Susan and the happy outcome of my visit to County Hall.

'So you're pleased about it,' said Ma. 'You fool. Don't you think it's time you grew up and stopped allowing people to exploit you?'

'What the hell are you talking about?'

'"Thou has never in thy life
Show'd thy dear mother any courtesy"'

Orde quoted.

'Oh, shut up!' I wished I hadn't come. 'All I'm here for is to ask you about peas and beans and Ludo, not to listen to *Coriolanus* or insults.'

Ma had the grace to look embarrassed. This contrition had nothing to do with her last remark, because we were both remembering her manipulation of me, all that time ago...

When I was four, she developed a curious habit. She was unfortunate enough continually to muddle the dried peas with the dried beans. The first time I recall this happening was shortly after she had borrowed *War and Peace* from the library. How many afternoons did I spend, while my sisters were at school, sorting out into large tins her tediously repetitive errors, while she fought at the battle of Austerlitz. The nature of her malady became more grave as rice and lentils were carelessly combined. If I occasionally mentioned that I had nothing to do, more examples of her disturbing behaviour would manifest themselves. Strands of hairy string would be produced, dozens of them, that she had accidentally cut and they needed tying together. Meanwhile she read *Les Misérables*, and by the time I had tied the string with large ugly knots, she had muddled the peas and beans again. One dark winter's afternoon, when she was deeply engrossed in *The Moonstone*, she irresponsibly promised that after I had finished sorting she would play with me. Today it was split peas and lentils. 'Just look what I've done!' she fumed. 'Be a good girl and sort them for me; you're so clever and quick! I'll play you Ludo when you've finished – two games,' she added recklessly.

Lentils, split peas and firelight may sound a fearsome combination to anyone less practised than I. Whilst she was still in the middle of a chapter, I produced the perfectly separated items. 'O, Christ!' exclaimed my mother, with ill-contained frenzy; 'You're the most marvellous girl! I'll put them away; there might be just a few more.' She didn't know that I had followed her into the scullery. To my amazement, I watched her place two handfuls each of lentils and split peas into the tin and stir them around. Then she turned and our eyes met.

'O, Mam, you are daft!' I shouted. 'Look what you've done! You've gone and faffled them all up again!' On that memorable afternoon she played four games of Ludo with me. Years later, I came home from school to find Orde sitting on the step sorting out rice and barley. 'I'm helping Mam,' he announced proudly, 'then we're going to the swings!'

Sweet, sweet innocence! How powerful and corrupting you are! How heavily it lies upon us who have passed out of its terrible gaze. She was at the table, bent over *Bleak House*. How we exploit that tender artlessness with our crookery and guile! How mortifying to be so duped at the age of thirty! I was childish; ridiculous. Miss Sanderson had been playing Ludo with me, waving me out of the way with peas and beans and easy flattery; fobbing me off with a few exercise books and a glass of sherry; not taking me or my work seriously. How dare she assume that I should spend yet another term with Susan, after she had harmed me with malice aforethought? Why should she try to make me feel guilty and a nuisance because I had had enough? No one else had been able to confine or tolerate her for more that three weeks, let alone teach her for a term. I would no longer be deceived by her dry, casual behaviour or patronised by psychiatrists who sat importantly at their clean office desks, handing out unsmiling advice; using their talents to make me feel uneasy, awkward and stupid.

I felt hurt by Ma's attack on me, although I knew it to be justified. A little revenge would be sweet. 'Orde, do you remember how Ma used to give you peas and beans to sort out when you were little? She used to muddle them up on purpose. I saw her.'

'Myrtle! You old fraud! I've always thought you were going through a bad patch!' Orde had been slow on the up-take, like me. He would be raking up the past for a long time to come.

'I'm only telling you this because exploitation is a habit we learn in infancy and it can stick with us if we're not careful.'

'Those tiny little orange things in the semolina!' screamed Orde. 'Do you mean to say it wasn't accidental? Tell me it isn't true!'

'I've never bought semolina in my life. Never!' She was doing her best to avoid the subject. 'Those sort of people are the parasites of society,' she said, referring to Susan; 'they're not for you to waste your time on, with your talents. Filthy little beast! Putting that stuff in your drink and ruining your dress. You always looked marvellous in it,' she lied.

'You're right, Ma,' I said, softening, 'I'm not going to teach her next term. I'm glad I came; I'm going to be firm and decisive from now on.'

'She told me that the lockshen squares were too big. She gave me a pair of blunt scissors to cut them all in half!'

'I'd actually forgotten that,' giggled Ma, totally unrepentant. 'It kept him quiet for hours.' I reckoned that she was going to have to make massive reparations.

It was quite late when I arrived home. Ranjini's luggage stood in the hall. The moment I saw it, a tiny pulse began twitching in my eyelid and twenty or thirty ulcers leapt to life under and around my tongue. A mini-cab driver came up the path behind me, asking for Mrs Jordan, and George pounded down the stairs, fulminating horribly, not caring about the open front door and that he was lowering the tone of the neighbourhood at every word.

'Go upstairs and see if you can do anything with that madwoman,' he shouted at me.

Mandy was standing in a blue plastic bowl, ironing her nightdress which was wet, frizzled and scorched in more or less equal parts. There was a strong smell of burning in the room. Ranjini was kneeling on the floor, stowing toilet articles into an overflowing suitcase. She greeted me, trying to suppress her hysteria. I knew straight away that we were still friends. 'I'm not going without my nightie,' wept Mandy.

'Yes you are,' I snapped, marvellously authoritative, pulling out the plug from the wall socket. 'They'll give you one there. It's ruined anyway.' I didn't dare to contemplate why she was standing in a bowl. If the baby was about to take up residence outside the womb, I wanted it to emerge in the right place. 'The mini-cab is waiting. Put your shoes on and get going before George has a stroke.'

Ranjini pulled two sexy nighties out of the case. 'Look, Mandy, these are beautiful. Come!'

'Why didn't the silly bastard tell me he had bought me a present? How was I supposed to know?' She stepped out of the bowl and into her shoes, and then, by the look of her, into the last stage of labour.

'Lucky Mandy!' said Ranjini wistfully, after she and George

had driven off. I doubted if Mandy was thinking on a similar wavelength just now.

We went downstairs, leaving the mess for George to face, and sat in front of my fire, drinking tea. I wouldn't rush things: I had plenty of time to bring up Rosenfeld's name. She looked well and happy, less nervy and more beautiful than ever – a living example for all would-be suicides, except for those who were plain and fat. If I brought a mixture of pygmies, Stone-Age cave dwellers, wild men from New Guinea and members of a Siberian sect who had never set eyes on a woman all their adult lives, and asked them whom they liked best, she or me, they would point unerringly towards Ranjini. This was quite a recent fantasy in which I permitted myself to indulge when making comparisons with people less fair than she, in order to upset myself.

She told me about the convalescent home, the friends she had made and the help and support she's received from psychotherapy. It sounded exactly the kind of holiday I needed. I waited for a pause in the monologue when I could decently introduce Mr Rosenfeld. No, not yet. I always take particular pride in showing interest and being more than commonly agreeable to people who are boring me intensely.

'I had a visitor last weekend.' I could detect confidence and coy complacency in her voice. Her pretence at a casual tone didn't fool me. So this was it! Off with the old and on with the new! Good for her!

'Who's this then?' I twinkled at her nauseatingly. 'What's he like?'

'What's the matter? Am I boring you?' Questions like that make me unwell. Ranjini should know better. I remonstrated with her. Now, I wouldn't be able to mention his name for hours.

'What are you asking *me* for? You've always been an authority on the subject.'

So it was Sarath. She'd made it up with him, taken him back. They were going to try to repair their marriage. He'd confessed to her about him and me; he was feckless; totally unscrupulous. And Ranjini was no better, playing this cat and mouse game with me. I would, of course, deny everything she accused me of, then ask her to leave my premises. 'I don't know what you're talking about,' I said coldly, and with a singular lack of originality.

'Look, is there something bothering you? You must admit you've always had plenty to say about Mr Rosenfeld, but I never realised you disliked him so much. You should see your face! I thought that reading his letter would have changed your opinion about him; that's why I gave it to you. I'm sorry now. Just let me have it back, and forget that you've read it.'

The letter was in my bag. I looked through the pile of mess on my table and then sifted through it again, carefully searching. 'I can't find it, but I'll be tidying up tomorrow, and I'm bound to come across it then.' I felt shattered at how close I had come to betraying myself, and my only thought was to build up my defences. 'I thought it was someone special; someone dashing and romantic. What a disappointment! So he came all that way to see you. Dear, faithful, old Rosenfeld!'

'Don't sneer – I hate it when you do that. I don't want to fall out with you, so let's not talk about him any more.' I must remember to remove my Hedex tablets from the bathroom cupboard; they were torpedo-shaped, for easy swallowing. She seemed unreasonably upset and irritable. One couldn't be too careful.

'I'm sorry, Ranjini,' I mumbled. 'I like Mr Rosenfeld, really I do.'

She giggled. 'You're such a liar, but since he'll be at my New Year's Eve party, you'd better start pretending it's true. I hope you're not going to be away. I need you for moral support and help with the preparations.'

'Of course I'll be here. I'm looking forward to it already, mentally sorting out my dresses and jewellery.'

After she had gone, I locked the door and took the letter out of my bag, devouring the bits that affected me most.

'Dear Ranjini, if you are reading these words it means that your curiosity has overcome your apathy and that you are not entirely indifferent to living. To tell you that I know how it was for you, before you took what you thought to be your final decision, would be pointless, for you would remain silent and separate. Other friends will shed tears at their inability to help and comfort you, and perhaps they will feel angry with you, too, for making them seem useless and impotent.

'I don't want to be angry or useless. I want to tell you about myself, for no one else will hear me with greater accuracy. I have no mother or father; no brother or sister; no relative or friend of my youth. They are all dead. I witnessed the murder of my father and brother and knew in what degradation my mother and sister died. My brother was a violinist so they cut off his hands. My father was hanged as a public example for his part in a "plot". All people that I loved were starved, mutilated and gassed. I saw unspeakable horrors and devilish cruelty. But I lived. I was little more than a child. Later, while I walked, drove, listened, spoke, worked, slept, I heard their shrieks and saw their terror and pain, not occasionally or often, but incessantly. I would close my eyes and cover my ears and howl like a mad dog, but I could not blind or deafen or drown myself against it. I sought death as a relief, and like you, I failed. I have seen you looking at my scars and the number tatooed on my arm: they are a perpetual and unnecessary reminder of those years of despair. I saw your misery, but was unable to speak of it; that is why I recognised a fellow traveller, when I saw you lying there, cold and forsaken.

'After my physical recovery, I knew that I would never attempt that same escape route. I suffocated my feelings in order to live sanely within society. I closed my mouth and shut off my emotions; but a change came over me. I found that I had deeper perceptions – I began to discern wretchedness in others, however well disguised; I saw sweetness and warmth, even when covered by layers of cold bitterness, but I remained untouched.

'You will fall in love again. You are young and animated and impulsive, and basically, full of gaiety and merriment, and now you have wisdom, maturity and experience. I am glad that I did not die, and so it will be with you. It is worth keeping alive in order eventually to live. I told you that I remained alone, and for many years I existed like this, and then my work brought me to London and to the house in which I met you. I never intended to stay – only until I found a place to myself, away from strangers who might intrude on my isolation; but these strangers became part of my life. I delighted in being of use and in being accepted by you all. Before that, the impossible happened. I fell in love.

'I drove up to our house in the early hours. I was tired and hoped that I would sleep. I remember wondering what it would be like if there was someone to greet me, and immediately cancelled the image as a stupid fancy. A young woman stood at the door, frightened and on the verge of panic. She called to me without speaking and held tightly to my ugly wrists, touching my wounds, healing them as she did so. Then she put her arms around my neck, straining me to her, making my heart ache for what I had missed. She released the bolt that detained me, probed into my being and restored me to life. She gave me passionate, eager youth at the age of fifty, and swept away the horror that had submerged it.

'I thought I was incapable of being affected by scorn or indifference, and while I burn and writhe from it, I am paradoxically happy to find that I am still, after all, a creature of the human race. If I expressed myself to her, she would find me ludicrous; perhaps pity me. I am not afraid of her compassion;

only of exploiting her through it. It is her vulnerability that restrains me; not mine. I am in the living stream again, cold and salty, yes; but buoyant and invigorating.

'Another person may think that I still have nothing. But you will not. Life holds so much for me, now that I can feel and want, when all seemed dark and hopeless. Come back to us soon. Everything waits for you.'

I wished he was here in this room with me, so that I could tell him that he was neither an object of pity nor ridicule. I wanted to embrace him and to show him that I loved and wanted him. The knowledge of having this opportunity so soon gave me such delicious anticipation that for a few minutes I wallowed in the pleasure of it. But how could I approach him; make him see that I was available without admitting that I had seen his letter? I would have to work myself up into a nervous attack and gasp for breath, so that he would come to me and comfort and minister to me. With a little subtle encouragement, I could arrange for him to stroke my neck again, and then take it from there. He would forgive me for having reviled and rejected him.

I marvelled at my past repulsion and dislike of him. I remembered the afternoon we had spent in Grantchester, picnicking by the river, lying next to each other. I had told him about my disastrous day, while sprawled on my stomach, greedily consuming the goodies he had provided. He lay on his side, his head propped on his hand, and when I had turned towards him, suddenly, I had caught an expression on his face which I had not understood, because no one had ever been in love with me before. I conjured it up for myself now, and saw the tenderness and longing blurring his features. I had taken another scone, washed it down with cider and then had fallen asleep on my back. When I opened my eyes, he was lying in exactly the same position, with the same bright countenance.

'Your arm must be aching,' I had said, not knowing, not caring.

'Not my arm,' he had answered, 'only my heart.'

I had told him that he should see a doctor. He had stood up then, quickly and easily while I scrambled clumsily to my feet. 'Perhaps you should have practised medicine,' he had answered, and I had taken his remark to be irrelevant and irritating. We had walked through the trees behind the Old Vicarage, watching for ghostly shadows and listening for a soft step, and I had cancelled polite concern for his health from my mind.

Now I thought of him constantly, eagerly stirring up all my memories of him, and when I discovered some half-forgotten detail, I prodded it until the ember burned, bright and lively again, and delighted in the extra warmth and pleasure that each one gave. In eight days I would see him again. Of all the wild men in my fantasy, he was the odd one out who would hold out his hand unwaveringly, towards me.

Chapter Nine

All my indecision and vacillating behaviour dissolved with the fading year. I could not remember when I had felt so confident or when I had looked so well. Ranjini dressed me in a sari for Cassy's party, who when she saw me, shrieked satisfactorily with surprise and admiration.

'Darling!' she gasped. 'You look absolutely riveting. Go upstairs at once and do something. The party's dreadful! There's no atmosphere. Rina is rushing around making everyone ill and nervous. We think the ceiling is too high; it makes them all feel so subdued and impotent and nobody's *trying*! That awful Peter is being nice to his wife and upsetting Rina terribly. Do something, dear one, do!'

I entered the room and waved my magic wand. The Queen of Sheba shrivelled; Handel was momentarily silenced. Guests sitting tightly against the walls moved towards me, and within a few minutes I was the pivot of merriment around which the party gained momentum. I was tireless and radiant and amusing. What an irony, that ever since Joseph had left me, I had never been so popular; yet now I was looking forward to claiming Rosenfeld, and wanted no one else. The most urbane, clever and attractive people clustered round me and clamoured for my attention, and one of them escorted me home at five a.m. on Christmas Eve. I was a huge success at Beryl's party too, and with my new-found self-assurance, courageously admitted to being called Leah, and no one took offence.

Who can explain such a metamorphosis? Why should one be

so charged with magnetism merely because one is anticipating an event? Why cannot we be thus when we are miserable and lonely and without hope? Try as we will to disguise or hide it bravely, depression must emanate from us and perhaps those amongst us whom we would so like to interest and befriend, have some primitive intuition regarding our unhappiness, and edge away from us in unconscious self-preservation. The hope and joy which I experienced during this short time buoyed up my spirits to a level hitherto unknown or forgotten. I was gilded with happiness.

Mandy's Holy Babe arrived in the early hours of Christmas Day, and George, Ranjini and I visited her like the three kings, carrying far more appropriate gifts. George sat beside her, holding her hand, in an aura of alcoholic fumes, considering the joys of having a son. His wife and three daughters did not enter into his consciousness that day – except when Mandy forced them there.

'If it weren't a lad,' she said sourly, 'he'd be off to that bitch, decorating their Christmas tree. I reckon he's done it anyway, while my back's been turned.' George smiled at her fondly, denying nothing. I wondered how long such benign good humour could last. There was none of this lying back on the pillows, exhausted after the birth, Madonna-like, Christmas Day or not. The vinegar in her was as potent as ever.

I told them about the party after Ranjini had left, and that Mr Rosenfeld was coming back for it.

'You'll have to put him up, then; you don't expect us to put the baby in a mangy old manger on the corner of Finchley Road. End of January is our time for leaving, so until then it's up to you to give him bed and breakfast and make him comfortable. If he fancied you in that dirty old dressing gown you picked out of the bin, he'll be mad for you when he sees you like this. She looks quite sexy in that outfit, doesn't she, George? The skirt only needs a wash and a press and a couple of inches taken in.'

Ranjini's preparations for the party were formidable. I wielded a duster, arranged the rooms and kept steadfastly out of the kitchen whenever I heard the hiss of oil. After being on my miracle diet, I slithered into a borrowed gown of Rina's, without untoward torment, and once safely enclosed, I began to eat and drink, frenziedly. I told myself that if I was sated by the time the guests arrived, I would be able to take nourishment with delicacy and restraint. Ranjini had organised the sleeping arrangements – I should stay with her in her room, and Mr Rosenfeld was to be booked into mine. She trod on my nerves continually, but I meekly complied with her arrangements. My mind ticked away, crazily, working out all the possible connotations of this romantic meeting. I was a princess who had always been nasty to the frog, but who could now be relied on to be sweet and charming to the prince.

The room was crowded with guests. Dinah and Walter handed round drinks and Ranjini was fluttering hither and thither like a beautiful butterfly with pretzels and peanuts. A police sergeant from Ceylon was observing her with his invisible net at the ready. George and Mandy were deeply engrossed in their drinking; they had thoughtfully offered the services of their child as cloakroom attendant, and he was sleeping in a drawer in my room. Judging by all the noise and bustle, the party was a blazing success and no one stood awkward and alone – not counting me, so I made myself useful by answering the door, introducing everyone and not allowing myself to become involved with any group of people, so that I could sneak into our temporary cloakroom at five-minute intervals and look out of the window.

Now Orde had commandeered the room. I wished I hadn't invited him. I find it most disagreeable to have to observe members of my family trying to ingratiate themselves in a non-platonic way, with a new acquaintance. An empty wine bottle stood between them. I was banned from the room by their selfishness so I resorted to standing on the doorstep letting in icy blasts and no one else, for all the guests, bar him, had arrived by now.

It was ten thirty and time for us to serve supper. Where is he? No phone call to explain the delay, but he is bound to appear by the midnight hour; for 'Auld Lang Syne', when everyone holds hands. It is not in Rosenfeld's character to promise to come to an event such as this, and not let his hostess know that he cannot. He is too correct and severe to allow this lack of manners. I heard that there are some roads in the North which are snowy and treacherous. Perhaps he is lying injured or dead somewhere, his head stuck to the gravel, the car upside down on top of him.

But I had no time to think things over properly, because Ranjini was shouting to me to come and help her. Why didn't she ask the others or that policeman, Gamini, who was hovering over her? There was no doubt that she was enjoying his attentions. Why didn't she ask him to investigate the whereabouts of Mr Rosenfeld's body? How incredibly shallow and uncaring she is! Has she already forgotten how he saved her life? Does nothing more important than serving hot food register with her?

I hated this party and despised all the guests, and I was giving myself a ramming headache by drinking this sour red wine. I really dislike New Year's Eve parties. Last year I welcomed in the year at the 'Open 24 hours' launderette and felt upset because no one had invited me to a party or asked me out for the evening. How radiantly happy I was, compared to now. I wondered, if I dragged my laundry bag and packet of Daz down the road, whether I could recapture the infectious excitement of the swirling suds! Better, perhaps, that I should rot alone in the kitchen, washing up all the greasy plates. At least I'd have some peace here. No one would dare to interrupt me, for fear of being drawn into helping; perhaps a useful occupation would benefit me and ease my state of anxiety – and who knows! Life might hold so much tedium that when I was in my dotage, looking back on all the milestones which marked it, 'tonight' might glow like a beacon through the bleak future. 'Heh heh! What a time I had! I only had a slight rheumatic condition then . . . the right knee, I think. The fifth lumbar caused occasional agony which must have been the start of this crippling arthritis. Oh, I was young and active then; fifty years ago to the day and only on the brink of senility! I remember how I washed up a great pile of greasy plates and forks in this here kitchen, spooning left-over trifle into my mouth, while all the young people danced and flirted in the back room. Silly fools! I never was a one for running after the men and showing myself up; I just liked to be of use; helping quietly in the background. Just put a little warm bread and milk into my mouth, will you, Nurse, before you jab me with my final morphia injection. Then take me into the bedroom so that I can fade away peacefully, comforted by that wonderful memory of a New Year's Eve, long ago.'

'What are you doing here?' Ranjini, the Queen of the Cuisine, entered the kitchen, my kitchen, putting me on the defensive and expecting me to give an account of myself.

'I'm only doing a bit of washing-up and wondering why Mr Rosenfeld hasn't come.'

'He should be here any minute. I'm just about to heat up his supper. Put a bottle of wine in the fridge for him; and the trifle, if you've left any. He said he'd be very late. For heaven's sake, come in and mix. Everyone's asking where you are. You've done nothing but skulk around being unsociable.'

'You could have told me he'd be late! How mean and thoughtless of you! I've been frantic all evening!' I felt like smacking her over the head with the wet rag I'd been wielding over the sink, and I was especially annoyed by the way she was looking at me – as if she were watching a dormouse hibernating in my hair. That Gamini was certainly having an effect on her.

'So that's how it is! I don't believe it! The others were right, then!' She started to laugh, quite hysterically, and had to dab her eyes with a paper towel. 'Help me to refill these glasses. No, wash them first! And take off that disgusting apron!'

Every time she attempted to do anything but give orders, she became incapable; exploding into childish giggles, and I was bound to cope with all the jobs, although I, too, felt none too steady. I joined her in a prolonged wine-tasting session, then she tottered off to effect her duties as hostess. I needed a few hours to sort out my thoughts and my bedraggled appearance, but instead, I leaned against the draining board, sipping an unknown mixture from someone else's discarded glass, considering my reflection in the dark window.

'Remember!' I admonished it, not knowing what I meant. Then I saw his image next to mine.

'Good evening. I was told to come to you for my food and drink.'

What is this delight? It is you; only you. Familiar and totally recognisable, yet an interloper, making me a stranger to myself, probing into my soul and discovering its extraordinary lightness and joy.

'Hello, Old Acquaintance!' I said, and I embraced him because he was here and I was glad. 'I've missed you so much. Where have you been?' I couldn't stop smiling and for a few moments I held his hands and watched his bewilderment and doubt change to amusement, pleasure and affection.

'Here,' he answered. 'Here, all the time.' His riddles were so utterly charming – I would save this one for future careful consideration; 'I will tell you about the other places too, but later.' It didn't matter that Ranjini was coming down the passage, for I had enough to dwell upon to carry me through days of interruption.

'I knew she wouldn't give you any refreshment,' she said spitefully, pushing past me in order to turn up the oven.

'But she has! Let us leave the food until later and join the party.

I have not yet greeted all the guests.'

'I want you to meet Gamini – he's heard so much about you.' She took his arm as if she owned him, but he waited politely for me to precede him.

How jolly it was in here and how popular I was! Mr Rosenfeld wasn't doing too badly either, sitting on the armchair over there, with Gamini and Ranjini perched on either side of him, and George, Dinah, Walter, Orde and his new friend, Donna, sprawled on cushions, at his feet. I was getting remarkably drunk and kept forgetting people's names, but it didn't seem to matter, since I was teaching the active set how to dance to 'Zorba the Greek'.

Mandy bore Mr Rosenfeld off to meet her son and some of the guests were preparing to leave. Orde and Donna got up to dance and canoodle and then flopped down next to me with another bottle of wine. He really was drinking far too much and as his older sister, I should tactfully try to put a stop to it.

'Pour me a large glass, please,' I said, altruistically, since there would then be less for them.

'I think you've probably had enough. You know what you're like when you've got a migraine.' He handed me a bread stick and fixed me a tumbler of soda water. Minute silver stars shot past my left eye, the precursor of that dreaded malaise; avoidable if I didn't lose my temper and took my tablets and his advice. I slyly dissolved three Aspro Clear, while he was busy with Donna's glass, and then, as punishment, sat down between them, like a block of jagged ice. Unperturbed, he patted his knee, and Donna promptly placed herself there.

'Are you enjoying the party?' I asked them sweetly, itching to get on to the subject of Mr Rosenfeld, but knowing Orde's subtlety, taking things carefully.

'It's the best one I've ever been to,' said Donna, happily kissing Orde's eyebrow, making me feel melancholy and aged. 'When I first came, I thought, O Jesus Christ, I've come to an over-sixties club, but it's been really great, mixing with older people for a change. Young people can be so immature and boring sometimes.' You said it kid. 'I mean, that tenant of yours, Mr Rosenfeld, must be at least fifty, and he's so clever and knowledgeable, and yet he treats you as if you were his equal, if you know what I mean.'

No, I don't know what you mean, you soppy little girl. You're nobody's equal as far as I can see. Mr Rosenfeld's merely playing one of his games with you, and as for Orde, who's so intelligent and perceptive . . . well! But I mustn't forget that he's still a child. I looked at him cautiously. He seemed preoccupied with Donna's shoulder.

'He became amazingly animated once he'd discovered I was your brother,' said Orde softly, looking towards where he stood, talking to Gamini and Walter, all three totally engrossed.

'I can't stand it when you're so enigmatic,' I said irritably. 'What do you mean?'

> His nature is too noble for the world;
> He would not flatter Neptune for his trident . . .

'It isn't a popular habit, the way you keep showing off about knowing lumps of *Cymbeline* by heart. It makes one wonder whether you've anything original to say.'

'Yet he got very animated when he discovered I was your brother,' he repeated, as if I was daft or deaf. 'That's me, not Shakespeare. You can always tell the difference between me and him, because he's stuck on iambic pentameters. And, really, you're slipping. Not *Cymbeline* although Neptune does get a mention there, too.'

'Show-off!' I couldn't help smiling; or thinking over what he'd said. Donna squeezed his hand comfortingly. She had a lot to learn. A wave of nostalgia engulfed me. The child, the lad, the youth had gone; and if I listened to him, I must recognise his manhood and maturity and acknowledge it as irreversible. 'You know me, Orde,' I said, not caring whether the novelty of crabbed age was beginning to wear thin with Donna. 'Shakespeare didn't.'

'He's always spot on, though, and it's no light matter, trying to improve on him; but keeping what you say in mind, and assuming that it's an advantage that I've known you all my life, the fact is, you're of the world; this world. I knew that about you when I was two. You look at people and ideas and things from where you and they stand; jostling next to one another. Not from the horizon or from another planet. Those places are for observers and thinkers. You *think* you think, but you don't; you *feel* that you think.'

Donna had fallen asleep, and if it wasn't for a rusty saw, covered with migraine powder, attacking my left temple, I would probably have been in a similar blissful condition. 'Before you tell me what it feels like to live on Mercury, just give me that bit of easy old Shakespeare again. You're a bit beyond me. Thank you. How do you know all that about a man you met tonight for the first time?'

'Just observation and thought,' he answered complacently. 'He really listens to people and doesn't pass anyone over. Donna saw that. It's very complimentary because he's the sort of chap you respect a lot. But I get the impression that he's covering up a sort of disinterest, because he's too meticulously attentive. When I was talking with him, he was different; more lively and careless – and not because I'm fascinating Orde; but because I'm your brother. He really let himself down. He let himself down again while you were teaching the dancing, and kept looking over your way. You fancy him too.' He'd become cocky and patronising. I'd soon put a stop to that. He wasn't used to being taken seriously.

'You're right out of your depth, my dear. If you continue like this, you might become a psychiatrist in thirty years.' I mustn't be too hard on him. He's only a boy, after all. 'I'm afraid you're jumping to infantile conclusions, regarding whom I, or he, "fancies" as you so crudely put it. Mr Rosenfeld and I haven't exchanged a word in your presence.'

'Now isn't that something! I wonder why, since neither of you have stopped talking to everyone else. "Are you enjoying the party?"' he mimicked, 'Meaning: "What do you think of that man over there?" You've been watching him practically all the evening, like an amateur private eye. Donna knew exactly what you were after, within five minutes, and I've known you a lot longer. Come off it! You're so transparent when you're trying to be devious. It's quite embarrassing! And what's so crude about fancying someone? I fancy Donna, and I think she fancies me. Is it too basic a word to use about that exalted gentleman?'

Oh, what the hell! I'd get even with him another time. 'Why don't you like him, Orde? He's so thoughtful and kind and helpful to everyone. He's not rigid or almighty in the way you think and he's just as vulnerable as anyone else.'

'You're putting thoughts in my head that weren't there. I *do* like him. He's unreal and unfathomable and you're just the opposite. He's not your *type*, which sounds daft. I knew we should stick to Shakespeare.'

Poor Orde! What was I about, trying to shift my problems on to his immature shoulders! Never mind! I'd made him feel grown-up and important for a while. He didn't have the faintest idea! After all, why should he? Look at the twit, who was now just waking up, whom he'd chosen to spend the evening with.

'I'm so tired,' she whined. 'Is it time to go home yet?'

They went to fetch their coats and all the other remaining guests began to take their leave. Now that my bed was cleared of coats, I longed to lie down on it, but Mr Rosenfeld was booked in it for tonight and there was still a lot of clearing up to do before I could go to sleep in Ranjini's room. In fact she was calling from the kitchen for me, already. She just never let up. I trailed in. Ranjini had prepared a beautiful supper. She handed the tray to me and placed a second glass on it.

'Take this into your room for Mr Rosenfeld. And I've got plenty of help in here; you've done more than your share. Keep him company, and once we've cleared my room up, you can go to bed whenever you like. Bye bye!'

My feeble offers of assistance were firmly rejected by everyone, so I swayed into my room and placed his supper on my table. He had removed his jacket and loosened his tie. His violin case stood against the bed, and his cuff links, wallet and razor were on my mantelpiece. His belongings, placed next to mine, made me strangely happy.

I sat on the chest of drawers and drank his wine while he ate. I gave him a blow by blow account of the antics of my household; my setbacks and victories at work and the state of my family. How easy it was to talk, to shine, to scintillate, when his eyes were on me; when he laughed at me; when he leaned back a little, to take a sip of wine, looking at me with attention and affection.

'The house isn't the same without you. You managed us all for so long. It's irresponsible of you to just wander off, and not to tell me where, or for how long. I mean, what if we had a crisis here, and me not knowing where you are! What if Dinah got sick, or Ranjini decided to make a thorough job of completing her life cycle? We've come to depend on you, you know!' A little gentle reproof would do no harm.

'Like an uncle? Or like a friend?'

'An uncle?' At some time or other, I must have used that term derisively, irritated by everyone's reliance on him. 'No. Not even a friendly one.' I suddenly felt ashamed and terribly shy, as if I'd been caught out being mean to the cat.

'Look at the time! Nearly four thirty and you've got to drive back in a few hours. How selfish and thoughtless of me, keeping you up like this! Why don't I ever learn? You must be longing to go to sleep.' I slipped off the chest and began fumbling clumsily for my shoes. 'I'll say goodnight now, Mr Rosenfeld. Is there anything else you need?'

He stood up, but instead of clicking his heels and opening the door, he took my face in both his hands, and I felt no anxiety and no shame, and I did not turn away. 'There is nothing else; I have everything.' He kissed me on the forehead, like a father bestowing a blessing on a wayward child, and spoke my name for the first time. It became an endearment when he uttered it as if it was a strange new word that I wanted to hear over and over again.

'Is this possible?' he said as if to himself, and I thought that a little reassurance would not come amiss, for I had such an abundance to spare. I would kiss him in a minute or two; disperse his doubts, restore his youth and invest him with confidence; but not yet. For then the subtlety of this moment will go; the protector may need protection; the rock will reveal that it is made of sand. I am not ready to give consolation to my comforter, or to allow my hero his frailty. I cannot combine romance and reality with him. Not yet. Let him continue to repeat my name and to stroke my hair, and to hold my head against his chest as if I were a child and not a woman. I do not have to tell him that I am tired and want to lie down, cushioned on his lap, so that my repose is complete. Nothing can disturb or alarm me, for he is here, and knows exactly what I find sustaining and restful. There is no challenge for me to meet. Not yet.

'Give me my name,' he said softly, 'Morris.' Morris. How did Jane ever bring herself to call Mr Rochester Edward? Charlotte didn't explain this daunting leap into intimacy. Morris. How strange it sounds! How pleasant, unusual, if only I could pronounce it! Why is it so singularly difficult, as if it were Chinese and contained ten unfamiliar syllables? I needed time to practise and would make an effort; but not just yet. Mr

Rosenfeld is so much easier and safer. It is he who is caressing my shoulders, neck and back, dispersing the tension, the headache, and all responsibility. And if I am aware of his turmoil and hear him sigh, I am secure in the power of his restraint.

How beautiful, sharp and pure the light was; how startling the colours and objects were in the room! What loveliness! What hell! I had woken up with my contact lenses intact, and must suffer for it all day. But sometimes it is worth the discomfort to open one's eyes to such clarity. I was lying in bed, between the sheets, warm and comfortable, yet dressed to kill, in Rina's gear.

Wait! Close your eyes! Allow the head to clear along with the perfect vision! What have I done? Where is Mr Rosenfeld? He should be lying here, and I should be with Ranjini in the next room. He must have sat up the whole night. What folly! What selfishness! Can't I do anything right? I'd get up at once and look for him. But first, I'd just slip off this dress, turn on the radio, return to bed and close my swollen eyelids for three or four minutes; perhaps they won't feel so awful once I press a cold compress over them.

'Good morning!' It was he, my hero, my friend, my magician, bearing a tray, and I could smell something hot and crisp and delicious. He had already been to Grodzinski's because the croissants had just come out of their ovens. He put the tray on my red stool and poured the coffee. Two months ago I should have felt irritated and embarrassed, but now his smile erased all discomfort, and the odd intimacy of the situation, his chivalry and care, delighted me. As if I wanted nothing more.

'I'm sorry. You can't have had a wink of sleep all night. Why didn't you wake me? I feel so ashamed!'

'But I was not tired and I had much to think about. I was too elated to sleep and that is perhaps your fault. Your head was resting on my knee. It is only half an hour since I went to find breakfast. I spent a night full of happy dreams.' He handed me my coffee. I knew that I looked like Medusa, but seeing myself reflected in his eyes, I could have been Cleopatra.

'How changed life would be, if every day I could wake up to your gallantry and breakfasts and the vanquishing of all my problems!'

'And would you change?'

'Yes.'

'Into what? Into someone careful of what she says? Into someone discreet and conventional? In short, into someone else?'

'Anything's possible; you should know that! You're the magician!'

'If that were so, I would exercise all my powers into keeping you exactly as you are.'

Remember, I thought, closing my eyes and swallowing my coffee. Remember, and never be wretched again. I loved him. I needed his support, his attention, his enormous moral strength and that ability of his which could now make me feel clever and lovely. With a little effort, I could call him Morris and draw him close to me, and make him happy. I knew that. With any other man for whom I did not care half as much, it would have been the easiest, most natural gesture. But with him I could not. It was as if we stood on rough and uneven ground, and I was unable to smooth the way to him. Any attempt would cause me to stumble and somehow lose my footing. Freud would have plenty to say about me. I preferred fantasy to reality. Thinking about this was vaguely distressing, so I would stop at once, and assuage my only appetite by eating a croissant. I opened my eyes to find it. He was looking at me with an expression of such tenderness, that for a few moments I could not quit its contemplation, and I felt tears in my eyes.

'I fell asleep wearing my contact lenses. My eyes keep watering.'

He fetched two icy cold flannels and pressed them to my eyes and forehead. I put my hands over his. I needed them to shelter, comfort and indulge me. 'I'm sorry,' I said, 'forgive me!'

'Forgive you? For what? For exploding my self-made barrier by the generosity of your greeting? For bringing me out of my hibernation in order to show me the sunshine?' He wiped my face and handed me my cup and plate, and everything was all right again.

The castaway on *Desert Island Discs* was playing 'Songs my Mother Taught Me' and he sang along with it in a glorious bass-baritone, until Roy Plomley interrupted. I'd once heard Hermione Gingold ask if she could take along 'a rather charming gentleman' for her 'one luxury', but no living creatures were allowed.

'What would yours be?'

'My violin. And yours?'

'I don't know. I wish I did. I've no special talent and any consuming interests I have are totally outweighed by my consuming antipathies; so I'd settle for a tanker of spray which kills all spiders stone dead.'

'And if you could only take one record?' I gave him my choice, and he reached for his violin. I watched him tuning it, and then he played, wielding his bow effortlessly, the instrument an extension of himself. Yet all the muscles of his face and body moved with the melody, and I thought that I had never heard or seen anything so sweet and so sensual. His exclusive devotion to his music overawed me, and I glimpsed something which I would henceforth always yearn for, yet would always be denied, and I did not know what it was.

He placed his most precious possession on the table. I could not speak. Then quite deliberately, he walked over to my open suitcase, which was lying in the corner, and looked down at the riot of papers within; notebooks and half-filled torn pads, dealing with my discarded novel. His back was towards me and he beckoned me to join him, without turning. I fumbled around for a dressing gown, unsuccessfully, and settled for last night's dress. I stood next to him, looking at the mess.

I'd given up trying to write. I'd been kidding myself and everyone that I was capable of completing this work, but now I saw with absolute clarity that this was a conceit. Henceforth, I would not waste my time entertaining illusions. I dragged the suitcase into the middle of the room and knelt down to examine the contents more closely. The sight of all those words depressed and embarrassed me and I felt a strange pang. Once I had thrown them away, I would feel better, guiltless and cleansed, but I'd leave that worthwhile assignment until later, after Mr Rosenfeld had gone.

'Why not take this to your desert island?'

I shook my head. 'I'd rather take an animated model of a tarantula. I'm going to destroy all that rubbish. I need an empty suitcase.'

What a marvellous, marvellous idea! I would go with him to where he was playing this evening. I hadn't been to a concert for ages, and a breath of sea air was exactly what I needed. I'd easily find a place to stay. No one went to the seaside at this time of year. We'd be able to get to know each other; drive out to the downs. After all, he'd only be busy in the evenings. He'd made it quite obvious that he found pleasure in my company. I was just about to inform him of my plans, when the image of his playing the violin a few minutes ago halted me. He wouldn't want me with him. He was sufficient unto himself. A second fiddle would be an encumbrance.

'Why?'

'Why!' I repeated, snappishly. 'Why what? Why am I going to destroy all my rubbish or why do I need an empty suitcase? To which statement are you referring?' I didn't give him time to answer. 'I do not like waste paper – it clutters and bothers me to have it lying around. And an empty case is useful; one can fill it with more mess.' I lingered indulgently on my own misfortunes, a pastime in which I was experienced.

'Why are you so defensive about your gifts and unstinting about your acknowledgement of those in others? Why are you ashamed of what is valuable and unique in you? Why do you diminish yourself and thus allow others to exploit you? Why do you think I do not want you to come with me?' The man was a clairvoyant. I'd given absolutely no indication of what was in my mind.

'I just thought a little sea air would do me good, and since you're going in that direction, I decided to thumb a lift from you. I haven't had a holiday for ages.'

He pulled me to my feet as if I was as light as a feather. I'd never feel fat again. 'I would like so much to take you to my desert island, but it's not allowed. How well this violin would work for me, if you were nearby; but why should I develop my skill at the expense of yours? I will not do this; it would be unjust. It is not rubbish in this case – it is part of you, just as my music is a part of me. You must finish what you have set out to create – it would be immoral to destroy it. And what about your teaching? Your term starts in two days. Would you ask me to give up my work?'

How stuffy he is. I'd forgotten about my tedious job, probably because I hated it so much, and I'd thrust it into a dark corner of my mind. The holidays had barely started. 'How can you talk about your work and mine in the same context? I've heard you play; I'm untutored and ignorant, but I can at least perceive great talent. You know nothing of my calibre as a teacher or as a writer. I fail at both, constantly!'

'And succeed – constantly! And are exploited – constantly! No one is exploited in a creative profession who is untalented. And as for your writing, did you imagine that I would wait patiently until you offered me a sample? I was not called a bloodhound for nothing. Dinah had the magazines in which your stories are published, and I have read them all – many times. I found you there, and relished them, as you relished my playing. How many more words have you to write?'

'Thirty-five and a half thousand,' I lied. It was the first large number that came into my head.

'So! Even allowing for gross inaccuracy, it is manageable. When we next meet, you will please show me the completed manuscript.'

I was right. He didn't want my company. I'd been stupid to believe that he really liked me. Why the hell should he? I'd not been the sweetest person in the world. 'How long do you think it might take me? Twenty years?'

He pretended to make a quick calculation. 'Six weeks. Remember the ticket I gave you? February fourteenth at the Festival Hall. If you are there, I will know that you have done yourself justice for once.'

'And if I fail? Don't you understand that certain tasks cannot be done to order? Go and tell a farmer to harvest his corn in the spring! How can I be expected to write without inspiration?'

'I understand that your analogy is incorrect. With you, it is your attitude and application which will bring in the fruits. I speak from experience. For years I worked without a light; then I found one and after that, there was an edge to all my endeavours. Let me, in poor exchange, be your discipline for tethering your talents and finishing your book. Please!'

'Then I shall have to begin all over again. I'll die of old age and boredom if I try to carry on with this. I've got to apologise to my non-existent audience and admit to having started in the wrong key. I feel foolish, embarrassed and exposed.'

'It takes courage to play it to the end, and then to listen to what you have done. After that, you can correct and adjust, but end it you must. I imagine you have begun many times. Commit yourself. I have such confidence in you. You won't let me down. The date is agreed?'

'And if I fail?'

'If you have not done your homework, you will not have the temerity to face me; and then I would be disappointed, and my evening would be spoilt. And you will be one hundred per cent to blame.' His expression was so soft, so benign, that he seemed to belie all his show of authority; but I felt renewed hope and excitement in the challenge.

'I'll be there!' I said. 'You and me in Row C!' I'd check in the *Guinness Book of Records* on the number of words contained in the shortest novel in the world. 'And I'll bring the last chapter. It's a deal, Mr Rosenfeld. I'll start finishing the book today!'

He smiled and then sighed. 'You sound as if you're lamenting my decision.'

'Only that I must leave now – and on my own; for my forfeit; for my Fielder's Choice; for the *Desert Island* rules. Make it worthwhile!'

I could do anything. Anything! My novel would be fatter than *The Moonstone*. I was seized with inspiration. 'I'll amaze you. I'll sort and sift all my papers, and spend every spare minute scribbling. I won't go out – except to work; I won't write letters or talk to strangers. I'll write and write and write. I'll call my book *Memoirs of a Teacher* – a kind of reference book for training colleges. To hell with everything else!'

'To hell with everything else!' he said, holding me to him, and leaving me with nothing and no one but him in my thoughts.

Chapter Ten

Goodbye, Mr Rosenfeld. I will not spend another minute staring into space; examining, gramme by gramme, the unique quality of our relationship. You miss me as I miss you, and so I can endure this separation without agitation. For loneliness has little to do with being alone in the physical sense. It is to do with isolation of the soul; the horrid knowledge that no one is aware of your predicament. In a very short time, I will overturn the suitcase, and shuffle through the half-finished notebooks and the shameful sheaves of repetitive scribble; and I will be steadfast. I will seek out the last known page. I will not be critical of my past efforts for that would impede my progress. I will shelve all my plans and ignore the telephone. I will not be overambitious, but ration myself to twelve hundred words a day, and be satisfied with that output. That accomplished, I might possibly allow myself the indulgence of society and leisure pursuits, and try to be in bed by midnight, so that I would awake, rested and revived, ready for the next three pages. In two days I would have to avail myself for work and all my talents, energy and insight would be used to the full. Thus inspired and vitalised, I would repair homeward, indulge in a light, healthful lunch and seven or eight minutes of total relaxation, and settle at my table on which would rest two fibre-tipped pens, a clean notebook and my typewriter with a nice new ribbon in it. My carbons and foolscap typing paper would be already inserted, and those waiting to be filled, lying on my red stool.

I cleared my table and sorted out all my relevant papers – a most horrid and mortifying task, which left me exhausted. Nevertheless, I gathered together a notebook, my pens and my thoughts, and looked out of the window. There was my charming, friendly postman. I'd seen him once, on a bus, and he'd said 'Hello'. His face being familiar, I'd asked from where we'd known each other.

'I see you in your nightie on the morning I bring you a parcel!' he lied, on purpose to make mischief. 'Your postman! Your postman!'

God forbid that someone I've known for years should shift his habitat: the librarian in the cinema; the hairdresser wheeling a pram in the street; the Queen at the laundrette. 'I'm terribly sorry; I just can't place you!' I'd just look to see if there were any letters for me. Only one, enclosed in the Inner London Education Authority's dull brown envelope.

Dear Miss Lazarus,

Home Tuition of Handicapped Children

I write to confirm that you have been engaged to give tuition to:

1) Susan Tiffin
2) Muriel Towey
3) Jacqueline Homer

Tuition should commence on 4 January, etc.

What malice! What confidence! What cunning! That Sanderson woman had twenty times the normal dose of each. 'Grist for the mill,' she was always saying. If she cropped up in my book, I would not change her name. Let others know her for what she was. And I would teach these children. After all, what I wanted for my book was an in-depth study of a few individuals, not a multitude of rather shallow case histories. Susan and Muriel would be of particular interest, and maybe this new girl,

Jacqueline, would prove to be a worthwhile addition. I'd use Miss Sanderson's vindictiveness for my own ends. I wished Mr Rosenfeld was here, so I could discuss my book; but I'd discipline my thoughts and plan out my regimen.

I'd give myself small rewards. After every three hundred words, I'd have a cup of coffee and two chocolate fingers. I'd make a flask – now – so that I wouldn't have to disturb myself at intervals, by going into the kitchen and being held up by Ranjini's chatter. This proved to be an excellent idea, for as soon as I had put the kettle on, she came in on the pretext of wanting tea, and detained me. I succeeded in hiding my irritation; she wasn't to know how busy I was, and really, I'd given her no opportunity of discussing the party with me. I'd indulge her for half an hour – no more – and make it absolutely clear to her that I had work to do without offending her. I'd be assertive rather than aggressive.

'Hello, stranger! How long are you going to be in the kitchen? Gamini is coming and I've got some cooking to do.'

'I'm just making a flask, so that I can keep going with my book. I've got a deadline to meet; less than six weeks.'

'Haven't I heard that song before? Anthony Hope finished *The Prisoner of Zenda* in a month. You've been finishing your great work ever since I've known you. You haven't the faintest idea how to take your work seriously, and frankly I'm sick of hearing about it. You're always busy doing something else. You can't stay in your room for more than an hour at a time, when you've got that writing to face. I bet you'll be going out of the front door before you've strung a hundred words together, on some trivial errand, like buying a packet of biscuits or because you've run out of milk. Well, don't bother, because there's plenty of stuff in the tins and the fridge – and you're welcome to it – cake, biscuits; all that you need for your staple diet. And there's plenty of cigarettes too; Gamini brought a whole lot of duty-free ones for the party and they're your brand. Half of them are left, since you were only at the party for half the evening. Come on! The kettle's boiling and I share the gas bills, remember.'

This attack on me was because she felt I'd let her down, and she was trying to upset me. Nothing doing.

'It was a marvellous party,' I said. 'That's all I want to say.'

'If it was marvellous, it wasn't entirely due to you.'

'But I didn't spoil anything. If you'd really needed me to help to get things going, and to keep them ticking over, I'd have made more effort, but my presence wasn't necessary.' Whatever was bugging her, it wasn't this. She'd have been nasty to me last night, but in fact she'd been quite gracious, and I hadn't seen her since, to have a chance to give offence.

'You deserted, though; and what's more, you've been secretive and odd with me, and downright deceitful.'

I was engaged in pouring boiling coffee into my flask. My hand trembled so violently that the liquid poured all over the table and floor, and I barely avoided a serious scald to my foot. I realised, in that moment, that I had a secret enemy who had fed her with information regarding myself and Sarath, some time between the end of the party and now; some vile creature who was jealous of my relationship with Mr Rosenfeld and who wanted to do me harm. Let her come out with it then! I wasn't prepared to live under this threat any longer. She was tutting and fussing, because I'd made a mess, and was already busy with the mop, jabbing at my feet.

'I'm sorry,' I said, humbly. Now what had I done! She'd probably think I was apologising for spilling the coffee.

'I don't like being made a fool of, that's all. You might have told me that you planned to spend the night with Mr Rosenfeld – particularly after you so pointedly pretended you couldn't stand the sight of him. Last night was your first indication to me that you liked him. You purposely misled me, and I feel very hurt. Did you think I'd be jealous?'

'No!' I had to sit down. The relief of reprieve dissolved my knees, and sharpened my wits. Nothing works like a counter-attack for bringing your opponent to heel. 'I've felt lately that you didn't respect me and that you were scornful of me and thought me shallow. You've been very critical of me,' I whined, 'and I've not been inspired recently with an overdose of self-confidence.' O hell! Why had I to say 'overdose'? 'And as for making a fool of you – you should know me better than that!' Let her think I'd spent a night of abandoned passion with Mr Rosenfeld. It would keep her off dangerous ground.

'Put the top on your thermos, and stop making me out such an ogre. You don't deserve him, you know. He's much too good for you!'

'Really.' That word; that dull, meaningless adverb, modifying an absent verb, if articulated without expression and with eyes averted, succeeds in quietening a stream of clichés, and brings the contender to a grovelling position.

'Of course not! I'm absolutely delighted that you two have got together at last. He looked happier and younger than I've ever seen him! But I'm still reeling under the shock, you being at one end of the spectrum, and Mr Rosenfeld at the other. He's quite a lot older than you, too; about nineteen years.'

'Twenty. But since I'm young for my age, and he isn't, it widens the gap to at least thirty-five, but we've managed to bridge it quite effectively.' She looked so crestfallen that I softened. 'Look, Ranjy, I'm in a hurry, and so are you. Let's continue this conversation when we're both less edgy and distracted. I'm now going to get out of your way. Have a jolly evening and don't throw away the leavings from your meal!' I smiled cheerfully, and left her to the pleasures of the kitchen. Ranjini; gloriously beautiful, exotic, feminine, charming Ranjini, was jealous of *me*! I settled myself at my table and addressed myself to my work.

The temptation of going back and being abjectly apologetic

for my harshness was overwhelming, and the resistance to it occupied a full half hour of writing time. Why was she jealous? Was she in love with him? How satisfactory! How disgustingly small-minded I was! I read an old comic and two stories from a *School Friend Annual*, dated 1959, which I'd found in the bottom of my suitcase, tidied my room, closed the curtains and adjusted my lamp. How short the days were! Nearly three hours to go until *Coronation Street*. I'd watch it, if I'd written my daily allowance by then. I ignored the door bell, knowing that Gamini was expected. I hoped they'd enjoy their evening so that she'd be less sour tomorrow. I could hear Ranjini answering the door, and a few seconds later, someone rapped sharply at mine. 'I do begin to have bloody thoughts' along with Stephano. 'Hello!' I trilled, hiding my malevolence.

He came in, closing the door behind him and stood where he was, looking at me – the perpetrator of my grief and exile; my humiliation, wretchedness and wasted youth; the physician who cured others' ills but who had caused mine; the lover who had bantered and cast me aside, without care for my suffering. 'Hello, Nehama,' he said softly, soberly. He knew better than to smile, yet his caution was insufficient. He had last used this, my second name, when I had encumbered him with my love.

'Joseph! What a surprise!'

'I pass this house so often! Last week I had a call at number sixteen, and saw you come in here. I couldn't believe my eyes – I thought you'd emigrated! I checked the telephone directory and found your name, so . . .'

'You thought you'd include me in your rounds. Well, put your bag down, Old Fruit; there's no plague here!' Only the squalor of bitterness and the sickness of revenge. I took his outstretched hands and he kissed me insolently on the cheek. I smelt his aftershave lotion. I had searched for that smell in the drug stores of New York, crazy for one sensual whiff. The air reeked with the shameful memory, suffocating and sickening.

Something horrid was happening to my pyloric sphincter muscles, as if I had lately dined on caterpillar sandwiches.

I pushed him away, playfully, begging leave to get a glass of water, as if being overcome by the delicious shock of seeing him again. I fled to the cloakroom, and filled the dirty toothpaste glass with cold water, and drank it down. The peppermint taste refreshed me and cleared my system; and I looked in the mirror and didn't give a damn and smiled at myself and re-entered my Consulting Room.

Doctor Joseph ben Ezra was at ease in the rocking-chair, almost sure of himself and of me. I would not make him wary; not yet. I must allow his arrogance full range before I prick it with the contaminated syringe he thought he had disposed of three and a half years ago. But I carry in my blood stream every infested drop.

I thought back to that miserable day, when I had read *Washington Square*. I was Catherine, pitilessly biding my time for when Morris Townsend, alias Joseph ben Ezra, should pay the forfeit for what he had destroyed. Total admiration, with a dash of the wanton, was my poisoned tonic for this particular patient. I attended to his symptoms for a full hour. I held his hand. I laughed uproariously at his wit. I looked into his eyes and allowed mine to linger suggestively over the length of his body. My bedside manner was masterly; now was the time to start probing gently; tenderly.

'Why didn't you come over to me when you saw me? Aren't we old friends?'

'Absolutely! But I wasn't sure you'd see it that way. I had to find out whether you were still single and free.'

Mark that down – the impudent assumption that single equals free. 'You might have had a jealous husband. I'm so glad you haven't – wise, wise Nehama! Marriage isn't all it's jacked up to be.'

'You and Marjorie; you're happy, aren't you?'

'Of course. She's a marvellous girl. I don't have to tell you how clever and gifted she is. After all, you were at school together.' Or how deadly dull, uninspired and treacherous. 'No one could wish for a better wife. But I'll tell you the worst-kept secret; the esoteric knowledge of every married couple. As soon as you make the relationship legal, you stop laughing at each other's jokes; the liveliness and zest is there, but intermittently, and – well – you cease paying full attention to one another. A kind of healthy neglect develops, and that's fine.' Really! How could I have been deaf to this man's clamouring mediocrity?

'Yet sometimes I get a yearning for single-minded devotion; you corrupted me, you know!' Attend later to that twinkle in his eye. 'I can't remember exactly when – about six months ago, I should think – we were watching a programme on astronomy, and throughout it, my mind was fixed on you. When we discussed it afterwards, I kept hearing you and seeing you. Weird, obsessive. I pretended that there were a couple of patients I was very worried about and that I wanted to see, and late though it was, I went for a long drive. Guess where?'

Could it be to Hertfordshire, you stupid, faithless bastard? How shall I answer? Is it time to stamp him to death? Do I hear the bell toll? Not for thee. Not yet. He does not know the trick I have for making my eyes water. It's easy with contact lenses. All I have to do is raise my eyebrows and open my eyes to slightly more than their usual slits; and then the tears flow satisfactorily. I'd never had to use this ploy with him. My tears had rained without assistance; in the street, on the bus; in full view of my family, friends, pupils and strangers. He had bereft me of dignity and eclipsed all gladness; blocked all paths and discouraged all my endeavours by leaving me to flounder in paralysing wretchedness.

Joseph. Clever, kind; superbly, wonderfully funny! You made me smile; shriek with mirth until my sides ached. You were the funniest man I ever knew. I used to wish that I had the pen of a Boswell to catch forever the nimble word; your strange, unusual turn of phrase; your contagious delight in brevity and understatement; the elegant irony of your mutely accurate observations. A bar of iron became a cobweb with one twist. You stretched my horizon and peopled it with new and fantastic aspects. I never tired of your capering conversation, or the movements of your face; the wide, sweeping gesticulations of your arms and the dancing of your fingers. How you enlightened and refreshed me! My ignorance and youth never hampered you and you joyously pierced the comparative dimness of my intelligence, lighting it up with gay paper lanterns. 'I love you!' I'd said, holding you in my arms, careless and not knowing; not looking at you properly. 'I love you. I'll love you all my life.'

For a few moments my fake tears became real, as not the mere memory, but the woe itself, engulfed me. 'Morris,' I called, looking towards the window. 'Morris!' He looked disconcerted, and smiled nervously.

'What? Who's Morris?'

'A character I read about in *Washington Square*. You reminded me of him.'

He took it as a compliment, without query. 'I drove along the A 41 to that place in Hertfordshire.'

'Why?' I asked, softly, knowing in that instant that I should have made acting my career.

'Because I missed you; hungered and thirsted for you! There I was, sitting in front of the telly, feeling tired, comfortable and middle-aged, and a few minutes later, I was haring across country in a masochistic sweat, recalling Romance. I went to the same place where we stargazed, and I lay on the grass for God knows how long, thinking of you, and how we'd made love.'

Wrong. Remember to correct him later. I changed the subject adroitly, making him think that my emotions were uncomfortably disturbed.

Marjorie couldn't have children, he told me. She'd been terribly ill shortly after their marriage. Possibly due to the power of my Evil Eye, I thought. They'd both wanted kids, but had come to terms with their disappointment. She was lecturing in English history at City College and he was still in general practice, although he now did quite a lot of private work. I told him what I'd been doing, and that I was writing a book.

'Do I feature in it?' he asked. Dear me! He really was scraping the bottom of the barrel with his asinine comments.

'Naturally. You've been an immense influence in my life.'

'Bless you for that! Come and stargaze with me again. I won't let you get cold.' He lunged forward and jammed his lips against mine, to show me how disarmingly sexy and mischievous he was.

I extricated myself, but apologetically, making it clear to him that I needed all my frail self-control to subdue the passion he evoked in me. I courted him; I upstaged Delilah, relishing the imminent climax of his total defeat.

'You showed me Cassiopeia's Chair. I still recognise it. I still remember. It always looks like a "W" to me.' I drew the shape of it on his chest. 'W for Wet. W for Weak. W for Weasel. W for Wrecker. Alas for Andromeda! Nasty old Neptune and his Nereides! But surely we didn't make love? O, for total recall!'

'Don't be bitter,' he said, unsure; afraid.

'Bitter, ben Ezra? What do you mean? I'm trying to recollect accurately, that's all, you Romantic Old Romeo! I made love; not you. You just took the opportunities when they arose, but mostly you were too tired or had more pressing distractions. I was young and foolish and did not understand, but I'm older and wiser now, and entirely sympathise; so if you'll excuse me, I have an urgent appointment in *Coronation Street*.'

'Is there someone else?'

'Someone else? No. Someone. Yes. Go home to Muswell Hill and Mendacious Marjorie. I like to watch the adverts before the programme – they invigorate me – and prefer to do so when my surroundings are pleasant. Keep in mind the fact that they are more efficacious than your medication, which tends to irritate the lining of my stomach, so exclude me, in future, from your nasty little private rounds.'

I turned on the telly and adjusted the aerial, picked up his bag, and held it out to him. He looked up at me. His face was horribly white and haggard. He did not move, and when he spoke his voice was cracked and wavering and old.

'Please ... Don't act like this. I need you. Can't we talk a little? Why have you changed? I want to explain ... to ...'

'Exonerate yourself?'

'If you like.'

'I don't like. Absolution is uncalled for, because all I feel is gratitude. And gratitude is such a weary burden for me; so I'll take the opportunity of shedding it now, by saying "Thank you". Thank you for leaving me when you did. I only regret it wasn't sooner.' I actually yawned, but I could feel another knife in my belt. 'You bore me. You always did.' Will he manage to rise and open the door, or will he, perhaps, crawl under it and make his shameful exit?

He took the bag from me and placed it on the floor between his feet. He sat slumped in the chair, as if unable to rise. 'May I have a drink?'

'There's coffee in the flask. Will that do?' He nodded, and I poured him a cup, handing it to him with my steady left hand. I watched him sipping it, listening to his loud swallows; mesmerised by the sight of it slopping over his shoes and bag. The music of his weeping invaded my soul and renewed my energy. I rescued the cup and placed it on the mantelpiece. Revenge! How sweet you are! Never before have I indulged in so much of your bounty! I am swamped and cloyed by your honey. Cease feeding me at once with your giant ladle, for I cannot digest another teaspoonful! Forego your zealous generosity, before my guts indecently protest.

He sat with his head in his hands – my Joseph; my Dreamer; my Funny Man, believing all the things I had said. Didn't he realise that I wanted to punish him for making me wretched, and that it wasn't his fault that I'd loved him? Had he no idea that he'd given me unimaginable joy, and that misery wasn't as memorable as I made out? I examined the top of his head carefully. Twenty per cent white hair; eighty per cent black. No grey. Did I have any subtle shades of feeling for this man, this stranger, who jeopardised my self-knowledge and faith in myself? Did I loathe or love him or feel total indifference? Why, no! The word spatters my vocabulary, but remains meaningless, while I irresistibly strive for it. Let me say, 'I am indifferent to you, Joseph. Your existence plays no part in my life. The mention of your name is a hyperbole.' He raised his head and looked at me. His face was wet with tears.

'I love you,' he said; 'just as you once loved me. I know now, what my rejection of you meant.'

'Do you?' I said, knowing only that this was my revenge, and his acquittal. I walked over to the window and drew aside the curtain, and saw the stars, pricking the cold, clear sky. I thought of Perseus delivering Andromeda; of the Morris who was Mr Rosenfeld; of the delicious, outrageous response that this man had once provoked in me, and which had come to life again. But so rearranged, that he had now, no longer, anything to do with it.

'The "Someone" you asked about has taken over. There's no place for you here. It's time to go, Joseph. Goodbye.'

I shook his hand and watched him as he left, and went towards his car. He turned, and I waved, closing the door, without malice and without regret.

Chapter Eleven

The snow was thawing and the pavement was glossy with watery ice. 'This way for the sorrowful city. This way for eternal suffering. This way to join the lost people . . .' This was to Jackie Homer's house; padded cell against me, you and the rest of us. Here is the mauve front door out of which this thirteen-year-old girl has not emerged for over two years. I pressed my choppy finger on the bell, and heard Oranges and Lemons chiming within.

A fat, middle-aged, highly nervous woman opened the door for me, and apologised for the painting and decorating going on in the hall. We squeezed past a small man on a high stepladder. Mauve was the new colour on his roller – and mauve was the old colour, too.

'He's mad, you know; take no notice of him,' said Mrs Homer, referring to the painter, who could hear her unless he was profoundly deaf. 'He starts on the top landing and works his way down, and when he gets to the front door, he starts again. Like that bridge in Scotland.'

I was ushered into a living room cum mortuary. Every possible neurotic tendency betrayed itself at once. Carpet, curtains, cushions, ceiling, walls and lampshades were spotlessly mauve. The armchairs and settee were black, and scatter cushions residing on them stood in upright diamonds, as straight, hideous and symmetrical as jack-booted soldiers. 'Tea or coffee?' asked my hostess.

'Yes,' I said 'Yes, please. What a pretty room!'

'We love it. Our Jackie chose all the colours. She's very artistic. Let me take your coat.' She wanted to watch my skin turn the same colour as the curtains. The cold was terrible, and there was no means of heating the room.

'I'll keep it on for a few minutes until I warm up,' I said with a gay smile, shivering, to prevent the onset of rigor mortis. 'What a lovely perfume you're wearing!'

'That's our Jackie! She's been spraying. He will keep on painting and painting and we have to use two cannisters a day in here.'

'Where *is* Jackie?'

'Her nerves are bad. She's got herself into a state about you, but I'll try to persuade her to come in. You sit down and help yourself to biscuits.'

I crammed two into my mouth, before I realised that they were contaminated by African Violets Perfume Spray, and emptied the chewed contents into an exercise book from my bag. New Ideas for Dieting.

I listened to terrified screams coming from somewhere near at hand: 'I won't see 'er! She'd better fuck off! No, no, no, I won't!'

Mrs Homer returned, bearing a tea tray. The cup rattled in the saucer long after she had handed it to me. I must pull myself together.

'She'll have a peep round the door soon, if I stay in here with you. She won't be without her mum for more than a minute.' How proud; how gratified she sounded!

Her judgment was spot on. I heard floorboards creaking, and looked up to see a face peering round the door. I expected the word 'SANCTUARY' to explode from it and went numb with horror. The eyes, nose and mouth were distorted; diminished by balloons of fat.

'Hello, Jackie,' I quavered.

'Mum! Mum! Come 'ere!' howled the apparition. The noise

she made was deafening and made me gasp. The mother jumped up like a jack-in-the-box in perfect working order, and rushed from the room to comfort and reassure.

Right! If the Mountain wouldn't come to Mahomet, Mahomet would go thence. I followed the row and found it in the kitchen. To report on the colour of the fridge, cooker, kitchen table and vinyl would be repetitious. Jackie had fenced herself between the wall, cupboard and ironing board and was gripping her mother with both hands.

Fellow Hullensians, you all know of the Fair which visits every October, turning the city into the strangest in the world, for one bizarre week. It is the biggest fair in Europe and is renowned for its side shows. Thousands of pounds are offered to anyone smaller than, taller than, fatter than, more tattooed than, hairier than, spottier than the poor wretches who exhibit their deformities to the public. Their reputation, as far as I know, has always remained unchallenged. Where were you last October, Jackie Homer? You could have made yourself rich in your own side show, if you'd been transported to East Yorkshire. So wretched! So sorrowful! So lost! Direct from London Town! Fifty thousand pounds for her equal!

Miss Sanderson, of course, had failed to forewarn me that my new pupil was twelve stones overweight. She had quoted bits and pieces from the psychiatrist's report – 'school-refuser; agrophobic; a symbiotic relationship between mother and daughter' – I thought that meant a mutually beneficial dependence; but this? This was horrible! Every time I tried to speak, the girl drowned my voice with her screams and insults. The mother asked me to leave the room, but I sat on a kitchen chair and refused to budge. At least it was warm in here and she hadn't drenched the air with spray.

Mrs Homer finally disengaged herself, assuring Jackie that she would try to get me out of the room and then make her a 'nice bacon sandwich'. Wise woman! The smell of frying bacon, which so many otherwise normal people enjoy, disgusts me. I've never understood Adam succumbing to the Forbidden Fruit. I withdrew to the overpowering embrace of African violets while the pan in the kitchen hissed venomously.

The painter joined me and introduced himself as Jackie's father. He was puny and undersized and put me in mind of a carelessly sexy, male spider. If a wicked magician had given me the choice of lifting a dumbbell equal to one Jackie, or two Mr Homers, I would unhesitatingly have settled for the latter. The three characters in this house were absolutely repellent.

'Why won't Jackie go to school?'

'She won't leave the house. She don't know the colour of the front door.' I bet she does, though!

'What happens when your wife goes out?'

'Oh, when Mum goes to work at the play centre, Nana and Auntie Iris sit with her. She won't be left with me.'

'She hates him,' smiled Mum, walking in with a Desperate Dan sandwich on a large plate. 'You must be hungry! Jackie's had her two. She's not so upset now. She always feels better after a snack.'

I refused the monstrous offering.

'You'd better have it then,' she said spitefully, handing it to her husband. 'No! Not in here! I'm not having bleeding crumbs all over, and don't go in the kitchen. My Jackie's in there, and I'm not having her getting all upset again. Have it on your ladder.' He scuttled away on his eight nasty little hairy legs while Mama licked her mandibles and led me to the kitchen. On the way, I looked over the banister and saw him sitting on the second rung. This was a madhouse.

'Piece of toast, Jackie?' called the Black Widow gaily, forestalling my entrance with a bribe. The monster howled, but I sat. She urged the wall to move, wriggling against it like a grounded whale. The smell of toast, however, seemed to calm her. Mother knows best. Where the hell did they buy mauve paper towels? They must have combed London and the home counties. While she was mopping the butter from her chins with one, I spoke.

'Jackie, I have come a long way, today; from Golders Green, and it took me over an hour. I don't want to waste my time. You don't have to go to school, as long as I come here.' A veiled threat wouldn't hurt. 'But you have to stay in the room with me and listen to me.'

'Mum! I won't go to school,' yelled the child idiotically. 'Don't leave me with her, Mum! I want to go to the toilet!'

They went off together, the child barely able to move. It was a frightful sight. Five minutes later, I heard the toilet flush, and the two of them swam back into the kitchen. 'She's got something to show you, Miss Lazarus, haven't you, Jack?' Jack glowered from her lodge behind the ironing board, unable to meet even the eyes of her mother while a foreign organism was within sight. From the cupboard Mrs Homer pulled a bulging plastic bag and placed it on the table next to me, with loving care.

'Let's put it on the ironing table; then Jackie will be able to show me, too.' She immediately orbited and faced the wall but she remained quiet, although quite obviously distressed by my proximity. The contents of the bag were placed lovingly on it.

'Who gave you these for Christmas, Jackie? Mum did!' cried the wretched woman triumphantly. 'This little lot cost me more than a hundred pound, one hundred and five pound, to be exact, and that was without postage!'

The most exquisite clothes covered the table – all hand-made. The dresses were silk, hand-embroidered and decorated with tiny seed pearls. I had never felt underwear like this in Marks and Spencer's. Each item was trimmed with creamy lace. There were two fur coats with matching hats and a cashmere sweater. Dread and horror swamped me so that for a few moments I could neither move nor breathe, and my heart was beating like a drum. The clothes were designed for a sophisticated, adult female, around twenty inches high. A midget lurked somewhere – a midget with expensive tastes, whom Jackie looked after. The inhabitants of Brobdingnag and Lilliput resided here. I must take a nerve pill as soon as possible.

'What beautiful clothes! Who wears them?'

'My Jackie's sister, Caroline,' the woman twinkled. 'She's in our bedroom. Do you want to meet her?'

'Yes. Yes, please.' At least I didn't have to queue up and pay.

Jackie actually emerged from her hidey hole, once I had withdrawn to the other end of the kitchen, and I followed the two of them across the landing into an adjoining room. I noticed that our lovable painter was back at his duties on the icy stairway, and I wondered whose genes were responsible for these tragic offspring. The colour scheme and temperature of the bedroom registered a familiar mauve zero, but I hardly noticed. I was convulsed with absurd trembling. A tiny figure lay on the bed and I realised with stunning shock that it was a doll. Why had it not occurred to me before? I must be going crazy. It was clad in an exquisite nightgown and bed-jacket. There was something painfully poignant, as well as grotesque, about this family.

I remembered an anecdote my mother often related, about an encounter she and my father experienced, a week before the birth of my eldest sister. They were resting on a seat in a country lane, when a middle-aged lady joined them, wheeling a pram. She prattled dotingly to the baby, adjusted the sun canopy, placed a bottle and a rattle on the pram cover, and began knitting a half-completed pink shawl. She engaged my parents in friendly conversation and my mother peered fondly under the canopy, dreaming of the pleasures of motherhood. A dog, dressed in a pink bonnet and coat, and secured in a baby harness, lay against the pillows. Although her nerves were completely unstrung, she cooed and clucked and went along with the pantomime, through cowardice and pity, until she was able to take to her heels, with my father in tow. She had horrid nightmares until Jean was born, a week later, in human form. She dressed her daughter in blue, and to this day dislikes dogs and pink. Dolls and mauve are probably not going to be my favourite things.

I would have to tread most carefully with Jackie. I must show my authority and gain her confidence. In a sense she was in more desperate circumstances than any other child I had been requested to teach. I would surmount one hurdle at a time. Her obesity was her prime problem, and a diet was essential. I knew myself to be a specialist on the subject. Jackie's luck was about to change. We would diet together; compete; count calories for maths; write out menus for English, cookery and biology – whatever subject I cared to call it. She would lose weight like an avalanche. I would need her mother as an ally, lunatic or not, yet there was no way I could speak to her alone, since the child would not permit it.

'I wish I had a figure like your Caroline! I'm going on a diet, but it will be a lot easier and more fun if we all try together. Will you join in, Jackie?'

She didn't have a chance to answer. Her mother spoke up too quickly. 'No one is going to take my Jackie away from me! They wanted to take her into Great Ormond Street Hospital. They said they'd get her weight down, but I told my Jackie that I would poison myself if they took her away. And I will too! I'll kill myself! I can't live without my Jackie!'

How odd, I thought, that 'they' hadn't seen fit to take the mother away, somewhere safe and isolated, so that a halt could be called in the destruction of the daughter. I detested this woman so much that I wished she would drop dead at my feet. She reaped misery and horror with her bacon sandwiches, doll's clothes and man-mashing. She must be eliminated before Jackie could be saved. I longed to strike her.

'Don't talk like that!' I said crisply. 'You know quite well that what you say is dangerous nonsense. Your daughter will not go to hospital if both you and her father forbid it. However, I would appreciate it if you would co-operate with me. You've no option. I'm here to teach her how to lose weight, not for English or maths or geography or history. My subject is dieting. It is my profession and I intend to follow it and insist on doing so with integrity. Do you hear me, Mrs Homer?' I shrieked. 'Do you understand me?'

'No one speaks to me like that in my house,' snarled she.

'I do. Is that clear?' I walked towards her, and put my face two inches from hers. She sat down on the bed and Jackie cowered next to Caroline. 'Now where do you suggest we have our lessons? The kitchen seems to be the most suitable place, since there's a table for us to work at, and it's warm. I don't mind you being present for the time being, since Jackie isn't used to me yet, but I'm afraid I'll have to insist that you don't interrupt us. If this is not acceptable to you, then I have no alternative but to telephone the local authority.'

'I only want what's best for my Jackie,' whimpered the woman, vanquished by my gibberish.

'Good! That's exactly what I want too. Have you any bathroom scales? Jackie, go and fetch them.' The child howled like a trapped animal and actually wrung her hands in terror and grief which was ghastly to see.

'Don't cry,' I said softly, although my voice was completely drowned. 'I'll get them, then all of us can go into the kitchen. Caroline too. I'd love to see her dressed in her day clothes!'

I withdrew to the bathroom for a five-minute rest and checked my own weight privately. Ten stone exactly. Only twelve pounds overweight compared to Jackie's twelve stone. I was a sylph; a siren, and when I looked in the mirror I was immensely impressed by the way my features emerged so clearly and cleanly. I picked up the scales and returned cautiously to the kitchen. Jackie was there, wedged in her usual place behind the ironing board, Caroline was perched thereon and Mama was sorting through the clothes. Round One, and I had won. Now I must ingratiate myself with Mrs Homer and Caroline.

'Mrs Homer, I beg your pardon for speaking to you so rudely, but I felt quite upset by what you said, and I think Jackie did too. I know you want what's best for her,' I lied, 'just as I do, so please let's be friends and forget our misunderstandings. While I continue to come here, and all goes well, Jackie won't have to go away.' I smiled winningly at her and grasped her hand. She immediately burst into tears.

'My Jackie is my whole life,' she blubbed; 'she's all I live for!'

'I know, I know,' I clucked, 'that's why you want her to be well and happy, and Jackie knows it too, doesn't she, Caroline?' O, clever, intuitive me! The child turned away from the wall and picked up the doll and began changing her clothes.

I put the scales on the floor and ostentatiously stood on them. 'Good God! My diet starts tomorrow, first thing. Now you, Mrs Homer!' She giggled and heaved herself aboard.

I extracted a few small notebooks from my bag, made a space on the ironing board, and wrote my name on the cover, date and weight on the first page. '5 January, 18 stone, 7 pounds' in thick ink and handed the second book to Mum. She looked at what I had written and smiled happily.

'Goodness, Jack, your teacher does need to lose! She's a lot heavier than me or you!' She wrote, 'Mum, 14 stone 10 pounds.' 'Now it's my Jackie's turn!' She edged the scales under the ironing board; Jackie glanced shiftily at what we had written, while I pretended to be involved with the doll's clothes. Then she placed her two bulging little feet on the platform and stood there with her back to the dial. I had guessed accurately. 'Jack, she weighs more'n you!' yelled Mum, 'Look! Look!' The girl lumbered round painfully, but was unable to see, since her stomach blocked the way and she had no room to bend forward.

Eighteen stone exactly. Not bad for a girl who wasn't five feet tall. While I replaced the scales in the bathroom, Jackie wrote her name, date and weight down.

'Okay Caroline! You're the only one who doesn't have to start watching her figure, you lucky girl! We three are going to write down everything we eat and drink from breakfast tomorrow, and next time I come, I'll bring my calorie-counter books, and perhaps your clever sister, Jackie, will add up our mistakes for us, and we'll check our weight again next Thursday. One day, we'll be able to wear beautiful clothes like you.' The doll was dressed in the fur coat and hat. It sickened me to look at it. At least the dog-baby, to whom my mother babbled, was animate. 'You're all dressed up to go out!'

'No she ain't. That's what she wears when she looks out of the winder.' I was momentarily stunned with shock. Jackie had actually spoken to me. She shuffled along the wall and stood before the window, holding her doll, just as the marvellous winter sun shone through to us. I saw that the child was weeping. The silence and bitter sorrow of her tears were more disturbing than her screams. I could not witness or understand this anguish.

'She hates the sun. It makes her miserable because she can't go out in it. She's ever so cheerful when it's pouring down with rain. Come on, my Jack; I'm going to fry us up some potatoes. We'll put lots of butter and grated cheese over them. Miss will be off soon, then we'll pull the curtains and watch telly. All right?'

No. Not all right. There isn't a thing or a person or an idea in this house that's all right, you ruinous madwoman.

'You know, Miss, I didn't think you weighed that much more than me. Course, I could see you was fatter and heavier, but I reckoned on you being about sixteen or seventeen stone.' She wasn't being malicious; her confused mind produced a distorted mirror image through which she viewed the world, and Jackie was her product.

I would depart before I had to witness them gnawing at potatoes, squashed against each other on the black couch, the frightening Caroline dressed in her thirty-pound outfit, reclining on a mauve cushion, the three of them watching *Home This Afternoon* and *Jackanory* in their suffocating security, no chink of light allowed admittance.

I left them with their homework notebooks, and saluted the wretch at work on his ladder, as I fled down the purple passage and out into the exulting street. Its life and colour and beauty washed over me like a blessing; the energy of my youth was restored to me and I leapt and ran along the slushy pavement towards the bus stop, undeterred by my forthcoming visit to Muriel. If I was unable to succeed, then I would triumph in defeat.

So I went to Muriel's house, optimistic and full of hope. I reached the front steps, and behold, I looked at the place where the dustbins belonged, and I saw that they were half-drowned in a sea of rubbish. 'Hath not the potter power over the clay, of the same lump to make one vessel unto honour, and another unto dishonour?' I waded through the rubbish and lifted the dustbin lid. I looked at its shining, spotless interior, and saw my face reflected there. I recalled the labours of the Filthy Squad. I did not have their stamina.

Muriel, I no longer have a rendezvous with thee. Susan, I will read about you in the papers one day, but I will take no further part in your life; for I have glimpsed my face in a dustbin while my ankles are lodged in muck. Mother Dear, you are right. This work is not for me. My destiny lies elsewhere. Sanderson cannot threaten or bribe me into playing it false. I'll complete and sell my novel and pay back Auntie Sarah. Perhaps I will have to start afresh; an entirely new theme that has nothing to do with teaching. I went home.

I took only one coin to the house phone box. I would not waste time arguing. She could call me back when she'd found a clever, clean, pleasant girl or boy with a broken leg. I was gripped by a strange power – a kind of enlightenment; and as I stood there, glorying in it, the phone rang, and I lifted the receiver, unencumbered by guilt or worry.

'What a coincidence!' I cried, on hearing Miss Sanderson's voice. 'I was just about to ring you. Thanks for saving me the trouble. Are you, by any chance, checking up on me to see whether I'm slouching around instead of busying myself at Muriel's? Ten out of ten, Miss Marple.'

'Listen,' she said, 'I want to ask you a big favour. Cancel any appointments you've made for tomorrow. I'm sorry to mess you around like this. Shut up. Don't interrupt; I'm in the middle of a meeting. Come here tomorrow at ten, and then we'll discuss what I have in mind. Yes, I'll pay all your expenses without questioning your honesty. We'll also pay for your time. What? No, I haven't got any broken legs for you; they go to teachers with less experience to offer. See you in the morning and try to be on time for a change. You'll be able to cover fifty pages with this one. Bye!'

It was no use wondering what that woman was cooking up for me. Whatever it was, it was sure to be cunning, devious and laced with flattery to which I must not succumb. I must be resolute and refuse all work which was demanding or demoralising. Teaching Jackie Homer three times a week was quite enough to keep me in migraines. No more Muriel and no more Susan. That was that. I must imagine that she was a spider trying to enmesh me.

The next morning I arrived at the door of her web. I was shown into a private office; one which I had never seen before; carpeted, with armchairs and curtains. Miss Sanderson didn't sit at the desk, but placed herself in an armchair next to me. Someone brought coffee in on a tray and I was handed an ashtray and cigarettes. This was cosy. I must exercise extreme caution.

'I don't have to tell you what we think of you here,' she began.

'You're not the run of the mill; that's why you've been asked to teach very difficult children lately. It would be irresponsible of me to place a Susan with a dewy-eyed idealist straight out of college, or to expect a teacher nearing retirement age to cope. I promise, though, that if you want it, in a few months' time, I'll get you a job teaching O levels to industrious middle-class kids. It'll be a doddle.'

'I want it now. Compliments don't mean anything to me any more. I've caught on to your methods. Whenever you say anything nice to me, you've always got a piece of rusty barbed wire behind your back. I'm through with Muriel and Susan for good.'

'Agreed. The job I have in mind for you is in a local hospital on a permanent basis, with paid holidays. But it doesn't fall vacant until April.'

'What am I supposed to do until then? Sit here and drink coffee while you pay me for my time? Even you can't wangle that!'

'I've brought you here to meet Celia,' she said. 'She'll be arriving in a few minutes with her social worker.'

'And what's up with Celia. Is she on a murder rap? How many people has she maimed or killed? Do I have to wear protective clothing and carry arms? Or is it that she's got an I Q of twenty-five?'

'If you'll allow me a word in edgeways, I'd like to tell you about Celia before you meet her.'

'Good. I'm listening. Try not to miss anything out – the way you did with Jackie Homer. You forgot to mention that she had a slight weight problem and insane parents.'

'You never listen; that's your trouble. Could we drop her for the time being? We're discussing Celia, now, please. It won't take long. She's been totally deaf from birth and is registered blind. She's got pinpoint vision, but it's deteriorating rapidly, and she'll soon lose her sight completely. She tried to express what she was feeling by wringing her own neck, but apparently you can't put an end to yourself that way. She's twenty-five and has been living in a home for elderly people for the last three years. The residents can't speak to her and the experts have given up, so it was decided to get her together with a non-expert. You. Take your fingers out of your ears and open your eyes. And bloody well stay where you are and stop behaving like an ill-mannered child. They're here.'

My knees were shaking and my mouth was dry with fear. I walked towards the door, but she was blocking my way, talking to someone in the doorway.

'This is Celia,' she said, drawing a young woman into the room, and putting her hand in mine. 'Introduce yourself while I show Penny the toilet. She's in a big hurry. We'll be back soon.'

Now I knew the meaning of desertion and the panic of absolute helplessness. This irresponsible and cruel action was unforgivable. I could disengage my hand quite easily and leave the room – it was as simple as walking out of Alcatraz.

'Hello, Celia,' I said. 'I'm so happy to meet you. Come and sit down next to me.' I knew that she couldn't hear or see me speaking, yet the sound of my voice helped me to be calm. I felt her hand shaking, and squeezed it. There was no response and her beautiful, green, dead eyes looked past me. I placed her hand on my chest and wrote my name on her back as if it was a self-erasing blackboard. She started at my touch, then looked puzzled. I 'wiped' the 'board' clean with the palm of my hand and wrote my name again. Perhaps no one else had ever used that space before, but after a few seconds, she laughed and nodded, and felt for my back and wrote 'CELIA' on it. I placed her hands on my head and nodded, and then shook hands with her, drew her to me, and hugged her. 'TEACH ME DEAF LETTERS' I wrote.

Where we stood, she began a ballet dance with her fingers, using her right hand as the active partner, and the left as the recipient. I understood not one single gesture. 'SLOW . . . A . . . B . . . C' I wrote, and put her hand on the armchair. We sat down next to each other, and she began again, slowly, patiently, to teach me the deaf-blind manual. I don't know how long it took, for the time seemed to be of no consequence. Nothing mattered to me but learning the signs. I wrote 'A' on her back, and with her right forefinger she touched the ball of her left thumb, and I copied her, using my right finger on her left hand, which now became the blackboard. 'B': she bunched her right fingers and thumb and placed the tips in the middle of her left palm. After five letters, I stopped her, and she held out her left palm for me to revise. She raised her thumb and smiled as if to say, 'Well done! All correct!' and then taught me F, G, H, I, J, and stopped on her own initiative to enable me to practise them. Thus she engineered me through twenty-six letters, and when I forgot one of the signs, I tapped her knee and she replayed it for me. Stumbling, awkward and clumsy, I went through the alphabet twice, without an error, and was rewarded by the 'thumbs up' sign.

'You are a good teacher,' I said on her fingers. 'Thank you.' A two-second, mundane remark that gave me a two-minute brain fever.

While I was laboriously making my point, she was making strange squeaking noises, and I realised with a sense of shock, that they were not issuing from her throat, but that Celia was grinding her teeth. In that moment I caught a glimpse and heard an echo of her dark and silent world. It was intolerable.

'God!' I screamed crazily; 'Why?' But no one answered. I felt her hands on my hair and face and throat, discovering my tears and my shaking grief. Her face showed a mixture of wonder and distress. Where was my self-control? This was awful.

I took her hand and pressed her finger against my forehead, in the manner of a child denoting madness. Celia rallied, understanding the gesture, and mimed her agreement quite delightfully, by pointing her finger to her head, and then to me. There was no self-pity here.

Miss Sanderson's voice in the doorway made me jump out of my skin. 'How are you getting on?'

'How the hell do I know! Where have you been?'

'We've been watching you through the one-way mirror; prying on you to see how you cope. This is Penny, Celia's social worker. She thinks you'll do. You'll have to read through this big fat file before our next discussion, when we'll try to answer some of your questions.'

I shook hands with Penny. She was young and pleasant and untidy, and I liked her right away. Yet she had been corrupted into spying on me. I asked her why she'd exposed me to such treatment.

'I'm sorry. It's the first time I've ever done such a thing. Miss Sanderson convinced me that it was the only way to get you involved and prevent any more time-wasting for Celia. We did it for her benefit.'

More coffee was brought in, and the four of us took refreshment, Penny attending and talking to Celia.

'I haven't the faintest idea what you want of me. I've no experience. What do you mean about thinking I'll do? Do what? I've never mixed with anyone with Celia's handicaps before. I'd need to attend special classes for ten years.'

'That's all we want – for you to mix with her. To have no experience and no goals. Just to be her friend. You don't need to be a specialist for that.'

'You're wrong, Penny. I've no opinions, no ideas. I don't know how to communicate with Celia – not on the crudest level. It takes me an hour to say a simple sentence, let alone understand what she's trying to say. My name isn't Annie Sullivan!'

'And hers isn't Helen Keller. She's twenty-five years old. You've got to read her file before you decide against seeing her again. I'm asking you not to dismiss her or commit yourself until you've done that. Please!'

'What does Celia say to all this?' She was sitting next to Penny, drinking her coffee and moving her head around and contorting her features, as if she was in the stocks and was trying to avoid the missiles being hurled at her. Penny took Celia's hand and spoke to her with enviable fluency. I watched, but could not follow. 'What are you saying?'

Celia nodded several times and smiled radiantly in answer to Penny's secret message. 'I asked her if she liked you. She hasn't liked anyone for a long time.'

So I said goodbye to her and went home with the folder under my arm. The dreary landmarks of her life lay within its covers and the mystery of her mind and soul latched on to mine. I knew that she was there for ever; that I would never be rid of her. There was no going back to what I was yesterday. When I arrived home, I put my typewriter and unfinished novel on the floor, put the file on my table, opened it, and began to read.

Chapter Twelve

That night I learned about Celia's life. I became obsessed with her; nothing and no one intruded. When I tried to rest my eyes, my inward ones took over, and pictures of her as a child, as a young girl, as she was now, streamed past them, like a noisy, unstoppable train. I came across a leaflet depicting the manual which she had taught me. I revised it, practising sentences on my own hand to try to speed up my conversation. The energy I expended, and my desire to succeed, exacerbated my frustration and gave me an insight into hers. I'd read of case histories, involving intelligent, enquiring human beings, forced into this mode of conversation. But Celia was in a far worse predicament than anyone I read about.

Her deafness was acknowledged by her distraught parents when she was two. She attended a day school for the deaf, but she seemed backward or lazy and unable to learn language or make friends. She lacked concentration. A school photograph, taken when she was eight, revealed her staring stonily into space, while her classmates looked about them in a lively way. Yes. There was something wrong with her. She had no peripheral vision. So she went through her school days, friendless and withdrawn, unable to do her homework, harrassed by her rapidly deteriorating vision, and in despair because she could not tell. Alternately mocked and ignored by the rest of her class, and because she was not troublesome, her impaired eyesight went unremarked.

At ten, she had the vocabulary of a three-year-old; her written work was muddled nonsense, and unable to understand or communicate, she became depressed and closed. Yet her embroidery, knitting and pottery were exquisite. She never questioned anything and did not attempt to make herself heard or seen.

At sixteen, when she left school, she didn't have a friend in the world. Deaf acquaintances had no patience to talk to her, because she would not or could not understand or answer intelligibly. The tunnel of her vision narrowed and clogged, and within that limited field, vast pieces of the jigsaw of sight were missing. She walked in an ungainly way, gesturing oddly, contorting her face. At seventeen she went to live in a hostel and worked in a factory making boxes; but her blind workmates teased her and used her for their scapegoat. She rebelled by attacking herself with scissors, scoring her arms and cutting off her hair.

She was moved from one hostel to another, given pills to allay her depression and other pills to make her sleep. Speech therapists, psychologists and social workers did their best, but to no avail. She did not learn Braille, for her meagre understanding of language rendered reading useless anyway. She went on holidays with groups of young deaf-blind people, but they had either been born with both handicaps, and had been taught in a specialised way to meet their needs; or had more sight and some hearing. Celia remained on the outside of the group, even though each holiday-maker had his or her own specialised mediator.

At home, her anguished parents were driven mad with grief, worry and irritation by her now evident, compulsive and neurotic behaviour. Their love for her dried up and they were unable to cope. She became a resident at a home for elderly people, but she caused distress because of the noises she made, and her inability to hear them approaching caused minor accidents, fear and hostility. The occupational therapist was amazed at her ability to learn crafts so quickly, but none of the residents had the desire to learn how to communicate with her.

She spent long evenings in her room, switching the light on and off, and during the day she would stand on the pavement gazing at the sun. On dull, cold days, she wandered around Woolworth's, smelling the soaps and perfumes, removing the lids from cold-cream jars and sniffing the contents, and was banned from the store. She had been taking bottles of nail varnish and cheap jewellery, which she never used or wore; rent-books, notebooks and chocolate bars. Her chest of drawers was crammed with these articles. She was considered cunning and selfish. Meetings were called on what to do about Celia.

Penny, the new social worker for the deaf, was compassionate and optimistic. People stole and hoarded when they were depressed and bored, she wrote. Perhaps Celia was frantically trying to draw attention to her plight. No one really knew her potential. She needed a companion-cum-teacher, who could, perhaps, cultivate some of her talents, stimulate her and guide her energies so that her life would become more fulfilled. Various authorities were approached, but only pupils under the age of sixteen could be allocated a teacher, and anyway, teachers of the deaf and blind were few and far between and were employed at special schools. Charitable societies became involved and a generous donor was found.

Penny wrote to Miss Sanderson asking if she knew of a suitable teacher. A copy of this letter was in the file, and so was the reply. It mentioned a teacher whom she knew well, but who, as far as she knew, had had no previous experience teaching adults with severe handicaps. She was aggressive, energetic and extrovert and followed no orthodox rules and was expert in nothing – except getting a response from her pupils. And if anyone was capable of extracting one from Celia, she was. She was at present engaged in teaching rather difficult pupils, but the Authority would be willing to forego her services temporarily in order that she could devote herself to Celia's pressing needs. I was that person.

Humility, a stranger to me, touched me now, more intoxicating than pride. Yet my commitment was sober and total. I would try to win Celia's trust and friendship, as I had never tried anything before. I would seek out ways of extending her vocabulary and expanding her view of the world, and pursue nothing else. In the folder was a book entitled *A Conference of Hope – Proceedings of the First Historic Helen Keller World Conference on Services to Deaf-Blind Youths and Adults.* The theme was the Deaf-Blind Person in the Community. I read it from cover to cover, adjusting all I learnt to Celia's case. But she wasn't a 'case' any more.

I must have fallen asleep with my head on the table. I woke, stiff and cold, to the clamour of the telephone. 'It's Miss Sanderson,' said a strangely gentle voice. 'Are you still on speaking terms with me?'

'Why? Shouldn't I be? I love you madly. Fancy *you* recommending *me* for Celia. I can't wait to see her again. Did you know that vibrations come out of the top of your head when you speak? I discovered that, entirely by accident, last night. When can I start? Are you still there?'

'Yes; and reeling over the shock. I thought you'd be furious with me – justifiably so – for commandeering you like that, and that I'd have to spend tedious hours flattering you and persuading you. Will you be able to read and digest the file by the end of the week? We need to know what you think as soon as possible.'

'I've read it – every word, and I've got a bad case of indigestion from all the horror stories.'

'You've done well, tackling it so quickly. I thought you were a slow learner.'

'I didn't stay up all night reading comics. Am I, or am I not, engaged to work with Celia? If I am, who's going to bring

Weight Watchers to Jackie Homer? Check up that Muriel and her baby are still alive; and delay Susan's plans for mass murder?'

'That's my problem from now on. No one's indispensable, so stop fishing and fretting. Celia can't stay in Dulwich with her parents just now – she's too depressed and difficult. She went back to the home today. Would you go and live with her there for a week? We'd arrange everything. There's plenty of space.'

'And after that?'

'Who knows? We've got to see how you get on. We can't jump over every hurdle at once.'

'I'll go,' I said.

'Good, but we don't want any slacking while you're there. Celia can't blow the whistle on you, so I'll want a full report of your activities and progress. When would you like to start?'

'Now, of course! Why waste time – especially talking to you on the telephone!'

'The day after tomorrow then. Catch the ten thirty-eight from London Bridge. We'll leave a travel voucher at the ticket office for you. The superintendent will settle your daily expenses, but don't get too creative about them. We'll pay you when you return. Then we'll talk about the future. But not now. Don't be overambitious; you'll only feel disappointed and let down. Enthusiasm's the thing, and you've always had plenty of that. Celia's going to have so much fun this coming week. Remember to write a daily report. Enjoy yourselves! Good luck!'

I needed an empty suitcase. It lay on the floor, ready for a week's clothes, paraphernalia and pills. A few days ago it had been crammed with papers to do with my novel. Only as I began packing did it dawn on me that Mr Rosenfeld was playing at the Pavilion Concert Hall, probably no more than five miles along the coast from where I would be staying. I glanced at my typewriter and discarded notebooks, picked one up and wrote

'CELIA' on the front cover. I'd have so much to write about. I'd keep my bond and justify his faith in me, both as a writer and as a teacher. I threw the exercise book into the suitcase and began to practise the manual.

'How long does it take for me to ask this question?' Three seconds – talking rather ponderously to myself; twenty-five seconds in manual on my hand, and fifty seconds in block letters on my palm. So the manual it must be, although at least eight times slower than normal conversation! I would shorten that difference in time, but Celia would have to bear with me. I would learn how to take short cuts; read her facial expressions and try to understand her movements. I practised for hours, sitting alone in my room, giving myself slow dictation, using simple vocabulary. Ultimately, I would need Celia with me in order to diagnose my progress. She must be my guide and teacher, and help me to assess my limitations. I felt that I was about to embark on a strange, exciting but lonely journey, and of all the pupils I had ever taught, she was going to be my greatest challenge and my most solemn commitment. The next morning I boarded the train at London Bridge, in a lather of trepidation, as if I were on my way to a new planet.

I wished that there would be someone to meet me; to breathe a little life into my fading confidence, but the taxi driver was friendly and told me that my destination was a mere two-minute walk to the sea. The weather was beautiful; cold and fresh and gloriously sunny. The superintendent had been told to expect me for lunch. We turned down a wide road, dappled with well-kept guest houses; took a turning off a lively shopping area, and came to a halt outside a huge house. The legend on the gate and the rails leading up to the front door told me that I had arrived – and the taxi driver added a word, too. I paid him, said goodbye and stood for a few minutes on the grass verge, like a refugee. Then I closed my eyes and felt my way, with the help of the rail, to the front door. Somewhere inside this house, Celia was waiting for me.

Report for the attention of Miss F. Sanderson

I arrived at lunch-time and was shown into the dining room. Celia was sitting at a table with two elderly people, and I was aware, without being fanciful, that everyone, bar her, was conscious of the presence of a stranger. There she sat, on her Desert Island, without her choice of discs; without the ability to answer the question 'How would you cope with loneliness?' How would she know, having never experienced anything else? I watched a helper place the soup in front of her and tap her on the shoulder. She felt around for the spoon, but my hand was there first, spelling out my name. She laughed aloud, then drew me down on to the chair next to her. No orator could have welcomed me more eloquently.

We talked all through lunch, and I had no problem in communicating with her. By this I mean that she generously accepted me as her friend. I wrote on her back when her hands were occupied with eating. I am left-handed in everything but the manual, where I have, of necessity, had to use my right hand. This has given me certain advantages, but I am painfully slow at 'talking' and intolerably so, at 'listening'. The grinding, nerve-racking patience which she has to maintain is not to be contemplated. Her companions at the table make no attempt to speak to Celia, but are not actively hostile, as I gather most of the other residents to be.

After lunch, she showed me to my room and then took me to hers, then gave me a guided tour of the house. She returned with me to my room and helped me to unpack, feeling the texture of all my rags and showing blatant disapproval when she discovered a loose thread or a missing hook and eye.

I asked her to come for a walk with me on the cliffs; she nodded happily, raised five fingers to denote that she would be back in five minutes, and returned at the appropriate time, bundled up like an old woman. She walks with a clumsy, jerking gait, swaying from side to side, as if feeling for obstructions with her feet and body, even though the guide rails and her familiarity with the house show this to be unnecessary. She is extremely tense, and although I reassured her that I would not let her fall down, she was fearful when we walked on the bumpy grass. I explained that if she fell down, it wasn't such a terrible thing, but that if she stood upright and kept in step with me, she would be quite safe. Each time I speak to her, we have to slow down to a snail's pace because I can't walk AND speak the manual simultaneously. Also, I can't talk with gloves on. Celia wears tight-fitting leather gloves, and that's okay, but my thick woolly ones are equivalent to talking with a set of loose false teeth in your mouth – plus a trapful of peanuts and chewing-gum. So my hands are perpetually frozen.

We tottered down the cliff walk to the promenade which was practically deserted. 'Run!' I said, and holding her hand, started off at a gentle trot. It was like forcing an elderly cripple into a marathon. She seems unsteady, weak and nervous, and has forgotten how to use her legs actively. 'You are safe with me. We will run thirty steps and walk thirty steps. There is nothing in the way. You will not fall.' (Do not allow yourself to forget, dear Miss S., that these few comforting words take a few freezing minutes to declare.)

When we sat down to rest, we were both hot and breathless. The sun was setting and the sky was aglow. She can't see it, or hear the pounding of the sea. I turned her face westwards and pointed her hand in that direction. 'Can you see the sun?' I asked. She nodded, but thinking that she might merely be trying to please me, I asked her what colour it was. 'Blue.' She was.

After supper we went to a large, well-lit pub overlooking the sea. A small band entertained and I placed her hand on the piano. She appeared to enjoy the vibrations, and could actually 'feel' the low notes when she was not touching the instrument. A group of young people joined us, and we made a circle and danced. I played the steps on Celia's back, using my forefinger as feet. She understood, and learned the movements quite quickly, although she has no sense of rhythm. Everyone was delighted with her and showed great kindness and friendliness. Her unselfconscious joy infected us all. It was one of the happiest evenings of my life.

Later, back in Celia's room, I found a small plastic 'venetian blind'. You place this over a paper, and it's possible for a blind person to write quite easily, by using the slats as lines. I tried it out with closed eyes, and the results were legible. Celia had never used it, but I showed her how and told her to write down what she did every day, and kissed her goodnight. It was well after one a.m. when I left her. Now, three hours later, I find it impossible to sleep. I'm so wide awake and excited. I've just realised something! She hasn't asked me a single question or made one spontaneous remark. Why?

Friday

She was waiting in the entrance hall when I came down, a few minutes before breakfast. I say 'waiting' because there was a look of expectation about her. She was sitting on the arm of a chair, twitching and blinking, aware, I think, of the residents and staff. The floor shakes slightly when you walk along and the carpet muffles the sound, but not the vibrations. Most of the old people use sticks and walk quite heavily. I said 'good morning' to several people, and introduced myself as Celia's friend. As they waited around for the breakfast bell, chatting to one another, I saw how completely solitary Celia appeared. No one turned her way or greeted her.

As I took her hand, she started, and her expression transformed to one of pure happiness. I wondered if she'd mistaken me for someone else, but no! That delight was on my account! I wonder why we, who can see and hear, hide our feelings from our friends, when it is so easy to reveal affection, and light the day for each other. We walked into breakfast together, at the tail end of a snail-like queue.

Edie, one of the helpers, came round to our table and said to me, 'She was waiting for you from half past six, getting in the way.'

'How was she getting in the way?'

'We have to vacuum, you know!'

'How was she getting in the way?' A sort of pleasurable silence invaded the dining room, as if the diversion of an approaching argument would be enjoyed by all.

'It's a nuisance when people are hanging around. We've got our work to do here. It's bad enough having to move chairs, and we can do without people sitting about downstairs at that time of the morning.'

'Are there lots of people hanging around at six-thirty?'

'Just her. She usually stays in her room until breakfast time, but now you've come, she's got it into her head that things are different. Tell her not to wait for you downstairs in future.'

'I will do nothing of the kind,' I said. 'If you have something to say to Celia, say it yourself.'

Edie took Celia's hand, and wrote something in capital letters on her palm. The tray of coffees that she had planted on the side table must have been quite cold by this time. Then she tossed the hand away. This woman is asking for trouble from me and I hope she gets it before the week is out.

Celia directed her face at the hateful Edie and looked at her as one would if, while eating a plate of spaghetti, it was discovered to be a plate of worms – and made the appropriate noise – a sort of wail of disgust. I wonder why we, who can see and hear, hide our feelings from our enemies!

'Edie is nasty,' I said mischievously to Celia, and received a marvellous 'hate mime' from her, which was so funny, that I collapsed into hysterical laughter. As I write this down, and recall her response, I cannot keep my face straight. Our table companions also started laughing. Perhaps Celia felt our gaiety, for she gave us an encore as Edie pushed open the swing door of the adjoining kitchen, and disappeared, in order, as I found out later, to curse and complain and to make more coffee for the impatient residents. She didn't approach our table again, but other waitresses did, smiling with malicious glee. I gather that they don't like Edie much, either, but are a bit afraid of her. I have told Celia to come down again at six thirty tomorrow. I'll be there, too.

I also told her that we were going to take a boat ride on the river. There are maps and lists of events pinned up on the notice board and there is no shortage of things to do. I said I would come to her room in ten minutes.

She was seated at her table near the window, writing in her exercise book. I switched the light on and off to signal my presence, and she immediately turned, and handed the book to me. This is what she had written.

'Leah came lunch-time. It was soup, meat, potatoes, peas, stewed apple, tea. Leah clothes suitcase, I helped clothes cupboard. We went for a walk on high-up rough. Cold lovely sunny. We went down to smooth. We walked ran very hot. After supper fish, chips, bread, butter, ice cream, jelly, tea. We went the pub. Lovely nice. Piano lovely music. I had a Coke, Leah cider. We dance friends in ring. Leah lost dark very late to house 11.48. Leah kiss hug love me.'

I gave her another kiss hug love and told her that her diary was very interesting and that she must write in it every day. Who said that Celia couldn't blow the whistle on me? We walked to the jetty which is about two miles away. During the season, tea is served in the Riverside Gardens, but today it looked rather a forlorn area. A friendly boatman was there, however, and I persuaded him to hire us a small motor boat.

We shoved Celia into the driving seat and I explained which pedal was for 'go' and which was for 'stop'. This took up a tenth of our boat-trip time, not because Celia is stupid, but because I am so maddeningly slow. Her breathing was light and uneven, her face twitched continually and her body was rigid. I asked her if she was frightened, but she shook her head. I think she was just excited by the vibration of the engine. I helped her to manoeuvre the boat into the open river, and directed her, only by tapping her right or left shoulder when it was appropriate to change course; and the right or left knee when a speed change was required. My hand in the middle of her back meant full steam ahead.

The river and sky were bleak, grey and beautiful, and the fields and trees looked sad and desolate; but I basked in the marvellous sun of her joy and achievement; a pleasure the like of which I have never before experienced, and I cannot adequately describe it. Her responses to my instructions were immediate, her body relaxed and her face became smiling and tranquil. Her trust has to be absolute, and she gives it because she must, and I find this terribly moving. I want her to feel equality in this relationship, despite her physical dependence. And, indeed, equality she felt, because while I was watching her face, I failed to notice the approaching bank. She drove into it, full tilt. She was only momentarily shocked, treated the incident as entirely her responsibility, laughed and set the boat to rights while I struggled to retain my composure and dignity. One doesn't have to be too protective with old Celia! She's used to knocks and shocks and bumps!

Once safely on dry land, I told her the name of the boat, and then asked her what she would like to do next. She looked worried and puzzled and couldn't tell me, perhaps because she has little experience of pleasant and interesting diversions. We walked along the towpath, following a sign to some riding stables.

'Do you like horses?' Yes. 'Do you want to ride a horse?' Yes. We approached the stable, I spoke to the girls there, and they brought out two enormous creatures for us to mount, and two riding hats for us to don. What is that strange noise? It is Celia!

She is caressing her horse's nose; fearlessly sticking her fingers into his mouth; talking; chattering; laughing; fondling his ears; standing on tiptoe and drawing his head down, so that she can make herself heard and understood. She reached out for me. What is his name? 'Snowball.'

'Snowball!' she exclaimed, as clearly as you or me. 'Hello, Snowball!' Why should an animal manage to elicit such a monologue from her, when I only receive hard-earned monosyllables? Is it because he is dumb, uncritical and doesn't insist on being understood? Or is it because he doesn't make her talk on her fingers, and that whatever she says will be acknowledged without effort? Do you want to know what it feels like to be jealous of a horse? Ask me about it when I come home.

The girls helped us to mount. I rode behind her, watching her straight back and the way she constantly patted Snowball's neck and spoke to him. Lucky, privileged Snowball! How confident and happy she was!

At lunch-time, the superintendent came over to our table and Celia, recognising his hand, told him all about the morning's adventures; about the boat and the crash; about the splendour of Snowball and the way she rode him and what kind of hat she wore. The conversation was conducted entirely in mime. I didn't know, until then, how exciting and rewarding her experiences had been.

This afternoon, I sneaked out to Woolworth's and spoke to the supervisor. She was co-operative and friendly, and explained why she felt it necessary to ban Celia from the store. Apparently, she has been in the habit of spending hours there, but not much money.

The superintendent showed Celia's haul to me. It is kept in a large suitcase which is hidden in a locked cupboard. The contents have to be seen to be believed. Piles of useless rent-books; notebooks of all sizes and colours; hardbacked files;

dozens of bottles of nail varnish and other cosmetics; pencils; pens; shower caps; soap; soapflakes; little bags; thirty bars of chocolate; kids' drawing books! I asked him, somewhat sternly, why these items hadn't been returned to the store; he replied that he didn't want Woolworth's to realise how much stuff Celia had pinched, otherwise they might take her to court. I like him. I persuaded him not to keep the things hanging about in the cupboard; rather that they should be put to some use.

'I can't let Celia have them back. She might be encouraged to believe it's all right to take things without paying.'

'Quite! I agree with you. I could do with a file, a few notebooks and a dozen pens. No doubt the residents would appreciate the chocolate and soap and the dinky nailbrushes and face flannels for prizes, when they play bingo.' He conceded the point, and we sorted out the swag into anonymous brown paper bags, then, as I told you, I laid my plans with the store supervisor.

I told Celia we were going shopping. She came very willingly, but as soon as we approached Woolworth's she froze like a frightened cat, knowing where we were. I assured her as clearly as possible, that it was okay. She was with me. No one would be cross. We sauntered round the store and then made our way to the vanishing cream. I unscrewed a jar, and got Celia to feel and smell what I was doing.

'MADAM! PUT THAT DOWN AT ONCE!' yelled the supervisor, as planned. All the shoppers wheeled round to stare at me, accusing, hostile. All, that is, except Celia, who, of course, had not heard or seen. I persuaded the supervisor to take hold of my arm and shake it.

Celia felt that, and gave the poor woman a good push. A crowd gathered. I explained to Celia that I was in trouble because I had messed around with the cream, and was taking it out without paying, but I had said I was sorry and wouldn't do it again. The supervisor had been cross and angry, but now we were friends.

None of the shoppers understood what I was saying to Celia, and they all thought I was a thief. It was a most harrowing experience. I now feel like a marked woman, and will never venture into the High Street again. I learned my lesson, but I'm not sure about Celia. I have plans for her to toddle round Patton's and Manley's for a few worthwhile goodies – one or two nice little portable tellies, perhaps; or a massive plunder of cashmere sweaters. Take that look off your face. I'm only kidding!

We took a bus ride into the centre and looked at the gardens and the concert hall. Then we went round Patton's and felt every article on every counter, including the TVs and fancy sweaters. As far as I know, we came out empty-handed. Excerpt from Ceila's diary:

'The morning 6.35 Edie cross shout me. Breakfast cornflake, milk, eggs, bread, butter, coffee. Leah cross shout Edie. Long walk river boats. I drive. Leah and man show drive me boat. Lovely nice. I saw white ducks on the water. Smooth, not rough. My boat is called *Sandpiper*. Bump thing water. Leah gave jumper me. I wear jumper Leah. Funny. We ride horses. My horse Snowball. Lovely laugh Snowball. I wear hat like hard egg. After dinner we Woolworth's. Leah take thing from Woolworth. People cross shout bad thing. We ride on bus 38 no roof. Big shop. I like the shopping. People not cross shout. We go in place gardens. Concert hall. Look for friend play violin not there. Lady in place give letter to friend violin in night. After supper pancakes, fruit, Leah show me words bump bed. Happy, pretty, passenger, frightened, naughty, nasty, friendly, kind, jealous. I learn all new words. I sit on the bed, she bump the bed. I see the words in the neck.'

I have been trying to teach Celia words that have come up in my conversation with her, but I am still not sure how much she understands. I got her to sit down on her bed, place her hand on my throat and write the word on her free hand, then bang out the rhythm of it on the bed and speak the word, which she tries to emulate. Her speech, however, is incomprehensible, and I believe that this exercise might prove futile. The effort she puts into speaking is beyond description. If we, in possession of all our senses, had her energy and commitment, what wonders we'd perform! I'd be teaching royalty and you'd be the Chief Education Officer! Perhaps the fact that we have sight and hearing diverts our attention into paths that Celia has no knowledge of. I long for her to succeed.

I am not attempting to correct her English. I feel that I would merely muddle and confuse her. At this point I just want to try to add to her vocabulary, giving her words that may be of use to her and finding out ways which will encourage her to ask questions. She's asked only one – the name of the horse. I'm sure you've noticed that she tends to list, in detail, food she eats and the precise time of events, whereas 'lovely nice' has to do to describe a very happy experience. The white ducks on the water reside in her imagination. There were none. No! Wait! The river was rough and foam-flecked. Were those white crests her ducks?

This morning, Celia and I came down very early in order to aggravate Edie. We made some coffee and sat at a small table in the corner of the lounge. Physically, we were not in her way at all, but her dislike of Celia is obvious and ill-hidden and she refused the cup of coffee that I offered her.

'You think the sun shines out of her! Just you wait till you get to know her! She makes faces at people; she switches the lights on and off and wastes electricity; she knocks into the old people. She's got no manners; she's like an animal, growling and making noises! She makes me sick! People like her should be put to sleep. She's no use to anybody!'

I swore at her and threw my coffee into her face and pushed her out of the room. She went to find the superintendent who was not yet on duty, leaving the vacuum cleaner in the middle of the lounge. I told Celia that Edie and I had had a fight, that she had run out to find Mr Maxwell, and that I was going to finish the cleaning. Five minutes later, the job was finished and Celia showed me where to put the vacuum cleaner.

'Get your coat, quick! We are going out!' She responded immediately, her face and movements showing tremendous animation. We sat in a shelter on the seafront. She thrust her hands in front of me, talking far too quickly for me to understand. I ignored her. She tried again, slowly, pausing between each word, awaiting a signal from me that I understood.

'You shout Edie. She shout you.' I refused to answer. She has got to ask a question. How the hell can I get her to do it? Only by withholding information she is burning for!

'Do you want to know what I did to Edie?' I wrote this sentence on her fingers, then very deliberately, I drew a question mark on the palm of her hand.

'You shout Edie,' she said.

I took her finger, and using it as a pen, drew a question mark on my hand. 'Ask me what I did to Edie. Ask! Ask! Ask!'

'You hit Edie. Ask?'

'Yes, I hit Edie. I pulled her hair,' I lied. 'I threw coffee at Edie.' No more information. Not unless she asks! I can actually see the news being digested; the shock; the delight; the excitement! Please, Celia, be curious! Ask some more! I will you to ask for further details, but not a word will you get out of me until you do! I waited. I watched the morning light strengthen and take over from the cold darkness. Her right hand hovered over her left, fidgeting, the tips quivering to express the need for involvement in the antics which had been denied her.

'Coffee hot Edie's dress ask?' She stretched her fingers out for an answer. I wanted to jump in the air for joy.

'Coffee not hot. Warm. I threw it in Edie's face. Edie shouted and screamed and ran out of the lounge. Edie is nasty. She says nasty things to me.'

Her face was agog with pleasure. 'Edie say thing ask?'

'What did Edie say?' I corrected, then pushed her right hand on to her left. She looked confused and lost. I hardened my heart and jabbed at her hand again. I repeated the words and actions four times, without result. Then I flattened her left hand, held the forefinger of the right and guided her into asking the question, 'What did Edie say?' She then asked the question herself, without any fuss or mistakes. Why hadn't I done this in the beginning? My stupidity and lack of imagination are without parallel.

'Edie said, "You are in the way. I want to clean carpet. You and Celia give me trouble. Make me cross. You are bad nasty people and I don't like you." Then Edie pushed me, so I threw the coffee at her. She went to tell Mr Maxwell.'

She was delighted with this piece of news. 'Max will cross shout you.' I think I have taught Celia how to gossip! Good old Edie!

She felt for the time on her watch. I knew and she knew that we should already be sitting down to breakfast, but I refused to take the initiative. I sat waiting. The staff would be put out if we were late, but I might as well hang for a sheep as a lamb. She began to twitch and grind her teeth. Why doesn't she say, 'It's time for breakfast?' Why is she so patient; so timid? Who would crack first? Ten minutes passed. We must have missed the cornflakes by now. Her anxiety was awful. I succumbed.

She jumped up at once when she felt me move. Perhaps she'd been thinking that I was afraid to return to the house. On the way home, I managed successfully to convince myself that any trouble I caused was entirely for Celia's sake, and it was all worth it. We walked into the dining room, cool as cucumbers. The atmosphere was electric. Edie was nowhere to be seen.

'Edie's up with Mr Maxwell,' I was told. 'She's very upset!'

'I should hope so! So she should be! It isn't everybody who is disgusting enough to have coffee chucked over them.'

We were served a hearty breakfast, cornflakes included. Celia folded her napkin and sat, waiting for me. Then to my delight, she nudged me and said, 'Where Edie is?'

'Edie is with Max. She is crying. She is naughty, nasty and jealous.' I might as well push in a few new words. 'She is not friendly and kind. She tells Max about the thing I did. We will run out of here very fast, before he sees us. He will be angry with me.'

Then this is what I did. As we were hurrying towards the front door, and hearing Mr Maxwell and Edie walking across the first landing, I grabbed hold of Celia and pushed her quickly into the linen cupboard under the stairs, holding her hand all the time of course, following her in and closing the door. I placed my finger on her lips and wrote, 'Max coming. We are hiding from him.' I could feel her hand trembling. This was far better than *Schoolfriend*! Edie, the school sneak, rushing off to tell tales to the terrible, but just, Head of House, that we had not showed up for lacrosse practice; Celia, the sweet, timid little fourth-former, being led into disobedience by a desperate prefect, fearful of being expelled! What a terrible fool I'd feel if Mr Maxwell discovered us there. Would he have believed me, as I certainly hope you will, that on impulse, I had decided to hot up Celia's life a bit and invoke some spice into it? I *think* that's why I did it, but on the other hand, I could have played this game without the superintendent being on the warpath. Celia wouldn't have known the difference.

Ah! But I would, and therefore, so would she! She senses, very accurately, other people's attitudes and feelings. I can't put into words exactly why I know this to be true, but true it is. I understand that much about her! I'm also beginning to learn a great deal about myself and it isn't all sweetness and light. I think Celia and I will eat our lunch elsewhere today. I'm not in the mood for a dispute with Mr Maxwell. You might call it cowardice; I call it diplomacy.

When I felt that it was safe to emerge, we crept out of the cupboard and scurried out of the house, running, walking, running, until we were well out of reach. Celia seems stronger, more sure-footed and confident about running and all I need to do is just hold her hand lightly. We sat down on a seat.

'I want to ask you some questions,' I said. Here are the questions, and her answers.

'How old are you?'

'Twenty-five. My birthday 12 April.'

'Have you any brothers and sisters?'

'I have sister Freda. Twenty. Her birthday 20 August.'

'What is your favourite food?'

She looked puzzled and repeated the question, then she spelt out 'favourite'.

I realised that she did not understand the word, so using her own finger, I spelt it out for her to do the same, on her own initiative; but she didn't. 'Favourite means what you like best. What is your favourite food?'

'Chips.'

'What is your favourite fruit?'

'Apple, orange, pear, and grape I like best.'

'Which one is your favourite?'

'Pineapple, lemon, strawberry nice fruit.'

I thought I would leave that subject alone for a while.

'Do you like Max?'

'Yes.'

'Do you like going in a boat?'

'Yes.'

'Do you like driving the boat or do you like being a passenger?'

'I drive boat. Leah passenger.' I gave that a rest too.

'Do you like Edie?'

'No.' She made terrible faces and wailed and sent me into paroxysms again. What a pleasure she is!

I then asked her to ask me some questions, and she repeated

more or less identical ones. I got her to use the word 'favourite' and in answer to the fruit and food, I gave her one answer, so perhaps she twigged. I was too tired to find out. I told her my favourite food was pepper, and she wailed and laughed and shouted 'Funny!' very clearly. Now, she probably has a confused idea of what 'favourite' means. I don't care. I'm heartily sick of the word, and so is Celia. I'm sure neither of us will ever use it again as long as we live.

We walked on, to see a lady who has kennels and who breeds dogs. I found out about this place from an ad. I read in the local paper last night, requiring a kennel maid. I thought perhaps that the owner would be so relieved that we hadn't come for the job, that she might let us look around. She did.

I think Celia has a natural feeling and love for animals. The dogs and puppies ran towards her. I told her whose mother was who, after Mrs V. told me. Then Celia shouted, 'Babies! Babies!' as the pups clustered around her. How clearly and beautifully she pronounced the word! She may not fully understand the word 'joy' but she knows of its expression and abandon far more profoundly than any of us who are curbed by the sophistication of language. No doubt this goes for grief and woe and misery and despair. I explained how the two big dogs were jealous of each other. She showed enormous interest and energy, running and stumbling around the field, stroking and playing with all the little pups. I told her the names of the classy dogs – all lunatic names, like Minka and Mr Blue, and she was able to feel the difference between a chow and a poodle. She lifted up the puppies and rocked them, calling 'Babies' and crooning and smiling. How loving she was!

I said, 'Call Posy to you. Remember how you shouted "Babies"? Shout like that to Posy and she will run to you, but she must hear you. Shout now! Loud!' But only a little, scratchy voice came out, and Posy, damn her, ran to the kennel maid instead. Ah, well!

There was also a goat there, which I was frightened of. Not so

Celia, even though he nibbled her coat and pushed his head into her chest. She kissed this creature, and bade farewell to all the dogs with a similar show of affection, when it was time to leave. I had to remind her to say thank you and goodbye to the humans who had so kindly accommodated us. With Celia, where animals are involved, people are merely incidental. Understandable, perhaps. I wish she could have a pet of her own. Are guide dogs trained to lead the deaf-blind as well as blind people? I hope someone will try to find out.

I telephoned the home and left a message to say we wouldn't be in for lunch, and we ate fish and chips from newspaper, sitting in the bus station. She can see the colour of the buses, but is unable to get the whole shape into her vision. She could feel the buses going in and out and could, of course, smell them. We then wandered around Marks and Spencer's, and I asked her the names of all the objects she felt on the counters and on the hangers. The shop assistants were very kind and let us rummage around, even though we had no intention of buying anything.

To tell you the truth, I felt a bit nervous about returning to the home. Celia, however, was quite excited as we turned in to the drive, obviously hoping for fireworks. Little cow! As we went through the door, she put her fingers to her lips, and I joined in this jolly jest, by making her sidle along the wall, then chasing her up the stairs as if a bull was after us. We rushed into her room and she slammed the door and locked it! Her cheeks were aflame and her eyes, no longer dead, were alight with a mixture of glee and fear. I sat on her bed and she pulled at the bedspread, released it and covered me with it, making little noises with her teeth as she did so. She was making a joke; pretending to hide me! Childish behaviour, you may think. Perhaps so, but why not? She was having fun, and I am giving her that fun, and I consider this a measure of my success!

When we went down for supper, all the staff and residents asked where we'd been, and whether we had seen Mr Maxwell or not. I referred them all to Celia, explaining how they could ask her, by writing in block letters on her hand. She responded delightfully, no matter that they hadn't hitherto bothered to talk to her!

A written message was handed to me. The superintendent wanted to see me in his flat, after supper, and Celia and I were invited to dine tomorrow evening with a friend of mine who is staying near here. Well, well! Our social life is looking up!

I told Celia that Max wanted to see me and that I would see her later. Yes, he was quite cross. Edie had apparently woken him up, screaming and raving and insisting that I should be given the sack. Since I am not sure who my employers are, this is a bit of a problem. I have assured Mr Maxwell that I will keep out of Edie's way, provided she keeps out of mine. And Celia's. No, I certainly won't apologise; it is I who should demand an apology. We then drank a lot of gin and talked about Celia and her need to be with young people. He feels that this environment is not suitable for her. I agree. Is she going to stay here, stagnating, for ever?

When I staggered out of his flat, the house was still and quiet. It was late and everyone was in bed. Then I saw Celia. She was standing at the foot of Mr Maxwell's private staircase, her notebook under her arm, and in a state of great anxiety. How long had she been waiting there? Three, four hours? What colossal percentage of her life is spent in waiting? Here, on this lonely little dark, silent landing, while I was lounging, talking and drinking, she had stood waiting for me, without bitterness or recrimination. And what was the reason? She was worried about me, because the night porter turns off the lights at midnight and she didn't think I would be able to find the light switches, and thus be unable to reach my bedroom without her help. I allowed her to lead me to it; we said goodnight, and she went off, quite calm and smiling. I feel deeply affected by this incident. While I am here, I shall not leave her alone again.

'... Sunday wet cold. We cook lovely chocolate cakes in the kitchen. Little ones and big ones. We cook ninety flapjacks to give old people with coffee. We put a cake in pretty box for Leah's friend. I wash her hair she wash my hair. We make pretty, curly. I wear my blue dress, Leah has red dress with white. Not torn. He come big car 6.27. His car white, nice. Leah say name Morris me. Morris her friendly. She hug love kiss him. We drive to a lovely place. Candle, sticks of bread, wine, soup, spaghetti and thing, trifle, coffee. I show Morris speak deaf-blind. Happy, friendly, kind. We walk the sea, dance the sand. We home late 1.52. They Goodnight to me. They holding the hands.'

Dear Miss S., I think Celia is quite capable of writing this daily report for me, and I enclose the diary itself for your perusal. Now that I am back in London, I write, as it were, a sort of summing up. Celia is a young woman with all the soul and body of a young woman. Her soul is starved, because she is deaf and uneducated and cannot see. This is not a double handicap. I hate and reject this term. Blind people have no parallel with Celia. Deaf people have no parallel with Celia. Two times x does not make two or x. It makes 2x, and x is the unknown quantity, and in my opinion, it makes a garbled, geometric progression of hell on earth, because no matter how we strive, we cannot conceive of it. It takes the imagination of a genius or a madman to reach a tiny echo of x, and even then, its message cannot be passed on to us. Could Helen Keller pass on a morsel of her thoughts to Annie Sullivan? These two names, I humbly acknowledge, are worthy of great reverence, and we learn 'shadows' from them, but never the image or the core of Celia's prodigious secret. But love and affection and sex are her right, and we know that these, when offered to us, reach our souls, and heal and comfort us. I beg of you to forget that I am arrogant and aggressive, as well as being limited and inexperienced in this work. Please give me a hearing on various points I wish to make, as a serious and thoughtful person.

She must be enabled to mix with young people of both sexes, handicapped or otherwise; be given the opportunity to choose her friends, and be rejected if necessary. It is the right of any brave human being, and Celia is brave. The night of our outing with my friend, Morris, was a happy, but poignant one. She told us, spontaneously, that she had a boyfriend and had kissed and hugged him. She met him on a holiday for the deaf-blind. His name is Donald Bright. He is totally deaf, totally blind, and works in Weybridge as a toolmaker. She has lost touch with him and would like to meet him again. I think it would be a good idea if we could help Celia to trace this young man. It would not be difficult and could do no harm, only good.

We must discuss her immediate transfer from her present home and she must be encouraged to exercise her body and mind. I feel sure that she is highly intelligent. This is unimportant, except for the fact that her suffering and frustration are exacerbated because so much of her feelings are stifled. I think she should be taught on a regular basis and encouraged to learn how to live a fulfilled and independent life.

During my stay with Celia, many people came over to me to tell me how she would miss me. When the time came for me to leave, after having said 'Goodbye' to everyone, Celia came out with me on to the pavement. I got into the taxi. She stood there, quite alone, waving. I watched her through the window, and I'm sure she was still there after I turned the corner. No one said to me, 'If you have tears, prepare to shed them now.' They said Celia would miss me. No one said, 'You will miss Celia.' Her image is still with me. I don't know how long it will take before I am able to ignore it or remove it. Perhaps this is what my time with her is all about.

Chapter Thirteen

February. The word alone is difficult to say and hazardous to spell. A strange, ill-formed month; the hyphen between January and March; the quick, sharp, painful leap from winter into spring; a small, lopsided package of fog, wind and drizzle. Yet here I was, halfway through it, and I felt merry and cheerful and kindly disposed to all Mankind. So I'd give Susan and Micky an uninterrupted session in bed; allow Muriel to devote her full attention to her baby; give Jackie the chance to eat her panful of fried potatoes. I wouldn't brood over Miss Sanderson's broken promises. I'd try not to think about Celia. I'd sit in front of the fire and listen to the radio and look at my Valentine card standing on the mantelpiece. I'd think about me, about this house and the friends who have shared it with me. But I couldn't indulge just yet; not until I'd made a couple of phone calls. County Hall first, just to report that I wouldn't be working today.

'No. I'm not ill.' Why waste my talents lying to a liar? 'I'm extremely well, in fact, but I've decided to take the day off; tomorrow, too, perhaps. Give myself and the kids a break. It's a total waste of time and money, anyway.'

'Why not? Good!' The last sentence was ignored. 'Let's call it the perks of the job. I've just written a letter to you. Celia's got a place in Torquay. She'll be there for eight weeks. They've been working on two suitable guide-dogs. No, you fool – they're not both for her, and please don't scream like that. I've written to you, because I can't stand the noise you make over the telephone. Guess who the other dog's for? Yes! Donald! You see, we do take you seriously. They're going to live for eight weeks in the same hostel, and then they're both going to this brand new training centre. Easily accessible for you to visit and act as matchmaker. Penny's already told her, and she's so excited. We'd also like you to consider being a visiting teacher for her. Your report has been discussed and has caused considerable interest – or, rather, Celia's report. I haven't forgotten about the hospital job I promised you in April, but it's up to you to choose. Think about it. I've detailed everything in my letter and planned a meeting for later this month to give the principal the opportunity to talk with you. Goodbye. I've got things to do, even if you haven't.'

I rang Ma. 'Why are you crying? What's the matter? Listen, is everything all right? It isn't . . . don't get mad . . . I mean, you're not still thinking about . . .'

'Oh, for God's sake, won't you ever unhook yourself from that rusty nail? It gets on my nerves, the way you go on and on about him! No! Of course I'm not mad. I'm happy, that's all! They've traced Celia's boyfriend; I thought you'd be interested. They're going to be together for weeks and weeks at the Guide Dog Training Centre – and I think I've been offered a job teaching her. She's going to live in London. Isn't it marvellous?'

'Marvellous!' she repeated. To the untrained ear it sounded as if she meant it. 'And you know why it's turned out this way? Because of you. No one could do what you've done. Not many people put their heart and soul into their work, but you've a life of your own, as well.' Why can't she ever leave me out of it? Why can't she celebrate Celia and join in my elation on her behalf? But I won't start an argument – not today.

'It's our anniversary, Ma. Exactly a year ago we decided to buy a house. We've come a long way since then. I reckon it was a good idea on the whole. You and Dad should mark the occasion by investing in a second-hand telly and a new radio.'

'Dad and I don't need a thing! Not a thing! Fancy! A whole year! Auntie Sarah wrote the other day, wanting to know what was happening – with you.'

'*Her* year isn't up yet; not quite. I don't want to think about her just yet. Tomorrow, maybe, not today. I'm celebrating this evening and I've taken today off.'

'Are you going out? With friends? Somewhere nice?' Why shouldn't I make her happy. Wasn't it about time she had a bit of nachus?*

'Yes. I'm going out somewhere nice with someone very nice. Morris. The musician who lives upstairs. You know, I told you about him. Mr Rosenfeld.'

'Mr Rosenfeld! I thought you couldn't stand the sight of him! Morris? I never heard you call him that before.'

'I never have. Count yourself honoured, Myrtle. You and Celia both. We bumped into him at the seaside; he was playing his violin there, and the three of us went out together. When I introduced Mr Rosenfeld to Celia, I had to call him Morris – you've got to use shorthand in fingertip language. We had a very jolly evening. We ate with a runcible spoon, then hand in hand, on the edge of the strand, we danced by the light of the moon.'

'So his name's Morris. Are you friendly with him now?' The casual enquiries didn't fool me. Her hopes, her dreams, made my heart ache.

'Yes,' I said. 'Not Uncle friendly or Tenant friendly. Owl and Pussycat friendly.'

'There's a pig in that poem. Remember the pig,' said she, sharp as a needle, sly as a mother with an elderly unmarried daughter.

'I'd forgotten, but I promise I'll keep that fact in mind from now on. Tonight we're just going to a concert together, though.

* Joyful pride – usually confined to the attainments of one's children.

I'll come over on Friday, Ma. I'll fill you in on everything. There's so much to tell you. I haven't deliberately kept you in the dark. I've been in the dark, too.'

'Goody! Wear your dark green velvet dress tonight. You look lovely in it. I'm so glad we bought the house. Happy anniversary! Have a wonderful time!'

The house was quiet, but not strange any more. I'd thought I'd miss Mandy and George, but I didn't. Not really. They're a family now, with their own home, and their absence has made this more my home – and his. Yet they'll always be a part of my life, along with Ranjini and Dinah. He'd asked me whether he could take over the two rooms upstairs – one as a bedroom, and the large double as a living room, so it would just be the four of us – and no more strangers yet awhile. How delightful to have him in residence again! How safe and happy it will be!

He wouldn't mind if I made his bed, cleaned and tidied the rooms and made them warm and comfortable. I'd buy a bunch of flowers and a plant. Ranjini had already loaded his pantry with food and Dinah had made the kitchen spotless and ordered milk for him. There'd be no need for them to feel left out and jealous. I'd got the whole day to think and plan and to arrange his rooms and sort out my clothes. I didn't have to leave for the Festival Hall until six thirty.

We'd have a late supper here – in my room. I'd buy something particularly delicious from the delicatessen and blow any change I had on a bottle of champagne. He'd want to see the novel, so I'd better leave myself two or three hours to draw it to a close; but he wouldn't expect me to bring a bulky manuscript with me. I'd had so many other more important matters to attend to, that he'd understand if it's not quite finished. He understands everything. But now I must write a shopping list. I'd be lucky if I'd have time to finish the chapter I'm involved with, let alone the entire book ...

The journey to Waterloo reminded me of the many occasions

I had travelled this route on my way to County Hall – angry; sick with myself; my heart like lead. How light, happy and pretty I felt now as I emerged from the tube and followed the arrows to the South Bank. I made sure that my seat ticket was still safely in my glove. C13. He'd be waiting for me in C14 or C12 – if I didn't arrive too early. I wanted him to be there first, so that I could watch him smile as I made my way towards him. He'd stand up, help me off with my coat, show me the programme; erase any discomposure I may feel, regarding the luxury of the seat and rubbing shoulders with the rich and celebrated.

The foyer was thronged with people, but I pushed my way towards the bar and bought a large sherry, to make my blood sing, and my confidence leap. The five-minute bell rang, and I showed my ticket to the usher, who escorted me part of the way and then left me after giving me friendly directions. C12 and 11 were taken by a couple of pedigree ladies and 14 and 15 by an elderly pot-belly and his wife. They were all dressed in sumptuous finery, and I was wedged in solitary confinement in my tawdry rag, wretched with disappointment. All the other seats on the row were occupied, and indeed, the entire hall was now packed to its capacity. The musicians were taking their places, the audience doing the coughing performance, prior to the hush of compressed, bronchitic lungs.

If I didn't know him better, I'd have thought he was paying me back for past offences. He must have known that I wouldn't like to be sitting alone here; that the arrangement was for us to be together. Perhaps he had found out that I hadn't written the promised thirty-five and a half thousand words and had given his seat to one of my neighbours. But they were both partnered. I asked C12 if I might glance at her programme and she passed it over with a pleasant smile. I'd start a conversation with her, during the interval; find out if she, too, had a ticket given to her. The programme was marvellous and included all my favourites. It was his loss, missing all this. I felt tears pricking my eyes. I mustn't start that; the Eyelure make-up would run and make a mess. The violinists were tuning up, and I watched them mixing their colours through a dazzle of water. The conductor mounted the rostrum and took his bow. Dvořák: Symphony No. 9 in E Minor from *The New World* was first on the menu and I felt the excitement of anticipation. No one could be miserable, listening to this music; no one disappointed and alone, while basking in the glory of those crescendos. I would have to be careful during Largo and Scherzo, parts of which are a catalyst for crying, but have little to do with sadness. Time, now, to give my eyes a quick wipe and clear my vision before the Allegro con Fucco, the Fourth, most familiar and dramatic movement.

I watched the front row of the violinists, focusing on one of them. His wonderful fingers danced on the strings and drew the bow as if the instrument were part of himself, the tail of his jacket dancing too, in time to the joyous movements of his hands. His long, thick grey hair fell over his brow and his eyes were shining below, though half-closed, in love with the music. His mouth was compressed, but sometimes twitching and stretching into a little smile. He knew the score by heart, of course; it was his joy; his consolation and his love. He was nearer to me now, than if he were occupying the seat next to me and I recognised that same blurred, yet oddly bright expression from when I awoke in Grantchester and saw him looking at me. I hadn't known what it meant, then.

Why had I not understood that he would be on the platform! How typical! My confidence, pride and love soared with the music. No one else in this vast concert hall heard it as I did. It was over. *Sic transit gloria mundi.* The orchestra stood acknowledging the applause and he bent his head towards me, as if I was the only one there.

Vaughan Williams next. How could he have known that these were all my favourites! *English Folk Songs*, and *The Wasps*, and then, yes, of course *Greensleeves Fantasia*. He had played this once before, just for me, when we were alone and now he was playing it again, just for me, and his eyes were twinkling with the pleasure of my pleasure. He must have been able to see the colour of my dress from where he was.

At the end, I wanted to stand up, and shout and wave; the whole row rose with me and continued to applaud, until at last, I was the only one left clapping. People were trying to push past me, for the interval drink and conversation, but by the time I was able to see the stage again, it had been vacated. I didn't need a drink or anyone to talk to. I left the auditorium and went to stand against the windows upstairs, and looked at the lights and the river. 'Happy anniversary,' I said to my reflection. Exactly one year ago I was crying over Joseph, depressed and dismal, running home to Mother, persuading my parents to help me buy a house because I'd had a trying day. I wished I'd kept a diary so that I could now understand, step by step, what it consisted of – this progress into joy and cheer. Tomorrow I'd try to write it down; investigate my memory about this past year; write a journal in retrospect.

I returned to my seat and smiled at my neighbours. A uniformed official leaned towards me from the aisle and said, 'Mr Rosenfeld asks if you would wait for him at the bar after the concert.' I told the lady on my right that it was a message from my friend who is a violinist, and she was suitably impressed, and I pointed him out to her as the musicians returned for the second part of the performance. I watched him all the time; unreserved; uncautious; abandoned; generously exposing his entire soul to me. How would I greet him, now that the music was over? How dull, flat and stupid my voice would sound; how presumptuous my praise!

The conductor and orchestra took their last bow to exuberant applause, then departed to a mysterious region, while I made my way, rather fearfully, towards the long queue in the 'Ladies'. I looked at my face in the mirror, as glamorous women jostled me. I washed my trembling hands and tried to wipe away the black smudges of eye make-up, dawdling until the cloakroom was empty. I hadn't planned what I'd say. Maestro! Thank you for a wonderful evening! I practised it in front of the mirror. It'd have to do.

Perhaps, if I hurried, I'd have time to swallow a stiff drink before he arrived, but I could see him there, already. He called my name and I ran towards him, forgetting everything but the pleasure of being with him again, and he dropped his violin case, almost as carelessly as I threw down my bag and coat, in order to embrace him. 'Morris! Morris!' I said, over and over again, unable to stop; as if I needed to make up for lost time.

The house was dark, and I was glad. Ranjini and Dinah must have retired for the night, so we whispered as we trundled his luggage through the door and up the stairs. I didn't want them hearing us, and coming running to say hello to him. We'd dump his things in his living room; I wanted him to see how attractive I'd made it – and to borrow a corkscrew, prior to going down to eat our late supper and to drink a toast to his homecoming. I showed him round, like a familiar concierge, pointing out the advantages of this fancy place, while he pointed out the disadvantages, with the corkscrew, and with equal extravagance.

'Supper is laid in the parlour downstairs. Would you be so gracious as to follow me? Now – before we both die of hunger and thirst?'

He gave one last look around, then turned to me, smiling. 'For all that you have done, it lacks the essential that I need. I shall not miss it unduly when I move, which I think must be quite soon.'

I stumbled down the stairs. My heart was still. So he was leaving. The house meant nothing to him. Nor did I. I had encircled everything he had written and said with the aura of my adolescent infatuation. My presence must have become an irritant to him. His heyday of falling in love had passed, while mine had remained. I stood in the dark hall. He opened the door of my room and turned on the light. I saw the japonica I had cut from the garden; the shining glasses, the gay paper table napkins, the salads and the bowl of oranges; the wine and the long yellow candle that I had stuck in the middle of the table. All seemed to be a pathetic, overblown, childish gesture. I felt bereft of dignity; ashamed to look at him. He lit the candle and the fire, while I stood, my hands hanging by my sides, an immobile, idiotic lump.

'Turn off the light, please.' I did so, grateful for the semi-darkness and the shadows which might hide my blundering thoughts and my wretched appearance, watching him pull the cork, hearing the pop, the clink of glass as he held it to the bottle. He filled the two glasses and held one out to me.

'A toast – to your anniversary and to the completion of your novel!' He touched my glass with his, waiting for me to take the first sip.

'And to your homecoming and to your going away,' I said, taking a great noisy gulp. I could feel my eyes and nose running. I picked up a soft yellow napkin and pretended to wipe my mouth. 'When, exactly, do you plan to leave?'

'That depends on you. And Ranjini.'

'You don't have to give me notice. And I'm sure Ranjini can manage now, without your financial help.' My voice was out of control, cracking and wobbling. 'Don't allow such trivialities to affect your plans. Have you found another place?' I drained my glass and put it on the bookcase next to me, and held the napkin to my mouth in a vain attempt to stifle the awful, creaking sobs which galvanised both of us. He held me in his arms, kissing my hair, straining my dreadful face against his chest.

'There is no other place.'

'Then why are you leaving? Why must you go? Don't leave me, Morris! Don't leave me!' I raised my head and kissed him, holding him to me, without reserve, freeing him of any doubts with deliciously injudicious success. I will not say 'I love you' and risk the loss of his tender and wholehearted embrace; I will not reveal my joy and desire for his passion, and thus avoid the flinch, the slight ducking away from me; I will not accost him with the knowledge of his weeping – his release from years of isolation.

'I love you,' I said, kissing his scarred wrists, feeling his tears on my neck, matching his delight with my own.

I watched over him as he slept. Soon he would talk to me; tell me about all the years before I knew him, so that I could be a part of them; help to dispel his woe and gather up his joy. I would be here when he woke, alert and efficacious. I lay my head on his chest, to share his heartbeat and respiration, and when I awoke, I was in his arms. The candle had burned low, and the room capered in its mischievous light. He bent to kiss me. Orde was wrong about him. The nobility of his nature matched my standards exactly. I wanted to ask him how he could be so ungallant as to leave me now, but he interrupted me, putting his finger on my lips.

'I was referring to the flat upstairs, wondering if it might suit Ranjini. I would trade both my rooms for hers! And then, my darling, if or when you are ready, we could make a permanent contract – nothing to do with such trivia as rent. The only move I ever wish to make is one which would take me closer to you.'

There was only enough wine left for a single glassful. It was warm but delicious because I shared it with him. We heard Ranjini's alarm ring briefly.

'I'll make her some tea!' I said, gleefully, 'and prepare her sweetly for the move upstairs. And if she's not utterly delighted by the prospect, I'll threaten to call you!'

'And then?'

'Then we'll have our supper breakfast; then I'll ring Ma, and tell her two for Friday night; then I'll remind Miss Sanderson that I'm not going to work today; and then we'll make up for lost time and iron out our misunderstandings; and . . .'

'Then you'll show me your novel?'

'I'd forgotten all about that! I've just got one or two more pages to write – the last chapter, in fact.'

'Then you'll write the last chapter?'

'No,' I said. 'Then I must write a letter to Auntie Sarah.'

A SELECTION OF FICTION FROM NEL

THE MARRIAGE BED	*Constance Beresford Howe*	£1.75
FAMILY HAPPINESS	*Laurie Colwin*	£1.95
BOYCHESTER'S BUGLE	*Alan Franks*	£1.50
A SELF-MADE WOMAN	*Ruth Harris*	£2.25
SISTERS	*Linda Lauren*	£1.50
RICHARD'S THINGS	*Frederic Raphael*	£1.25

All these books are available at your local bookshop or newsagent, or can be ordered direct from the publisher. Just tick the titles you want and fill in the form below.

Prices and availability subject to change without notice.

NEL BOOKS, P.O. Box 11, Falmouth, Cornwall.

Please send cheque or postal order, and allow the following for postage and packing:

U.K. – 55p for one book, plus 22p for the second book, and 14p for each additional book ordered up to a £1.75 maximum.

B.F.P.O. and EIRE – 55p for the first book, plus 22p for the second book, and 14p per copy for the next 7 books, 8p per book thereafter.

OTHER OVERSEAS CUSTOMERS – £1.00 for the first book, plus 25p per copy for each additional book.

Name ....

Address ....

....